THE MORE
A Journey to Sustainability

by Brent Leigh

TRAFFORD

[handwritten inscription] Pam, Thanks for your wonderful work on The More! All the best, Brent

There are hundreds of heated warehouses spread across the globe, each containing a forest of unpublished books. (It is estimated that 80% of all books published are never sold.) This book was printed at your request "on demand" and thereby represents one more contribution to sustainable living.

Front cover: this image was taken by Charles Guildner of Everett, Washington while cruising in the British Columbia waters among the Thormanby Islands. Although Charles has not titled the image, he notes: *"For me there is the bringing together of the beauty both man and the Supreme Being are capable of creating, with both always returning to the earth."*

Part 1 image: reproduced from *Squamish The Shining Valley* by Kevin McLane, showing the left side of the Split Pillar on the Grand Wall of the Chief.

Please note: The characters within this novel take the liberties of earlier hikers, camping at Tsuqanah Point, leaving the trail at Nitinat Narrows and visiting petroglyphys south of Whyac. Anyone using this book, in part as a reference to hiking the West Coast Trail, is asked to respect First Nation's lands by not duplicating any of these side trips.

National Library of Canada Cataloguing in Publication Data

Leigh, Brent, 1953-
 The more : a journey to sustainability
ISBN 1-55369-065-6
 1. Sustainable development--Fiction. I. Title.
PS8573.E468M67 2001   C813'.6   C2001-904154-3
PR9199.4.L43M67 2001

TRAFFORD

This book was published *on-demand* in cooperation with Trafford Publishing.
On-demand publishing is a unique process and service of making a book available for retail sale to the public taking advantage of on-demand manufacturing and Internet marketing.
On-demand publishing includes promotions, retail sales, manufacturing, order fulfilment, accounting and collecting royalties on behalf of the author.

Suite 6E, 2333 Government St., Victoria, B.C. V8T 4P4, CANADA

Phone	250-383-6864	Toll-free	1-888-232-4444 (Canada & US)
Fax	250-383-6804	E-mail	sales@trafford.com
Web site	www.trafford.com	TRAFFORD PUBLISHING IS A DIVISION OF TRAFFORD HOLDINGS LTD.
Trafford Catalogue #01-0467		www.trafford.com/robots/01-0467.html

10   9   8   7   6   5   4   3

The More

father inspired
mother nurtured
wife embodies
sons become

There was little I did not say when you were with us,
that I loved you was clear.
You called me forth, you honored my nakedness, my desire to dance.
In your presence I grew unashamed of my magnificence.
You encouraged my more rather than my less.
I'll keep the vow we made in jest,
and drink the wind and dance beyond the morning.
I'll honor you the best I can by being who I am.

Author unknown

THE MORE: *A Journey to Sustainability*
by Brent Leigh

Part 1: *Context*

The Life Wish: *Speaking to the core*

As Tomo prepared himself for the continued ascent up the face of the Chief, physical demands of split fingers and burning muscles yielded to a more pervasive calling. What James had just said spoke to the center of his being, and he sensed his future course had changed forever. Tomo forced their conversation to the back of his mind and attempted to concentrate on what James was saying about their route up the sheer rock wall.

"I'd say we've climbed about 300 vertical meters," James said, glancing casually over the edge, then pivoting to look directly overhead. "I would like to get past that roof above us. Looks like it's about a 30-meter climb. The overhangs we crossed this morning were a challenge, but that's got to be the crux of this route. Would you like to exchange lead?"

The two men had been alternating the lead position all morning. Tomo knew James was offering him the prize of the day by suggesting he lead over the toughest overhang. It was more his state of mind than the severity of the climb that found him declining James' offer.

James seemed to sense his preoccupation and indulged it, saying, "It was Rumi who said: 'Out beyond ideas of wrong-doing and right-doing, there is a field. I'll meet you there.'" James cupped his hand firmly behind

Tomo's neck. Their eyes locked. The moment passed, and James transferred the same firm grip to the rock fissure above Tomo's head. Lifting himself like a feather caught in an updraft, he drifted skyward on a current of intent. It occurred to Tomo that James was utilizing the intersection point of physical and mental prowess that occurs in late-30s age to his advantage.

Tomo watched James climb fluidly as before. He thought of how good climbers have great body awareness, like ballet dancers asserting every ounce of energy to the edge of their toes or fingertips. As James stayed in aggressive balance with the rock, there was a controlled efficiency to everything he did. It crossed Tomo's mind that climbers are referred to as having a death wish. Watching James was proof of a life wish.

As he approached the A3 overhang Tomo saw that, in relation to James's body, it was bigger than expected. Not a word was spoken as James free-climbed the overhang, clipping to successive bolts for protection. He smeared his rubber-toed shoes into the stone, hugging his way across the underbelly of the rock. A muscle and friction grip on reality.

Tomo's mouth was dreadfully dry, and he stared up as James neared the outer edge of the overhang. James spoke in caution for the first time as he approached the bolt where the horizontal ceiling broke once again to a vertical wall.

"Tomo, this bolt looks like my grandfather set it. I'm going to set my own nut for protection."

James clipped to the bolt with his left hand, then reached behind his back and pulled free a rock-jamming nut. Tomo could see him position it in a crack and test its strength. He wondered how James was able to continue holding his body horizontal against the ceiling and wished he had pushed through on the existing bolt. He watched James draw his arm back and gather some rope in his teeth to make a loop. Then, reaching forward to clip his rope, James seemed to freeze.

"Come on, James," Tomo whispered, trying to break the spell that held James' muscles locked in position—but his grip broke first. James' body peeled off the ceiling. Time stood still. Even as gravity took hold, each stretched second implied that James would float to safety.

Tomo braced himself to break the fall, James' warning about the last bolt fresh in his mind. Within the same few seconds, James recovered his lost balance in mid-air and was perfectly positioned with knees bent towards the wall in case he swung that far.

His weight hurled down, transferring a great force on the last anchor bolt. The rope sprang taut, and the anchor ripped out, violently spinning James around. Flying backwards, he continued on an almost uninterrupted arc towards the vertical wall that intercepted the roof.

Tomo could see that James was going to crash head first. He heaved at the line to fight the downward thrust of James' body.

As the full weight transferred to the line it slammed Tomo against the rocks, locking at the anchor set in the belaying perch. Tomo scrambled to regain his position, wrenching to see if James had also hit the wall. Tomo determined that James was in a 'hang-dog,' and prayed that his friend was in this laying-open position merely to rest his muscles.

Three calls.... Nothing.

The pendulum motion slowed as Tomo caught sight of James hanging face up in his waist harness, suspended directly above Tomo from the center of the overhang. Tomo thanked some unknown source for this coincidence and very slowly started to lower James. Bringing him to position, Tomo set James on the rock ledge slowly and knelt down beside him.

First he instinctively checked his airway. James was alive and breathing. Next, Tomo gently manipulated James' neck—it did not appear to be broken. Reaching to undo the chin-strap of the helmet, he saw a spider-web crack radiating from the top right-hand side of the plastic shell. As Tomo pulled it off, he watched James' face, which conveyed a look of peaceful sleep—a child-like quality that disguised the danger he was in. Tomo pulled out his water bottle and splashed James' face.

"Come on, James. Wake up—Oh, for...." Tomo threw his head back, trying to collect his thoughts. "Your hair isn't even messed up," he added in frustration as he refastened James' helmet.

It was only then that Tomo registered other noises, sirens. Looking to the parking area, he saw that people at the base of the Chief had realized what had happened. Emergency response units were moving up the highway from the nearby town of Squamish.

Someone was shouting from below and, as Tomo concentrated on the voice, he was surprised how audible it was. But before he could make out what was being said, the clap of a helicopter drowned out all sounds as it hovered in from the north. It flew directly toward the cliff, and the pilot nosed the aircraft toward the ledge on which Tomo crouched.

The pounding of the motor reverberated against the wall, and Tomo looked down at James, astounded that the noise alone did not stir him. Tomo smacked his own helmet with his hand and pointed to James, trying to indicate what had happened. The pilot spoke into his headset but made no further motion as he pulled on the controls and banked away.

Tomo felt an odd sense of detachment as the helicopter retreated to the parking lot adjacent to the highway. Within moments, he could see some equipment being loaded from the emergency vehicles to the helicopter. Then the helicopter lifted almost as quickly as it had landed.

Tomo realized this emergency response team was assuming the worst, and his mind raced to determine how he could confirm their assumption. He looked overhead at the broken black basalt, then realized the wall behind the ledge they were on had a large smooth surface. He stood up, gathered a fistful of climbing chalk in his hand and scrawled the letters "COMA" on the wall.

Tomo finished the last letter as the helicopter hovered within one hundred feet of the cliff adjacent to them. A man with climbing helmet and harness made sure Tomo was looking at him, pointed at the wall, and nodded deliberately to indicate they had Tomo's message. He then held up the end of a thick line coiled in front of him and pointed above, to Tomo and then to the base of the Chief. Realizing they were going to lower the rescue equipment from above, Tomo nodded back in the same deliberate manner.

The man in the helicopter signaled to the pilot, then turned back to Tomo with a thumbs-up sign as they lifted away from the face. As the drama continued, Tomo looked down at the calm expression on James' face, and the notion of a life wish took on new meaning.

Driving Passions: *Awakening the change agents*

Tomo stood motionless as though bound to the rock by the line that nested at his feet. The sound of the motor died off as he looked overhead, unable to see anything beyond the looming rock above.

Tomo stared out at the vast expanse, gripped by a sense of remorse. He realized he had never examined what passion had brought him to climb but, more so, had never identified what motivations truly drove his life. There was no resolution to his thoughts except for some quality that connected him back to James.

The connection brought him to a tangible concern for rocks falling from the rescue efforts taking place above them. He crouched down to straddle James' body, resting his elbows above James' shoulders and his helmet against James'. Tomo listened to James' breathing, measuring it against his own as his mind drifted in search of some psychological reference points.

He recalled James as he had first known him in graduate school 15 years earlier, where the two focused their concentration on study. In his memory he saw the first class they shared, international economics, debating how man-made systems work and why. James, always the provocateur, asking questions that challenged his peers and professors alike. Then he saw the final exam for that same class and James opening his paper, writing for just a moment, closing it and then sitting with his hands folded on the desk for the remaining two hours.

Tomo had approached him in the hall after the exam. "What were you doing in there?"

"I answered the question with the same level of respect in which it was conceived."

"But the only question on the whole paper was the word 'Why?'"

"And that's why my answer was 'Why not?'"

The only person to receive top grade point in that class was James.

James' spirit was an intensity welded to the strongest sense of judgment Tomo had ever seen. A judgment that discerned power is granted, not taken, and James never allowed others to assume authority they had not earned.

As their friendship moved outside the class, Tomo found these same qualities translated into an unbridled passion for life in general. It was a passion that seemed to fill James constantly with a vision of what was possible. As he set the vision, his focus would drive him to the end goal.

Tomo was not surprised that James' climbing style and lifestyle were the same: two drivers working in sequence—defining, pushing; defining, pushing.

The two men had not climbed together often, but their friendship instilled a foundation of trust they had often built on. Part of that trust was an understanding that their personalities had combined strengths. James knew Tomo was methodical, attentive, disciplined, and in superb physical condition. Tomo knew James was driven by adventure, with a character as compelling as it was complex. A mind and body that moved with supple strength.

Going separate ways after studies, they planned occasions together, usually through some expedition James had dreamed up. This one involved the big face climb on the "Chief" north of Vancouver, followed by a week-long trek with four additional friends of James.

Tomo regretted that his wife, Barbara, would not be joining them, but the demands of her work seemed to be pulling them apart. Tomo and Barbara had sat over breakfast on the day of his departure and tried to address the gap, but issues of starting a family, building a career and having a life seemed only to complicate resolution. Barbara had always seemed more clear about her goals, and her desire for a family was on his mind as he drove north from his home in Seattle the previous day.

Arriving in Vancouver to warm welcomes, Tomo shared a late dinner with James and his friend Kim. Tomo had heard of Kim, but her studies and work had found her absent whenever he and James had gotten together. Her fair hair and handsome features seemed perfectly complemented by James' dark similarities. Other than some knowing presence in their eyes, one could easily mistake their late-30s age for their late-20s look.

Tomo expected the conversation to be consumed with the ideas expressed in a paper James had sent to him earlier that month. But, true to style, James was basking in the sincerely held joy of being together. Tomo knew that he was the honored guest of James' living-in-the-moment, and his understanding of their friendship flowed back in place.

It was an honor heightened through Kim's being there as Tomo witnessed something more complete in James through her presence. When one of them spoke, there was a kind of serene attentiveness between them. As Kim watched James speak, her full lips held the smooth planes of her face in tension, and her large blue eyes amplified the quality of a presence that Tomo felt strongly. As Tomo watched James reciprocate his attention to Kim he wondered if they realized how much in love they were. Being in their presence Tomo felt as though he had been welcomed into a place of great peace. The evening passed through highlighted memories where their lives had intersected.

The next morning's start was early from James' home in Vancouver, but the summer sun had already risen on the beautiful boom town of the Pacific. Tomo reflected on the irony of his father growing up in this city then, returning from the war with a Japanese wife, moving to the more tolerant Seattle. Now as Tomo drove through this multi-cultural metropolis, it was apparent to him that Vancouver had done a lot of changing in 50 years.

Crossing the picturesque Lions Gate Bridge that links to Highway 99, they traversed the community of West Vancouver, noted for its rustic beauty and highest per capita income in Canada. Still early in the morning, they wove their way through the bottleneck of traffic at Horseshoe Bay, as vacationers jostled for position at the ferry terminal. Skirting the cliff edge, they stayed on the highway above the bay where they could see large and small car ferries staged in a jostling of their own. Tomo had seen this lineup to island retreats swell in the past—people traversing to other people's idea of paradise.

As they continued up the spectacular "Sea to Sky Highway," mountains towered overhead and the islands below scurried into light as the sun's rays tipped over the coastal peaks. Fifty kilometers of winding road and open vistas brought them to the head of the inlet and the massive granite outcropping known as the Chief.

As they stopped for a hearty breakfast at the Roadhouse Diner near the base of the Chief, Tomo brought up the subject of the coming week and his real reason for being there.

"James, this is quite a hiking party you've got planned for next week."

"It should be great fun, particularly if this good weather holds," James replied. "I've hiked the West Coast Trail in the rain, and it can be a pretty muddy, slippery affair."

"Everything I've heard about the trek sounds great, but I'm interested in why you've pulled together this five-person party and what your real agenda is."

"Agenda?"

"Well, of course, James. You send each of us a letter which introduces the group, and with it you include a hundred-page paper that proposes the global economy is poised to align with the natural world."

"So?"

"So are we supposed to show up with a book review or our hiking boots?"

James looked bewildered. "I guess I never thought of it as an either/or proposition. I know the people who are coming are grappling with change in their own lives and in the world at large. I also know the unfolding wonders of the 70-kilometer trek will decompress anyone having cultural cramps. I guess I just saw the paper as a mental fit to the physical hike."

Tomo felt abashed. Why did he have to keep relearning how this guy thought? He couldn't start back-tracking now and say it was an honor to be included, even though he knew that it was, so he moved to safer ground. "Tell me a little more about the party."

"Well, I've known Kim since we were kids. As she was saying last night, she has lived in Boston for some time. She did her Ph.D. there and has since become a meaningful voice in educational reform. I think Kim is trying to look across the spectrum of change and determine how it is shifting our learning priorities."

"Interesting. Did I detect a rekindled relationship between you two last night?"

"That's a subject I approach more carefully than that block of granite," James said, looking out the window at the 600-meter rock face. Then, as if addressing the Chief itself, he added, "I have a deep respect for her."

That intensity again. This time, Tomo decided to walk around the sacred ground. "Tell me about the other members of the group."

"Celine is French-Canadian, working out of Montreal in international banking. She has seen it all in the financial world and is big into economic reform." James paused like a jeweler who wants to acknowledge the quality of each gem.

"Paul left what was formally Czechoslovakia to attend university in the States in the '70s and never went back. He is the most progressive businessperson I know. I believe Paul is developing products and running his organization the way all will run in the next century.

"Zahir was born in Uganda and raised in the States." James' face softened, awash with some pleasant thought. "He is a software developer and a new breed altogether. He has accustomed himself to change that most of us have not even realized is taking place."

"This sounds like one interesting safari," Tomo said, having caught James' infectious enthusiasm towards each of these people. "To what do I owe the pleasure of inclusion?"

"You'll challenge us to stay honest," James replied. "Even the best vision needs to work from reality, and you're the most real person I know."

The sincerity of this compliment was clear, although Tomo was unclear how he was meant to live up to it. As they finished breakfast, he sensed that James was trying to define some common element, some hidden potential, he saw in each of these people—or maybe the world of which they were part.

Those things that drove James were at work again: defining, pushing; defining, pushing. But how did James' paper work into all this? How did the individual pursuits of the team relate to the thesis he had proposed? What did he expect to gain from the trek? What did he expect they would gain?

As they stood to walk out the door, James spoke with that same clear-eyed truthfulness. "It's a wonderful group. I'm just glad you're with us.... Let's go jump the rock!"

Jump the rock is exactly what they did. James had executed several of the routes on the Chief, including the Tantalus Wall, the North Wall, the Western Dihedrals and the Grand Wall. It was a vertical playground, a million years in the making. Its towering slabs of stone seemed evidence of the massive force still active in the Pacific Plate.

They drove Tomo's car a short distance down the highway, parking near the base of the Grand Wall. Tomo pulled out his copy of *The Rockclimber's Guide to Squamish*, wondering to himself if James, in fact, had a plan.

"I've always wanted to flash the Black Dyke," James said, pointing at the 600-meter vertical intrusion of black basalt that ran down the white granite slabs of the Grand Wall.

The term "flash" signaled to Tomo that James had never attempted nor studied this route. Flashing a rock face was a purist approach to rock climbing, let alone big-wall climbing.

Tomo looked up at the Black Dyke, which resembled a mammoth pencil line drawn through nature's cleanest sheet of rock. As he considered his own uneasiness, James explained that, after an attempt to free climb the whole route had ended tragically, several bolts had been put in place, converting some pitches to aided climbing.

Interpreting this as affirmation rather than warning, the two men made appropriate changes to their climbing gear, slung the racks over their shoulders, locked the car and headed toward the highly textured basalt strip.

From its base, where James and Tomo were standing, the Black Dyke, so well defined from the highway, became a 30-meter-wide mass of broken black rock. The flat planes of vertical granite on either side of the dark scar seemed as separate as the sapphire blue sky overhead.

—·—

As Tomo remembered standing at that spot with James earlier that morning, he became aware of a noise from above and turned from his crouched position over James and once again saw the sheets of stone and sky overhead. On the smooth stone off to the right, a man was being lowered with a stretcher balancing between himself and the rock face. Both he and the stretcher were suspended from a master knot at the end of a heavy line. As he neared, Tomo could hear him say, "Ten meters, five meters." The rope slowed. "Two meters. Good, hold there."

The man stopped level with the ledge ten meters along the wall and slipped a portable radio into a pocket of his vest.

"Hi, Squamish Search and Rescue. My name is John." The announcement was made casually as if he were welcoming Tomo to a convention. John walked across the wall, the rope pivoting easily from the overhanging face above. As he moved in directly below the ledge on which James lay, his tone and demeanor changed completely.

"Any change in his condition?" The slight man's intense eyes evaluating Tomo's psychological state.

"No, he is still unconscious," Tomo replied, rising from his crouched position over James, "but his breathing is even."

John had already taken James' wrist, and, as he gauged his watch, said "good" to both levels of evaluation. Turning his deep-set brown eyes back to Tomo, his face softened with a smile. "You've taken good care of your friend," he said, then reached out his hand. "Makes our job a lot easier."

"I'm Tomo. He's James." Tomo felt the relief of John's firm grip. "He almost made it across the ceiling, then he lost it."

"Muscles will lock up if you don't find a way to rest them," John confirmed, holding his eyes on Tomo for a moment, then looking down. "Well, James, how is the rest of your body?"

"His neck seems fine," Tomo replied. "I've checked him over—I don't think there is any other injury."

As Tomo spoke, John ran his hands deftly over James' limbs. His fingers had the square ends of a climber, but moved with the skill of a surgeon.

"Are you going to raise him?"

"No, this rescue line is 700 meters long," John replied. "The paramedics will be waiting at the base. An air ambulance is on its way from Vancouver. Best we move him quickly," John added as he pulled his radio out again. "Command, this is Rescue One. Confirming one injured climber, unconscious with stable vital signs, no other apparent injury. I will be putting on a neck brace as a precaution, then loading. Please lower one foot." The rope responded immediately. "10-4. Please hold."

John swung his backpack off, flipped it open and pulled out a collar of molded plastic. He gave Tomo instructions on how to help him secure and load James and, within minutes, James was cradled on the stretcher in front of John.

John turned his full attention to Tomo. "You're a little banged up yourself. I'd like to request a climber to come and buddy you down."

"I would like to work my way down," Tomo replied without a trace of bravado.

John seemed to sense his deeper need. "Very well. Search and Rescue will help you out with anything you need at the base. Our descent will be out of your line, so feel free to start any time."

As the two men shook hands, Tomo realized that this time it was John who was feeling reassured. John unclipped from the station and walked across the face with the stretcher cocooned in front of him. He radioed instructions and started to descend as if by elevator.

Tomo allowed his focus to shift totally to his descent and was glad of it. He packed his gear, reset his rope and set off to the successive rappelling stations pinned into the rock. The movement and freedom on the line offered welcome relief. Approaching the base rapidly, he set foot on the ground just as the helicopter lifted James toward Vancouver.

"They will be taking him to Emergency at Lions Gate Hospital in North Vancouver. He'll probably be up chirping like a magpie by the time you arrive," a man with white/blonde hair offered reassuringly. "I'm Jim and this is Ron. The way you came off that rock, I don't have to ask if you're okay. Probably the most help we can be is getting you past the press at the parking lot."

Tomo let his glance follow Jim's, toward the helicopter. As it disappeared behind the mountain, Tomo found himself staring at the same sheets of rock and sky, but with a vastly different perspective.

The Ascent: *A distant view of The More*

The men helped Tomo with his gear over the broken ground to the parking area. Knowing the press would create their own story, Tomo offered a quick account of the facts and ducked into his car, eager to catch up with James.

Reaching into his bag, he got the listing of hikers that James had provided and called Kim's day number on his cellular phone. Tomo explained briefly what had happened, and Kim said she would meet him at the hospital. Kim was clearly concerned, but did not seem surprised. She offered to call James' parents.

As Tomo drove back down the mountain-lined waterway, the geography took on a bigger-than-life appearance in the afternoon sun. His thoughts seemed similarly enlarged as he scanned back over the climb, searching to see if the accident could have been avoided.

He remembered having started at the base of the Black Dyke. Once they had agreed James would lead, he had gone quickly to the task of moving up the vertical mass. Tomo had established an active belay, feeding James line and making observations about conditions of which James might not have been aware. "Extend your rope with a sling," Tomo had said when he could see the potential of rope drag. "Flip the rope," he had instructed if the rope was going to impede upward progress or be sliced during a fall. "10 meters of rope left," he had reminded James when it was time to look for an anchor point pinned to the rock.

They had moved like this swiftly up the face as James acknowledged each piece of advice with a clear "thank you." In his private concentration, James had offered little commentary about the climb unless he felt it would yield an unexpected situation for Tomo: "climbing," "rope," "slack," "loose rock."

James had never once said, "watch me," a request often made by the lead climber when concerned about falling. Whether James had never felt the potential of falling or believed Tomo would be in position if he did, the effect was a mutual statement of trust of which neither spoke as they had reached a ledge on which they had agreed to rest.

All morning Tomo had been convinced that James' concentration could melt hand holds in the black basalt, but as James had offered his hand to help Tomo onto the ledge, James' face had been perfectly serene. His eyes, the exact blue of the sky overhead, had held a look that said something unconditional had been established between them.

Tomo and James had settled on the narrow ledge, the sun having just worked its way past the mammoth buttress of the Great Wall. The first rays of light had cast long shadows across the white walls of stone. As Tomo's burning muscles had fused with the cool rock, he'd wondered if risk to life and limb was necessary to establish some primordial connection to another human being.

As if sensing the same thing, James had spoken while casting his gaze down the chain of Coastal mountains now in clear view to the north-west. "This is an awesome time to be alive."

Tomo, not intending to be funny, had replied, "Do you mean after this morning?"

Unable to ignore the obvious truth, they chuckled. "This morning is part of it," James had said. "Pushing past limits is very liberating. I find it fascinating that people everywhere are redefining their relation to life."

Tomo had detected the generalization. "You're not just talking about the natural world, are you?"

"No, I see a redefinition that brings society to better purposes."

Tomo had stretched mentally to capture his meaning. "Are you saying society is at some unique stage of improvement?"

"Absolutely."

Tomo had gazed down at the parking lot where people were milling around like ants. He'd wondered if his car had been broken into yet. "I see the exact opposite."

"A cynic is merely a fallen idealist," James had replied as he coiled the climbing rope.

"Listen, James, when I first met you I was going to law school because, in my previous career as a cop, I had realized we were powerless against crime on the street."

"I would say that is a process of improvement," James had replied evenly.

"No, because, as I started to practice law, my ability to effect change was no greater than when I had been a cop. The very same crooks that used to laugh at us on the street, like us, graduated to bigger things. They still have the upper hand through a system that has become totally dysfunctional, choking both due process and the courts."

James had opened some trail mix had and handed it to Tomo. "Right, so what do you do next?"

"Me! What do I have to do with it? I'm talking about a whole system that is trashed."

"The system isn't trashed. It's just the structures devised to contain it are over supplied."

"Oh, so I make my contribution by being one less lawyer?"

"No. You've devised new ways to help resolve the glut within the legal system."

Realizing that James was talking about his current project, Tomo had grown frustrated, feeling James was avoiding the issue. "James, the anti-theft technology I've been developing is to nail these bums the instant they pick something up that doesn't belong to them."

"My point exactly. Cut the funding source for criminals, cut crime, society moves to better purposes."

"But it's like putting your finger in the dyke when you look at the mess the world is in today."

"Not so. What you are doing, although unique in itself, is part of the transition to the next society." James had paused, taking a long shot of water from a squeeze bottle. "Knowing the structures we live within are stretched to their limits, we look for ways to expand and reframe our understanding."

"So here we all are, standing together at the edge of our limits," Tomo had pleaded.

"Well, Tomo, I guess 'together' is the operative word. But it's not a helpless together; it's an enabled together."

"What do you mean by enabled?"

"We live with an awareness of the need to develop positive visions of the future. Visions that are capable of delivering us to a greater quality of life. This attitude is fundamental in allowing or enabling change to happen."

Tomo had been only slightly more willing to be influenced. "Are you saying our awareness of a more qualitative life is enabling?"

"An awareness of life as it could be resides in each one of us. In general terms, it represents a set of universal values that a broad cultural awareness moves to see as human rights. The knowledge that some of these rights have been artificially denied becomes a very powerful motivation for social change."

"Like the right to have my car in one piece when we get off this mountain or, if I had kids, to have them safe on the street outside our house?"

"Yes, in the broadest sense the right of those kids to inherit a healthy social, economic and environmental context from their parents. Our true rights fit within a natural system. We have mistakenly constructed our rights within a man-made system, which has put us at odds with ourselves and all other aspects of nature. As we come to see ourselves evolving as part of nature, we redefine our personal and thereby our social and economic goals."

James had turned to look up at the towering face of the Chief. "It took this rock a billion years to evolve, but at some point, the conditions were right to create the huge shift of molten magma from which it was born." He'd looked back to Tomo. "I think conditions are right to create a similar advancement in human affairs."

"What kind of conditions do you see?"

"Conditions where countless numbers of people, like yourself, are pursuing a redefinition of life-supporting values."

"But, James, on a practical level, I'm just inventing a product."

"I think if you look at the promise of what life could be, you will find you are doing more than inventing a product."

Tomo had struggled for an overview, hoping it would clarify James's proposition. "So the implicit promise of what life could be, compared to what it has become, has set up a kind of social tension that has motivated people to seek a definition of 'The More' as you call it."

"Yes, and there are other enabling trends that drive positive change."

"Such as?"

"Well, our increased understanding is coupled with the enabling technology to communicate that understanding."

Tomo had paused while checking the mechanism of a spring-loaded rock-climbing device. "I can see how technology has helped us scale mountains, but I'm at a loss to understand how it translates to real social change."

"Tell me about the technology of your anti-theft device."

Tomo had furrowed his brow as if the functioning of his own technology was evading him. "Well, it's kind of a by-product of plasma-physics, sub-micro-chip and photo-electron technology. We can encode any plastic or metal object with what amounts to an invisible bar code. These microscopic encoders have transmitting capacity, so if a receiver is tuned to that item's frequency, it will send an identifying signal that can be tracked."

"Why can't the crooks get a receiver and strip the codes off?"

"Short of burning them off, they won't come, but more importantly, the signal blurs when you're less than seven feet away. This means the code emanates so you can find the item via the transmission code, but it is impossible to pinpoint the code location on the item. Even if you smash the item flat, the code just lies there transmitting away."

"So, Tomo, tell me how long has this technology existed?"

"Well, it's totally emergent—it's not even a technology—it's more like the flowing together of several technologies at once. The specialists working on the project say the nature of its operation is complex in that it defies a logical, linear description."

"That's because it imitates nature in its complexity," James had said. "We are starting not only to see but to encourage the organic patterns of nature to develop solutions to complex social problems."

Tomo had been unconvinced. "That's fine for the development of high-tech, but how does that kind of thinking apply to social change?"

"As many of us question a loss in the quality of our lives, we represent a movement in social consciousness. These collective desires of society move us to insights that go beyond the framework of our current reality. This collective insight is organic in that the potential for change emerges from a broad network rather than a single authority. This interconnected thinking moves us from a narrow egocentric point of view to a broad world-centric view. The networks that allow us to communicate that world view will facilitate sweeping shifts of behavior."

"I don't see having better tools to communicate with enhancing the quality of what we communicate about," Tomo had replied.

"Well, take an issue like the concept of sustainability. On one hand, it's motherhood; no one would argue it's a global imperative. The events that shift us to sustainable ways of living will be enabled through our increased ability to communicate. But the events that trigger our will to communicate cannot be predicted in a linear fashion. They will arise from a broad understanding that networks to a new order of reality. Because, like your invention, that potential is beyond how we have framed our reality, we have trouble seeing how it will come into existence."

"You know, James, sometimes I think you understand the field I'm working in better than I do."

"I promise you, I don't." James had smiled as he'd looked down at the base of the rock face. "I can't even figure out why, with access to your technology, you're so worried about your car in the parking lot."

Tomo had looked up sheepishly. "The code only has a 200-kilometer transmission capacity, and I figure someone would be out of range before we could get off this cliff."

"You've got a value problem."

"No, I've got a distribution problem. To make the invention functional, it has to be pervasive on a national level—maybe even a global level—or the stolen goods will just get shuffled out of a protected zone."

"I suspect it will cost a lot to manufacture," James had challenged.

"Not at all. The technology has already paid for itself in supply to a few dozen specialized users. The coding itself is near zero cost. All the worth is in the intellectual property rights. I'll need an army of people to protect my patents alone."

"You do have a value problem," James had repeated.

"James, now I'm sure I don't understand you."

"Values endure because they uphold our life-supporting goals. Your invention is based on the fact that when these values become compromised by the structure, we must find ways to enforce them. Most of our organizations and institutions have been compromised to the point that resulting control mechanisms have become both the focus of their operation and the source of dysfunction."

"You're saying the traditional rules aren't working."

"We are a mature society living in adolescent structures," James had responded, staring out at the distant chain of mountains to the north. "We cannot establish our value goals by adding more complex control structures to existing control structures. But the patterns of nature are pointing us to new ways of being."

"This is the vision of the future you were getting into with the paper you sent us."

"Yes, that's right. By aligning man-made systems with the patterns of nature we can discover both physical and spiritual sustainability."

"It sounds ideal, but a transformation of this magnitude is too arbitrary to come together in sweeping change."

"I don't think so, Tomo. Many people are defining a new reality and as they act on those understandings, there will be a convergence of wills. We are moving to some universal understanding about our survival that must translate to action. The riddle is how this change comes about on a broader system's level. My sense is the answer lies in the kind of people we will be hiking with next week."

Tomo had grinned back at his partner. "And you said you didn't have an agenda."

James had smiled as he'd glanced at his watch. "I only said it was going to be an interesting meeting." Looking back at Tomo, he had added, "You all have the influence to be substantial change agents within the structures you operate. In effect, you have the enabling forces at your fingertips. The final enabler will be your decisions of value."

"So you're telling me that the success of my technology will depend on identifying an enhanced value based on the absence of control?"

James had not responded as he'd stood and stretched out his muscles; then, as though they had already refocused on their ascent, he'd added, "To me it should be approached the same way we do this glorious piece of rock. And to tell you the truth, we've invested too much time talking; let's climb."

As they had taken positions for the continued ascent, they'd agreed to go only as far as the next overhang. Then Tomo had remembered James' comment: "It was Rumi who said, 'Out beyond ideas of wrong-doing and right -doing, there is a field. I'll meet you there.'"

Now, Tomo saw that the last statement before the fall as more than a parting thought. Still immersed in reflection, Tomo was suddenly jerked back to the present when he felt the firm grip on the back of his neck.

—·—

"Sir, can I help you?"

He looked up, expecting to see James moving swiftly up the rock face. "Sir?"

Tomo attempted to respond to a stout woman in a white lab coat.

"Yes," he said, focusing on the 'Hospital Admissions' sign at the reception desk. "I'm looking for a patient of yours, James Garwood. He fell. I'm his climbing partner."

The receptionist punched the name into the keyboard and looked at Tomo as though she were going to observe hospital regulation, then appeared to change her mind.

"He's in emergency admissions, through there, second door on the left."

A Compelling Life: *Going without the leader*

Kim leaned over the bed in a light cotton dress, holding James' right hand softly. From his left hand, cables trailed over the stiff white sheets to a cluster of technology.

As the door opened, Kim's focus of concern moved to Tomo—to the thick wave of hair plastered against his head by a mixture of sweat and dust, to a rope burn across his cheek, to both his muscular legs blood-stained from rock cuts.

"Tomo, are you alright?"

"I'm fine," he replied without apparent conviction. "How's James?"

"They've just finished some tests. I don't know the results. He's stable, thanks to how you handled him off that cliff.

"It was on the radio," Kim explained, seeing his questioning look. Tomo had not told her the details of the evacuation when he called. "Eye witnesses said they couldn't believe how quickly you and the rescue team brought him down."

"They wanted to move him quickly." Kim noted almost a defensiveness in Tomo's voice.

"And they were right—if he had been bleeding internally or had stopped breathing—time is everything." Kim could see that her assurances were not making Tomo feel any better. She thought of the anxiety she had felt in similar situations, and a welling of resentment surfaced for both herself and Tomo.

"I've stood over this man too often as he has teetered between this world and the next," she said.

Tomo seemed as detached from reality as his unconscious friend. "He looks like a cherub," the climber replied. "Wherever he is, it must be very tranquil."

"Two years ago, we were back-country skiing," Kim said softly. "At one point, James went ahead to check out an exposed slope. His weight set off an avalanche. I watched as he stayed on the surface swimming with the sliding snow, but as it slowed, a thicker uphill mass overtook him and he was buried. I raced to where I thought I would find him and started probing frantically with the handle of my ski pole.

"Ten minutes later, through my exhaustion and despair, I hear a mocking voice say, 'I didn't know you cared.' I turn and this little head was poking out of the snow 50 meters down hill. After I had skied down and pulled him out, I said, 'How did you ever dig out of that?' He looked up as though nothing had happened and replied, 'Digging is the easy part. Knowing which direction to dig is tricky. I packed a big air pocket before the snow settled and dropped my glove in the dim light—it fell up—so I knew I had to dig down to get out of this pile.'"

Kim watched Tomo studying her face before saying, "I wish he would find his way to the surface now."

Kim looked down at James in silence, waiting for him to respond. Several minutes passed then Tomo said, "I guess we should phone the rest of the group and call off the West Coast Trail trek, at least for now?"

As he spoke, James' parents—he a distinguished gray-haired man, and she a handsome elder woman—hurried in. Behind them, a man in medical garb followed.

James' parents moved to Kim and hugged her as if they were greeting a daughter. She choked back the tears as Mrs. Garwood moved instinctively towards her son, and James' father approached Tomo. He raised his hand in acknowledgment, placing it at the back of Tomo's neck exactly as James had earlier. "We really appreciate how well you looked after James."

Kim watched Mr. Garwood's sincere recognition, and felt she could see Tomo's spirit being lifted as if on some platform made of security and trust. Kim had had enough exposure to James' family to know that they were the source of his positive vision—this proved it. She let the moment sink in, reflecting on the origins of James' inspired freedom, while the optimism swelled inside her.

Introductions were quickly exchanged between Tomo, Jean and Bob Garwood and the man who had accompanied them, Dr. Jeff Craig.

"What can we expect from here?" James' father asked Dr. Craig.

"We have completed x-ray and a C.T. scan of the head. There doesn't appear to be any clotting or physiological damage," Dr. Craig reported in a clinical manner that failed to hide the compassion in his eyes.

"Can you give us any indication of what we should expect?" Bob asked.

Dr. Craig took a measured breath as though not wanting to imply any promises in his response. "We rate unconsciousness on what is called a Glasgow Coma Scale. Three signifies deep coma, 15 represents an alert/normal condition. Right now, James falls in the deep coma range, because he is not responding to pain stimulus. His vital signs are strong, so we are not moving to sedate him or introduce oxygen support. Time will tell how quickly he comes out of it."

Dr. Craig turned his glance to Jean and then Kim. "I'll be on shift all night," he said before excusing himself.

As the door pulled itself shut with a click, all eyes had returned to James. It occurred to Kim a wait without schedule had begun; it erased the importance of all other schedules.

"Tomo was suggesting we should phone the others and call off the West Coast Trail hike," Kim offered.

James's mother looked up. "I understand you have people coming in from different parts of North America for this trek. There is little any of us can do until James comes to, and we'll be here when he does." She looked to Bob. "If the party is still willing, we'd suggest you carry on. We know it's important to James that you meet."

Tomo looked over at Kim. She had her lips set in a determined manner and was nodding her head.

"We'll make the calls now and see what the group wants to do," Tomo responded.

Being immobilized and unable to help James had made them anxious, and Tomo jumped at the opportunity to do something constructive. Within 20 minutes, they returned to the room, having spoken with Celine in Montreal, Paul in Denver, and Zahir in San Jose.

Each of James' friends had immediately said they would come to Vancouver. After hearing the circumstances and the recommendation of James' parents, each had agreed they would proceed as planned unless James' condition changed.

Two days later, final preparation had been made, and everyone was ready to go except James, who had shown no change. Bob and Jean Garwood were at the hospital when Kim and Tomo made their final visit. Allowing themselves to think only of James' absence in finite terms, they talked candidly about how different the trip would be without him.

As Tomo and Kim readied to leave, Bob took Kim's hand and spoke with empathy typical of his son. "James is a hard man to love. He compels us to live life to the fullest, and it's not easy at times."

She hugged the elder Garwood man and said, "That's why I'm going."

The Goal: *Seeing the journey's end*

James, Tomo and Kim were to have been the advance party for the West Coast Trail hike, which involved dropping a car off at the southern end of the trail. This would ensure ready transportation at the end of the trek. Tomo and Kim would now complete this task.

They started by catching an early-morning car ferry to the southern tip of Vancouver Island, a giant finger of land twice the size of England, which protects southern British Columbia from the open Pacific. Both Tomo and Kim were familiar with this island-dotted passage, so after breakfast they found a comfortable spot to read their books. The journey passed as they relaxed with the scenery that occasionally pulled their attention into new conversations.

In the middle of Active Pass, both Tomo and Kim looked up as the ferry, laden with 400 cars, listed during a sharp starboard turn between Galiano and Mayne Islands. The massive ship navigated so close to the shore it seemed they could reach out and touch the arbutus trees that curved over the low rock bluffs.

As the ferry slipped though the channel, the view opened up again to an archipelago of Gulf Islands.

"This really is beautiful," Tomo said. "I'm wishing more and more I could have talked my wife into coming."

"Is she not an outdoors person?" Kim asked.

"Oh, yes. She loves to get out in nature, but the demands of her work are incredible."

"Really. Where does she work?"

"She is with a large brokerage firm — climbing the corporate ladder," Tomo added with some reservation.

"Well, that's great, if that's what she wants," Kim replied.

"No, actually she hates the environment. What she really wants is a family."

"But not you," Kim said

"I guess that is something I am trying to work through," Tomo said. "It's not the added responsibilities or anything like that. My concern is just the kind of world we are bringing kids into today."

"I'm exposed to a lot of that world," Kim said with empathy.

"Is that through the educational program you've developed?"

"Yes. The program creates better teaching conditions for underprivileged kids. But there's a lot to do in the general population, I'm afraid."

"Yes, I guess so," Tomo said, sounding quite distant. "Population is the very thing that concerns me. With six billion people on the planet doubling every 36 years, we need to define some quick solutions, or nature's limits will define them for us."

Kim looked down at her reading, then thought better of it. "The population explosion is not going to be solved by the few who are concerned, denying themselves a family. We need to grow smarter and it seems to me any progeny of yours would be part of the solution."

"Thanks. I appreciate that."

Kim got a strong feeling that Tomo was no longer interested in pursuing the conversation. She looked out the window as they neared the ferry terminal. She thought of how similar she and Tomo were. Once you scratched the surface, you got to a personal life that was unresolved. She wondered if Tomo and his wife had been deferring the family they wanted because of some other pursuit or if they were really that concerned about the world they would be bringing children into.

Her mind wandered as she thought of the pursuits she and James had set as goals over the years. Now, with him absent in a way she had never experienced, she silently questioned what ends those efforts had been towards. To her mind surfaced the words of Richard Bach:

> When we come to the last moment of this lifetime,
> and we look back across it, the only thing that is
> going to matter is 'What was the quality of our love?'

The thought brought her a sense of peace that the goals she and James had set as individuals and the relationship they shared held some connected meaning.

As the ferry approached Swartz Bay, an announcement asking passengers to return to their cars interrupted her thinking. Emerging from the hollow cavern of the ship, she parked her car at the roadside and waited for Tomo to pull up behind her. They then drove in tandem for two hours to the east side of the island where they would leave one car near the government dock at Port Renfrew.

When they arrived, Kim locked the drop-off car, put her pack in the trunk of Tomo's car and jumped in the passenger seat. Kim looked out across the broad bay of Port San Juan feeling ambivalent about the journey ahead. Her mood stood in contrast to the bright summer day.

Tomo spoke first. "A week from now, we will have completed the circle back to this point." Kim sensed he was trying to ease the anxiety of beginning.

She looked to the far side of the bay and detected a fluorescent orange speck in the forest. She knew this was a signal at Thrasher Cove indicating that hikers had finished the trail and were waiting to be picked up by boat. "It's a switch to be so certain where things will end."

"There's lots of uncertainty, but the goal is clear," Tomo replied as if aware she was thinking of James.

Kim scanned Tomo's Caucasian features, and saw tension under his smooth olive skin. "I suspect life would be clearer if we examined more of our end goals," she said.

Tomo seized the lighter mood. "I guess that's why we're on this journey. Shall we get going?"

They left the southwest corner of the island on an abandoned logging road that cut back to the eastern shore, then headed north up the long slice of land toward their final destination for the day. They were to meet the others at Port Alberni the following morning. This active logging town, only 20 kilometers from the east coast of the island, was a major service port for the more remote western shores.

From Port Alberni, access to the west coast was accomplished through the 50-kilometer Alberni Inlet that emptied into the equally long and wide Barkley Sound. These were the waterways they would be cruising down to start the hike, disembarking at the small fishing settlement of Bamfield.

Each of the other hikers were reaching Port Alberni by different means of travel. The group had made arrangements to meet the next morning on the *Lady Rose*, a 1930s vintage cargo and passenger ship that plied the inland waterways. The *Lady Rose* took supplies to the remote communities on the West Coast, including an ever-increasing stock of hikers to and from the West Coast Trail.

Kim enjoyed the day driving through booming seaside towns. As the coastal scenery and conversation passed, they became less dependent on their common bond with James and started to form their own.

Leaving the sprawling coastal town of Nanaimo and turning inland toward their destination, Tomo directed the discussion back towards James. "Kim, you mentioned life would be clearer if we examined our end goals," he stated.

"Yes."

"That rings true to me particularly when I think of James and how he seems to squeeze the juice out of life."

"What are you getting at, Tomo?"

"He is clearer than anyone I've ever known," Tomo replied, obviously searching out some perceived contradiction, "but I really can't put my finger on what his life goal is."

"It's not easy," Kim replied. "James operates from a deep calling."

"Do you mean like a religious calling?"

"No." Kim laughed, relieved she didn't have to explain her statement. "James had his opportunity to follow the path of formal religion."

"Was he considering becoming a priest?"

"During his last year of undergraduate school, he got permission to live in the seminary at the University of British Columbia — that is, until they threw him out." Kim's broad smile beamed over at Tomo.

"I can just see James running amuck in a theological school," Tomo replied as they shared a laugh.

"I don't know if I ever got the whole story," Kim said, "but James wrote me when he was there saying he had entered hoping to find out why these people had received 'the calling' and he hadn't. I think he used the Socratic method, questioning the students about the nature of their calling and what they saw their mission to be."

"Trust James to be out there asking all the tough questions," Tomo replied. "No wonder they threw him out."

"He wasn't disappointed to get thrown out. He was disappointed in the answers he got from the students," Kim said. "I remember his letter saying, 'The only call these people have received is one from medical school or law school saying their application had not been accepted. Theology by default further institutionalizes dogma.'"

Tomo laughed hard this time. "James has had a long history of chasing charlatans. He hates impostors. I remember in the second year of grad school he asked me to help him set up a student court to impeach blatantly incompetent teachers."

"I'm surprised he didn't get thrown out again," Kim said, remembering the incident.

"I think the Board of Governors at the university welcomed the unrest because they knew the tenure system, set up to create academic free thought, had created academic entitlement." Kim noted Tomo's big smile of satisfaction. "How things have changed. Now professors are afraid to say anything controversial for fear of reprisal from some student group."

"Reinforcing even more pervasive mediocrity," Kim said. "I think the accountability James was trying to force on campus is now happening globally through the virtual campus and distance learning."

"Yeah, the fat is really getting cut out of the system, but I sometimes wonder if James himself has gone soft," Tomo said. "When he first got involved in corporate life, he used to be brutal on the pretenders sitting in board and senior-management positions."

"I think that's where he had to evaluate where his calling really was," Kim said.

"What do you mean?" Tomo inquired.

"James has always felt the "pretenders", as you call them, are in a position to inspire others to better ways. If you conclude they can but won't, then you spend your whole life exposing one pretender after another. If you believe that people will move towards a better way, when they understand it will solve limitations of the current way, then your orientation is to define that positive view."

Clearly absorbed by what Kim had said, Tomo was silent as they wound their way through the massive first growth trees of MacMillan Park. "So James' 'calling' is trying to define the vision to a better way, and that is the goal of the paper he sent us."

"Yes. That better way suggests the accelerated rate of change today is a precursor of society's readiness to move to a new standard. This is a point of view that interests me from a learning perspective."

"Do you think this new standard can be taught?" Tomo inquired.

"A standard which maintains we can both identify and pursue our passion means that which is most relevant to our lives is attainable. I know James has helped people find this authentic self, and I believe he is correct that it is an attainable goal on a systems level."

"Put in those terms, I can see why James has focused on the notion that society is moving to better purposes," Tomo said as they drove past the "Welcome to Port Alberni" sign.

Kim smiled, feeling Tomo had conceded the point prematurely. "In a sense, we are all pretending that the world as we find it today is simply a condition we need to accept. We have learned to be passive about our own deepest goals, so it follows we have become passive about our vision for society."

Tomo appeared vexed. "A pretend world?" he repeated, as though seeing a contradiction.

"Cheer up, Tomo. Where we're going it's very real."

Tomo chuckled as he spotted the hotel they had planned to stay at and drove in. "Completing the West Coast Trail has been one of my goals, but I must admit I'm glad you've experienced this trek before."

"I'm glad both of us have wilderness experience," Kim replied, looking back to Tomo as the car stopped, "because, once you've defined the goal, the real adventure begins."

Part 2: *Concept*

Surfacing an Awareness: *The endless field of light*

P arking close to the quay where the *Lady Rose* was moored, Tomo and Kim organized the last of their gear and helped each other on with their packs. It was an hour before the 8 a.m. sailing, and the sun shone warmly through the fresh high-tide air.

The quay was putting on its best tourism face with little help from its immediate neighbor, the largest saw and pulp mill in British Columbia. The latter marked its presence with tall effluent stacks that belched an endless gray cloud into the blue sky. On the foreshore, platforms of boomed logs lay like a chain of floating football fields.

As Kim and Tomo walked down the pier, Tomo caught an unexpected whiff of donuts cooking. While Tomo detoured for the indulgence, Kim allowed that hers would be calling to check on James. She dug into the side pocket of her pack and pulled out a miniaturized cell phone. Within moments, Tomo returned with a dozen sugar twisters.

"Well, there's five of us," he said defensively.

"Super," Kim replied. "I'm sure they'll go fast. I took a moment to call the hospital. There's been some improvement with James, but nothing that would find him joining us. Let's see if we can find the others."

Moving along the pier, Kim spotted the *Lady Rose*, the boat's classic lines recognizable immediately. Continuing to walk, they scanned the dozen plus people moving about with packs. "It would be nice to locate everybody before we sail," Tomo said. "What descriptions do you have?"

"Well, I once had dinner with Paul and his wife," Kim said. "He's probably pushing 40, medium height, athletic build, chiseled facial features and prematurely gray hair. Zahir is dark-skinned and very tall like a basketball player. He's in his early 30s. I remember James saying he had kind eyes. Celine is probably about the same age, I've only spoken with over the phone, but I did see an annual report with her picture in it. She speaks with a French accent and is very pretty. You'll be able to pick her out of a crowd—she has eyes the size of those donuts."

As Kim was speaking, Tomo had been looking about and had spotted a man with dark hair and complexion. "The tall fellow over near the gateway to the *Lady Rose* may be Zahir. Let's go check it out."

As they moved toward the end of the dock, Kim took Tomo's elbow. "I think I see Paul. Let me get him, and we'll catch up with you."

Walking across the dock it occurred to Kim that, in the short time she had spent with Paul and his wife, they had seemed to be a couple that utilized each moment of their lives. It was not a surprise to see him reading now. "Hi, Paul. Welcome to the West Coast."

Paul looked up. His steel-blue eyes had gray shards that matched the wave in his thick hair. He rose to hug her, ignoring the pack on her back.

"That James is always getting you to do his work," Paul said. "How are you, and how is he?" His Czech accent underscored his sincerity.

Kim knew Paul was acknowledging her strength. "Thanks, Paul. I'm fine. They think James is improving. Maybe doing his work is what we're all up to here."

Paul laughed as he nodded his head. "Where are the others?"

"I think Tomo and Zahir have connected at the head of the dock," Kim said as she helped Paul hoist his pack onto his back.

"I know Tomo and James go back a long way. How does Zahir fit in?" Paul posed as they moved toward the *Lady Rose*.

"He and James met running drugs," Kim replied with an impish grin.

"And to think my wife let me leave her at home with two little ones because she thinks James is a saint," Paul teased back.

"It's your wife that's the saint."

"Now that is the truth."

They approached Tomo and Zahir, who were discussing the kind of gear they had brought in preparation for the trail ahead. As Tomo and Kim shared introductions, Tomo noticed a striking dark-haired woman approaching their group. "You must be Celine," he said.

The others turned as she replied, "You must be the Garwood group. I knew we'd be easy to spot. We are the only ones doing first introductions at the start of a week-long voyage." Her French accent rolled across a broad smile, and everyone laughed at the issue already behind them.

Boarding had just commenced, and they decided to move directly onto the *Lady Rose* to find seating. Crossing the gangplank mid-ships, they passed between the wheelhouse and the covered stairway leading below ships. They headed to the stern, where two rows of high-back curved white benches faced out to ocean views.

The Garwood group settled into the smooth, sculptured seats that radiated the heat of the sun. Tomo and Zahir opted to sit on their packs and lean their backs against the railings, the water lapping against the hull directly below them.

As the comments died down about the physical adjustment they would have to make to the loads they were carrying, Paul spoke: "Kim, you mentioned James is improving."

"He is still unconscious," Kim said, aware of everyone's attention. "But they got a response this morning when they gave him a pain stimulus. If we are lucky, this may lead to voluntary movement and, who knows, maybe he'll come out of it."

"I can't help but think that James' determination alone will pull him through," Paul offered. "How are you doing, Tomo?"

"Half of me is still waiting on that cliff," Tomo responded, before launching into the story of the Black Dyke ascent and fall. As he stressed how supportive and understanding James' family had been, he looked at Kim, acknowledging her role without drawing attention to it.

Zahir asked, "What drives a person to accept such danger as a constant part of their life?"

The silence that followed made it clear the group needed to speak of James.

"You know, Zahir," Kim said, "I don't think it is a willingness on James' part to accept danger. It's a sense of living where decisions are actively engaged. I can almost pinpoint the time James became aware of how he could make these kinds of choices."

A whistle sounded as the Lady Rose moved away from the dock, but no one looked away from Kim's face

"When I was 14, our family rented a cottage on an island up the coast of British Columbia. James' family spent their summers there, and he and his buddies shared a kind of Tom Sawyer existence. Being a stranger to the place, I had no history and seemed to fit in better with the boy's activities, but there were still certain privileges held "for men only." I knew I had been accepted the day they asked me to run the logs with them."

Kim looked at the log boom as the Lady Rose did a large sweeping turn in front of the industrial complex.

"In those days, there was still easy harvest of first-growth timber on the south coast. The logs would be rafted and towed for processing at places like this." She pointed over the railing to the boomed logs and mill.

"During the east winds, the tugs would shelter their booms in the large protected bay where we camped. That's when the boys would go out, against their mothers' wishes, and run along the bobbing mass of logs. I joined in the races across the block-wide expanse of logs, where the reward was diving into the crystal clear northern water on the other side.

"One time, trailing the pack, I saw James fall in the water and the massive logs close off above him. We all ran about, trying to find or make a crack he could escape through. For a moment we saw his skinny arm poke through the logs, but we still could not pry the logs apart."

As Kim spoke, she watched the wake of the *Lady Rose* break over the boomed logs, causing them to undulate in a serpentine movement. A chill went up Kim's spine.

"We were stunned with fear, and I was sure James had drowned. Suddenly we heard the water break at the edge of the boom and looked up in time to see James' entire body leave the water as he surfaced.

"As we fished him out, it was clear something had happened to James under that boom. I think he made a choice in those few minutes about how he was going to live."

Kim's eyes narrowed as if viewing something in the distance. "I remember later, the adrenaline rush had subsided and the boys filtered home for dinner. James and I were sitting on the beach and he spoke of his revelation—of the victims that have no choice.

"He said that when he was trapped under the boom, he thought of the trees whose stumps stand in the bush like huge tombstones to consumption; of the deer that sink with a bullet, chased off the island in the name of sport; of the fish and seal washed up on the beach, oil-soaked by some coastal freighter that had exercised the right of God to create its own little natural disaster.

"It was seeing that we, unlike all the other creatures of nature, have a choice in life. That was what led him to a flash of insight."

"Insight about life?" Zahir interjected.

"Yes, his," Kim confirmed. "At the point of having expended any usable oxygen, he remembered he was only 10 meters from the edge of the boom when he fell in. He pushed himself deep in the water to scan the upper horizon of floating timbers. He saw shadows and the light from the south-western afternoon sun being cast under the boom. He scanned the length of the boom. Two mammoth arrows of shadow stood at either end like massive exit signs. He could now see the field of light before him and realized then that if he did not reach the light, he was dead.

"I remember exactly what he said on the beach that evening at the tender age of 15: 'I made a choice right then, I was going for the endless field of light.'"

Quality of Choice: *Transformational change*

The silence that had fallen upon the group, absorbed in Kim's story, was broken by a great belly laugh. Everyone looked over at Zahir, who was trying to regain his composure.

"That sounds like James," Zahir said. "Animal-wild one minute and priestly-wise the next."

Kim and the others laughed at the truth in Zahir's comment, but Kim felt as if James were close as she watched diamonds of light dance on the water just a few feet away.

"It's interesting how an awareness of choice plays such a large role in James' life," Paul said. "I think that was the quality that first attracted me to him."

"Are you saying that James helped you make some major decisions?" Kim asked.

"He helped me see choice in an active way that led me to a better quality of life." Paul squinted at the patches of second-growth timber across the narrow channel as if trying to capture some piece of history. "When I first met James, over a decade ago, my business was new. I was a fairly recent emigrant from what was then Czechoslovakia, and James seemed aware of the huge choices I had made in my life at that time."

"You mean the decision to leave your country?" Zahir asked.

"Yes. My parents were married in 1948, the same year the Communist Party seized power in Czechoslovakia. Their families had built substantial holdings, all of which were expropriated by the government. As I grew up, my parents were not bitter about the loss of their possessions so much as about their loss of choice. Their entire generation watched the bread basket of Europe in the 1930s become the waste basket in the 1950s."

"Didn't it start with the Communists getting voted in? When it proved to be such a damaging system, why wasn't there more resistance?" Zahir queried.

"The Communists had been treated harshly by the Nazis in the war," Paul said, "and the Czechs and Slovaks were sympathetic to the Communist appeal for social justice. Their movement to power in Prague was known as the bloodless revolution. But once the new regime was in control, the blood of political prisoners, who were our former elected officials, flowed freely in the Prague jails."

"Weren't people outraged?" Zahir persisted.

"Yes, but by the time the Communists had established military control, the ability to attain reliable information, let alone mobilize around it, was nearly impossible. In the spring of 1961, there was great speculation that the regime would be defeated, but the public was not able to break the hold of those who enjoyed party power and privilege. Nearly a decade later, I was old enough to get an exit permit for a vacation from which I have yet to return."

Celine had been listening intently. "In the late '80s, the bank sent me to Czechoslovakia to study the possibility of guaranteeing loans made by the government. I recommended not proceeding because the government told a very different story than the public. People would carry a Communist card because it was the ticket to the most basic privileges, but they speculated constantly about the fall of the regime. It really was the tyranny you say it was, but it took so long for the system to correct."

"Not unlike the systems we live under," Paul said.

"How can you compare them?" Zahir asked.

"I think whenever we become oblivious to choices, either by suppression or complacency, we are vulnerable to the tyrant—to oppression," Paul replied.

Celine was on Paul's wavelength. "Oppression is an appropriate description for the place I work," she said.

"How can you compare Western institutions with a former East Block dictatorship?" Zahir asked Celine, obviously enjoying his devil's advocate role.

"I'm not comparing the oppression, just the attitudes of the oppressed. We are card carriers in the sense that we comply to receive privileges from an economic system which increasingly fails to represent our real needs."

"But changing the economic system is impossible," Zahir responded.

"We seem to forget that the economic system is not divinely ordained, but simply a man-made set of rules," Celine responded without a trace of challenge in her voice. "It is becoming more clear that the way the system measures our well-being has left us with very few choices in regard to the quality of life."

Zahir looked around at the group. "Kim, what's your take on this?"

"To see the public as 'complacent' and the system as 'oppressive' is to see us having made poor choices," Kim replied. "I think we make the best choices based on our awareness at any given time. But we have reached a new understanding about the finite nature of the earth and are beginning to see ourselves capable of making judgments in how the system can be improved. That's where real transformational change is happening."

Kim knew she had not answered Zahir's question directly, but before she could continue their attention, the ship pulled into the small floating community of Kildonan. Paul and Zahir stood at the railing as the crew delivered bags of mail to the modest floating post office. Zahir made some joke about "sea-mail," and as fast as the ship landed, it was off again. As the group settled, Kim wanted to return to Paul's story because she sensed it would illustrate a quality of choice. "Paul, I'm interested to know why James' understanding of the choices you had made were so important to you."

Paul watched the little outpost disappear behind the headland. "When I came to America, the freedom to choose seemed so unencumbered," he said, turning back to Kim. "My first reaction was to try to find a way to fit in. As time passed, it seemed to me that the oppression I had sought to escape in the

East was being embraced in more subtle forms in the West. James put a lot in perspective for me by pointing out that humanizing forces will eventually address inequities in all walks of life.

"His positivist philosophy encouraged me to actively engage in my beliefs," Paul acknowledged to Kim as the ship returned to cruising speed. "We structured Beerman and Associates on democratic principles of shared decision making, collaboration and equality, and found that it quickly attracted like-minded people."

"My experience working with James as a consultant is similar," Celine said. "But for all he's done, our organization finds it easier to deny change and stay rooted in entrenched practices."

"There's a lot of denial going on," Kim offered.

"I can't deny my grumbling stomach," Zahir interjected. "Who wants a burger?" He quickly took orders and disappeared mid-ship.

Tomo had been watching the scenery as they cruised 40 kilometers down the Alberni Inlet, a sliver of water seldom wider than a canal. Now the *Lady Rose* had begun to rise and fall on almost imperceptible swells as the ocean reached up the protected waterway. Looking ahead, one could see the inner Octopus Islands and gaps of endless horizon beyond Barkley Sound.

Kim had noticed that Tomo seemed content listening to the conversation as the group got their cultural bearings, but at this point he appeared obliged to jump in. "Your discussion about change is starting to cross paths with one that James and I had the other day. I never got a chance to ask him why he is so confident that we are at the point of major cultural change."

"It's major because the choice we hold as individuals leads us to make qualitative changes in how the system works," Kim said.

"I don't know, Kim," Tomo continued. "Our generation thinks they're the first ones to experience everything. In the '60s, the boomers thought they invented sex, and now we are the first ever to experience change."

Kim knew Tomo was up for the challenge. "I was still playing with dolls in the '60s, but I think the baby-boom we are part of is the first generation to face *personal* transformational change," she said.

"Oh, come on, Kim," Tomo responded with the familiarity of addressing a sister. "Are you telling me two generations that got stuffed into World Wars have not seen change beyond anything we've known?"

"The decisions that guided the last several generations came from an authority that was unquestioned by the public," Kim replied. "Doctors, lawyers, politicians, teachers, heads of organizations and heads of state were all above reproach. The kind of choices that will support a new vision for society will not come from those in control of the old vision."

"What you're really saying," Tomo asserted, "is that we have dethroned that group we called leaders. We have replaced authoritarian leadership with no leadership. To me, it sounds chaotic."

"Leadership is just one of the things being redefined," Kim responded. "The price we pay for exercising the quality choice is to realize it means the individual retains power. Until a new system of understanding emerges, regarding our use of this power, we live with chaos."

Paul smiled at Tomo's unwitting assistance in proving Kim's point. "That's why it's correct to say society has never faced such fundamental *personal* transformational change," he concluded.

Zahir had returned with a tray heaped full of burgers and drinks. "Ah, Paul, sounds like you're back on the topic of wrenching systems. One look at the size of these burgers makes me hope we can at least count on the digestive system. I'm the only New Age, so I got a veggie burger—the rest are beef for you prehistoric types."

Everyone laughed as the burgers and banter mixed together and the Garwood group enjoyed their first perspective of the wide-open Pacific.

The Trailhead: *Living beyond old growth*

The last glance of ocean had disappeared behind Aguilar Point, and the *Lady Rose* nestled down the narrow Bamfield Inlet. The Garwood party was at the railings discussing options for the balance of the day when the captain's voice was heard over a loud-speaker system.

"Attention, passagers. Il est 12:55 heure Standard du Pacifique. Nous allons amarrer à Bamfield Nord pour decharger des provisions et, ensuite, continuer jusqu'a Bamfield Sud ou les excursionnistes de la Piste de la Cote Ouest vont debarquer."

"What did he say?" Tomo asked.

"That we would be stopping off at the north side of Bamfield to unload supplies, and then they will drop us off on the south side," Kim said, just as the captain began to repeat the announcement in English.

"I think we should declare English the official language for this trip," Celine offered.

"Good idea," Kim replied.

The small quay on the northern side of the inlet had just come into view. From the water, it looked more like a movie set than a working village. In an act of defiance to the wild surroundings, several well-maintained buildings dotted the shoreline.

"What a beautiful scene!" Celine exclaimed. As the vessel drew closer, they could see that the main road was a waterfront boardwalk weaving down the inlet the full length of the town.

"Bamfield is known as 'Venice of the North,'" Kim offered just before the ship's horn sounded its arrival.

The vessel docked, unloading and loading pallets of foodstuffs, mail, machinery and fishing equipment, underscoring the working nature of the small community. No one spoke of the feeling they shared watching a scale of life that was compelling because it had to be real and not because it was trying to look real. The good feeling was overlapped by the warm breeze that held the seagulls aloft and the gentle nudging of the vessel against the dock that created a dolphin-like sound.

As they pulled away and headed across the small inlet to its southern shore, the group agreed to push down the trail that afternoon, rather than camp and wait until morning. They had heard a rumor that a few locals stood by with their trucks to run hikers to the trailhead. When they disembarked at a government dock on the south side, the self-appointed taxi service was waiting. Most of the dozen or so hikers jammed into a vintage pickup truck well worn by heavy loads and salt air.

Zahir and Paul stood in the box holding onto the roof while the others crouched on fender wells or their packs. Careening down the gravel road with a great billow of dust rising behind them, they crossed the peninsula to Pachena Bay.

Along the way, Zahir turned and shouted back to Kim, his large cotton shirt flapping like a square rigger-sail cut loose on his long pole-like frame. "Kim, how far will we be flying at this low altitude?"

Kim smiled up at him. "About five kilometers."

"How far is that?"

"It's a little over three miles," Kim shouted back.

"Thanks." Zahir resumed his braced position, making the truck look only slightly less top-heavy.

Tomo was sitting on the wheel well across from Kim. Speaking at close to normal volume, he said, "How did you Canucks get on the metric system when your largest trading partner and neighbor still speaks in inches, feet and miles?"

Kim rolled her eyes. "Twenty-five years ago, the United States had a plan to move from imperial measurements to metric. Our government was being copycat progressive and decided to make the move before the States. Subsequently, the plan was dropped in the U.S., but Canada was committed."

"Leaves a lot of us south of the border wondering what you're talking about," Tomo said.

"Don't feel badly, Tomo. We have a few generations of Canadians who don't know what the temperature is even after listening to the weather report."

"Seeing that you guys have made English the official language, maybe you will go one step further and make imperial the official measurement for this trek," Tomo said.

"I'll go along with that," Celine said. "Forty-six miles through the roughest coastal rain forest in the world sounds a lot shorter than 77 kilometers."

They laughed as the truck jerked off the main logging road and onto a lane that wove its way through giant trees to an informal parking area.

Kim had forgotten that a magnificent stand of first growth marked the entrance to this end of the trail. She had privately speculated when the group would first be taken by the impact of the forest, and now she had her answer.

In those few moments, the scale of everything had changed. The giant fir and cedar trees, wider at their base than the truck was long, obliged everything on the forest floor to follow the pattern they had set. As the truck, now dwarfed in its setting, came to a stop, there was an involuntary silence in the cool, moist air.

"It's like a cathedral," Celine said.

The moment of wonder broke to excitement as anxious people and heavy packs slid over the edge of the pick-up. Squaring with the driver, the Garwood group walked disjointedly out of the towering cavern to a bright, grassy field. They dropped their packs on a marshalling platform constructed around a mammoth tree at the clearing's edge and checked in at the warden's station where hikers jostled anxious to get on or off the trail.

The warden offered brief warnings about the hazards on the trail as each group of hikers signed in. Returning to their packs, the Garwood group loaded up with fresh water and prepared to head off. To everyone's surprise, they were the only group that had decided to start on the trail that day. "What do they know that we don't know?" Zahir asked, pointing over to the other hikers disappearing through an opening where the sound of surf penetrated a thin ribbon of trees.

"They've probably decided to start fresh in the morning," Kim said. "But the first part of the trail is very easy walking through the woods. It's a little under six miles to the Pachena Point Lighthouse, which should take us about three hours. If we feel good when we get to the lighthouse, there are great campsites along the beach not far beyond."

Full stomachs and a morning of sitting still on the *Lady Rose* encouraged everyone to follow Kim's local knowledge. Eagerly mounting their packs, they adjusted straps and belts, trying to determine the friendliest position for this newfound weight. Satisfied that their loads were as comfortable as they were going to get, the group did a final check of each others' gear to make sure everything was secure.

Paul, looking over the outside of Tomo's pack, took interest in a metal object that looked like a multi-pronged pick folded neatly into a compact sleeve.

"That's quite a weapon," he said inquisitively.

"That's a rappelling hook," Tomo replied as they headed off. "I've always wanted to climb an old growth Sitka Spruce. This on the end of a rope should help me get there."

"I'll be satisfied just getting over the ground," Paul quipped.

Passing the sign that read "Camp Ross/West Coast Trail," they stepped immediately into old growth-forest on a path the width of a one-lane road.

The massive trees grew with towering independence. Some, cased with bark as thick as flagstones, tilted off vertically as if reaching for a patch of sun high aloft. Others grew straight and smooth for 200 feet before spreading their symmetrical branches. The sun filtered through the high canopy, casting an aura of light on the forest floor and its inhabitants.

"This is breathtaking," Celine said.

"This is old growth at what they call a 'climax state,'" Tomo said. "It's the forest's final stage."

"What do you mean by final stage?" Zahir asked.

"If this forest were cut or burned off, the first thing that would grow is fireweed, shrubs and alder," Tomo replied. "Douglas fir would grow next, but it can't regenerate in the shade, so it eventually gets replaced by a cedar and hemlock forest. That's what this is."

"So this forest lives on because the seedlings can tolerate the shade and reproduce themselves," Paul propositioned.

"Douglas fir is considered temporary, lasting around a thousand years," Tomo continued. "A climax forest like this is, of course, multi-age, and it can take up to 2000 years just to evolve."

"That's amazing," Zahir said. "I don't think I ever understood what 'old growth' really meant."

Kim remembered being equally impressed when first in an ancient forest. "You're right, Zahir. This is very unique, even in British Columbia. Here on the West Coast and in a few of the valleys we'll be crossing, high rainfall has allowed the forests to grow for thousands of years. Imagine, the Aztecs were just starting to build their pyramids when these trees were young."

"Unbelievable," Zahir said.

The trail crossed a mossy creek, then climbed the headland, leaving the sweeping vistas of the mile-long Pachena Beach and the sound of crashing surf behind. The bounding pace through the first stretch of trail slowed with their conversation.

Moving through the higher ground, the hikers relaxed their skyward gazes as their eyes now fell upon the rich forest floor covered with plants, mosses, ferns and lichens. They stepped over the rolling ground, pushed up by massive root systems, and started to notice how the trees supported their own vast colony of plant life and fungi.

Catching their breath, they moved down a flat stretch of trail passing a cluster of ancient cedars whose presence raised a comment from Celine.

"How can someone take a saw to a tree that is 1000 years old?" she asked.

"Forestry built this province," Kim offered. "But old habits are colliding with new attitudes."

"That seems to be happening everywhere," Celine replied, stopping to rest against the carcass of a wind-fallen cedar.

The others moved without question, relieving the weight of their packs against the thick radius of up-turned root. Tomo stood in the center of the path, obliging the need for a rest as he separated a thick clump of moss with his fingers.

"Society faces the same problem as this forest," he rebutted. "It's old growth at the final stage of maturity. Professional foresters refer to it as the decadent stage because it's susceptible to rot, decay and destruction by fire."

Resisting the analogy, Kim focused on the life of the forest floor and found herself becoming more uncomfortable with Tomo's implied conclusion.

Right beside Tomo, a great cedar tree rotting at the center balanced its tall body on long root legs. Beyond him, giants had fallen and nursed new growth from their decaying hulks. The forest conveyed a sense of majestic accomplishment and tired decay all at once, Kim thought to herself.

"Many argue that it is a time when nature creates a new dynamic of bio-diversity that is richer than the one that preceded it," Kim finally said, her comment grounded in feeling more than knowledge.

"This tree is certainly supporting a new dynamic," Zahir said, pointing his long arm down the direction of the fallen tree.

They followed his glance down the rotting mass that fostered no less than 100 small trees sprouting along its length.

Celine spoke in an uneasy tone. "If today's social structures are at the old growth cycle of full maturity and the movement of people exercising the quality of choice is the dynamic replacing an earlier vision, what ensures that this dynamic will rise above the over-bearing structure?"

"More importantly," Kim interjected, "when it does rise up, what ensures that the new dynamic is richer than the one that preceded it?"

Paul leaned against the horizontal bend in a distorted cedar. A sunbeam pierced the high canopy, framing the area in which he stood as though casting him in ascension.

"Scientists used to believe that natural systems ran down," he said as he threw his leg over the 90-degree bend in the tree trunk near ground level.

"Then we started to understand that nature is self-sustaining. The ecosystem as a whole is without waste because what is waste for one organism is food for another."

"Sustaining," Kim repeated as if the word didn't fit. "But nature doesn't run down; it runs up. Over billions of years of recycling the same molecules of minerals, water and air—somehow groups of organisms have evolved—this evolved—we evolved."

There was an empty silence as though the ancient forest was holding a secret they were trying to disclose.

"The Darwinian explanation of evolution does little to explain the infinite number of random mutations required to make a something as complex as a human being," Paul offered. "Somehow nature moves beyond in a manner that is more dynamic than we can explain in a linear fashion."

"From developing computer models, we have discovered that, through the chaos of countless iterations, patterns arise to demonstrate a new level of order," Zahir said. "System theorists refer to this as nonlinear dynamics, citing examples in which thousands of independent chemical reactions demonstrate the ability to transform into new patterns. It appears as though very subtle influences can trigger the system to massive forms of self organization."

"Like?" Tomo challenged.

"Like the rolling pebble that triggers the avalanche," Zahir responded. "Unstable systems that experience a high degree of feedback can move to dramatic new forms."

"You're suggesting this is evidence that natural systems self-organize to advance life," Tomo said.

"The spontaneous emergence of order arises from unique conditions," Zahir replied. "The organism is in a state of chaos, maximum amounts of energy are flowing into the system and it is very unstable."

"Are you saying life moves forward from its most chaotic state?" Tomo demanded.

"A new level of order underlying the seeming chaos," Paul proposed as he slid off the twisted tree and the others made a motion to get underway. "Every living thing on this forest floor is in some dynamic battle to live beyond old growth. Are we so different?"

As they moved back along the forest floor, Kim could sense that nature had achieved a new kind of living beyond old growth, but she was at a loss to say how it would take hold in the world of man.

A silent adjustment to the new environment took them to a bridge over the appropriately named waters of Black Creek, then up the meandering trail to higher ground. As they concentrated on catching their breath, Celine said, "Do I hear dogs barking?"

"Those are sea lions," Kim replied. "We can stop and view them from a lookout just up ahead."

In a short while, they reached the detour off the main trail and moved out toward the cacophony of honking. As they came to the edge of the cliff, Seal Rock and its several hundred inhabitants came into view.

"Holy Marine World!" Zahir exclaimed. "Look at the ruggedness of this coastline."

"It was the danger of this coast that first caught the attention of white settlers," Kim responded as a hundred sluggish brown seals barked skyward. "In the mid-1800s, the shipping trade had increased to the point where hundreds of sailing and early steam vessels would pass this coast each year.

"Due to the strong onshore winds and a heavy northerly current, several ships lost their bearings when heading for the passage between this large island and the American headland. As a result, there were so many shipwrecks on these shores it became known as 'the Graveyard of the Pacific.'

"After some heavy losses of life, this trail was put through around 1907, along with the lighthouse to which we're heading. By the 1950s, new radio and radar technologies eliminated the need for this trail and the telegraph line that ran along it.

"Funny thing is, Zahir," Kim continued, "it was the access afforded by the trail in the 1960s that got the public interested in the beauty and history of this place. If the trail had not been here, as part of marine commerce, development in the form of logging would have taken this forest."

"It still might," Tomo said as he rose from a crouched position. "I've heard they are logging so close to this trail you can see the clear cuts. That's the dynamic that rises above old growth," he added mockingly as he turned toward the main trail with the others following. "You're dreaming if you think our changing attitudes are going to reverse our habits of consumption."

Moving down the wider path, Paul seemed to be deep in thought. Kim and Celine walked beside him, and after some distance he spoke. "When resources were seen as expendable and inexhaustible, a consumption ethic made sense," he said. "They are habits we cling to even as new levels of understanding confirm our changing attitudes."

"The habit of consumption is tied to a system of measurement that resists our changing attitudes," Celine responded. "Our economic well-being is measured through our level of consumption or the number of dollars that change hands. We habitually measure success in ways that our changing attitudes reveal are detrimental to our well-being."

"Institutionalizing the wrong set of values is the source of the chaos," Paul speculated as they approached a clearing.

Zahir smiled back at Paul and repeated his earlier statement. "The organism is in a state of chaos, maximum amounts of energy are flowing into the system, and it is very unstable."

Paul returned the smile. "The consumption ethic was fine when man was taming frontiers, but habitual exploitation must be influenced by a new dynamic."

As Paul spoke, they approached an intersecting trail marked by a cluster of "Welcome" signs in a dozen languages. Tomo moved down the secondary trail several yards. "Speaking of taming frontiers, look at this."

Exploring an Ethic: *Caretakers with nature*

The group followed Tomo as the trail widened to a grassy field dominated by a red-domed lighthouse with white clapboard houses, and the sea beyond. Drawn by the tapered hexagonal shape of the lighthouse, they approached the settlement.

A covered area with a guest registry encouraged them along a concrete walkway, trimmed with flower gardens and a wide expanse of lawn on either side. Near the outer headland, they could see a man and woman crouched in a garden that rimmed the outbuildings.

The man rose immediately, waving as though the hikers were expected guests. "Good afternoon. You must be the lighthouse keeper?" Zahir said.

The older man smiled at Zahir, then rested his warm glance on Kim. "We are. I'm Mike and this is my wife, June. And you must be a fresh set of hikers moving south."

"It shows, does it?" Kim responded with equal warmth.

As June walked towards them with two freshly-cut roses in her hand, Mike said to Kim, "I don't know if I get more pleasure matching my roses to the beauty of the women starting the trail or to the magic held by those finishing." Mike smiled as if it were the first time he had said this line.

June handed the roses to Mike. "He charms all the girls with my labor, but he is such a sweet man," she said, putting her thin tanned arm around his thick shoulders.

Kim and Celine accepted their roses with coy delight. They all laughed as the refined exchange took place on the edge of the wild Pacific.

As they commented on the beauty of the settlement Mike's manner changed, as though some test of sensitivity had been passed, granting them entry to the grounds. His speech now seemed knowledgeable and assured. "This is the oldest standing wooden lighthouse on the coast. Please come, we would like to show you."

Kim exchanged a knowing look with June and accepted with an immediate echo from the group as they dropped their packs. "I'll wait here. I never fit in spaces like that," Zahir said, pointing to the curved glass wall at the top of the tower.

Approaching the lighthouse with Mike, they passed through a doorway in the flat stone foundation and climbed a labyrinth of wooden supports and stairways, finally entering the lens room. From the vantage-point at the top of the lighthouse, they could see beyond the undercut face of the cliff edge to the sea 200 feet below.

"This is unbelievable!" Celine said.

"Even moreso when you consider how dramatically nature can transform your meaning," Mike replied. "We've had hikers in this tower that we've revived from hypothermia, and seamen we've fished off the rocks. As they watch the storm rage on, yours is the one comment they all share."

"It's a very real existence you endure here," Paul said to Mike.

"The fact that it's real makes it less to endure," Mike replied. "As caretakers with nature, we've come to see the believable." Mike spoke in a tone of simple observation, and there was no response to what Kim felt might be his deeper meaning.

The hikers squinted as they looked down the coast they would be traveling. "It's hard today to see exactly where you're going," Mike said. "Your vision is not as clear as it could be."

Kim noticed that the mist from the salt air had obscured the view down the coast, but she couldn't help thinking that Mike was talking about a different kind of vision. She looked at him and he nodded. They shared a smile again, but this time his was more knowing than charming.

"How far will you be going tonight?" Mike asked.

Kim almost answered, "We'll probably explore the new dynamic," but she caught herself and said, "We thought we might head for Michigan Creek or one of the other campsites along the beach."

"Michigan's an easy half hour," Mike said. "It will be a beautiful walk in the late afternoon along the beach."

The inviting directions and a break from their packs found the hikers keen to press on. Leaving the dark tinder-dry cavity of the lighthouse, they squinted at the sun and blinked their way to where they had left their packs.

Zahir was over at the rose garden shaking hands with June. Within moments, they had their packs on, having said and waved good-bye.

Entering the trail, they found both the physical and psychological mood of the space different. It was after four in the afternoon and, although the northern sun would not set for hours, the light was lower now. Its reflection cast a warm radiance in the forest, and the colors blended together softly. They walked in single file on the narrow path that traversed around headlands, through gullies and between stands of leafy salal that grew in clumps 12 feet tall.

Zahir was in the lead, taking long relaxed strides. The mood was childlike as the others moved almost at a canter to keep up. "Did you find the meaning of life up there in the lens room with Mike?" Zahir asked.

"Somehow I think we missed it," Kim replied, "Why do you ask?"

"Old Mike back there has a Ph.D. in sociology," Zahir said. "June said he was dean of one of the universities here in Canada until five years ago when he packed it all in."

"Did June say why he left?" Kim asked.

"She said he had been working in social change theory but had reached some sort of impasse, believing people were not ready to move to what he calls 'The Ethic Shift'. She said that for the last five years he has been hosting hikers up in that lens room looking for some evolution in attitudes from people coming off the trail."

"I wonder what would have been said if we were finishing this trek?" Kim said.

"What do you mean?" Zahir asked.

"Oh, nothing," Kim replied. Then, changing the subject, she added, "June seems to understand his purposes."

"How does she feel about living out here?" Celine interjected. "It's a big sacrifice if it's just supporting his social experiment."

"I asked her the same question," Zahir replied. "She told me some remarkable stories about women who had come to this coast supporting someone else's dream and extended it to something beyond for themselves."

"What is hers?" Celine pressed as they moved together on a wider section of trail.

"I got to thinking as she told me these stories that service seemed to be a constant in leading these women to very meaningful lives," Zahir said.

"So," Celine said with a tone of skepticism. "Mike is attempting to define how society has to evolve, and he's married to a woman who lives the first principle."

"It seems Mike is living that principle also," Kim said. "I think that is what his 'caretaking' comment was about. Out here they can serve in an honest way without compromise."

"The whole idea of service has been turned into a marketing mantra," Tomo rebuffed.

"It's hard to reduce real caretaking to a public relations ploy," Paul responded. "I think Zahir is right. Women have traditionally been able to see service as a valid goal without a contingent reward."

"Women have been conditioned to serve, even though it was deemed second-rate to the development activities typically carried out by men," Kim said. "Now many people see the limits to development, and they're looking for other ways to find meaning. As men turn to service, they know it is a higher order, and they won't tolerate it being treated as a second-rate activity."

"We're hitting limits all right," Tomo retorted. "But I don't see a higher order; I see a feeding frenzy. Sort of a get-what-you-can mentality."

"Whether one's reaction is to help or to hoard, we agree on the fact that we are running to limits," Kim said. "It will take a different kind of applied intelligence to reverse this trend."

"I don't believe society will make that kind of change," Tomo said.

The conversation splintered as the group descended the headland, and moved towards the sound of the ocean. Stopping at a point where the trail neared the sloping foreshore, they viewed through the forest to the long white sand beaches beyond.

Paul had been trailing, apparently content to listen rather than shout his thoughts forward to the group. Now, as he stopped with the others, he said, "The Garwood paper acknowledged that, if society does not force us to replace the ethic of consumption, Mother Earth will."

"You know, Paul, you're right," Zahir said, "James said ecology has taught us that nothing we do is in isolation. There is no throwing anything away because there is no away."

"No local ecology. No local economy. No local society. No local ethic," Paul added. "Somehow, a new dynamic arises."

They stood in the filtered sunshine, immersed in the wild beauty as they made their first conscious connection to the ideas James had expressed.

"Mine is a world of old growth in decay. I don't see the new dynamic," Tomo said.

Kim knew they lacked the understanding to redress the reality Tomo spoke to, but she sensed some pattern was trying to present itself. The feeling lingered as Kim tried to raise the thought clearly enough for words, but she found none of her own. The feeling connected with something Mike had said back at the lighthouse: "As caretakers with nature, our vision will be clear."

Quest for Meaning: *The new reality*

Navigating through broken ground and exposed tree roots anchored in the side hill, the group made its way down to the derelict wooden bridge that spanned Michigan Creek. The beach sand moved up both sides of the creek, drawing the forest to a V-shape that ended at the decaying structure.

As they left the bridge and walked along the far side of the creek, they could see campsites hollowed out of the forest. No one seemed tempted to consider these locations, having viewed the inviting beach ahead.

The open expanse of white sand and crashing surf brought cheers from everyone. Tomo dropped his pack in the soft sand and started helping others lower theirs. A cool south-west breeze suspended the waves and the weight-less hikers in a refreshing mix. Cameras were dug out for photos of views in all directions, and trail mix of nuts and dried fruit were shared with long shots of water from a squeeze bottle.

"Sitting here in the middle of this high-pressure weather system, it's hard to believe how ugly the storms can get," Paul said.

"If you look at how all the trees at the edge of the shore are swept back, you know just how lucky we are to get this weather," Tomo added, glancing at the foreshore growth brushed back like a massive crew cut.

"Makes you want to take it all in," Zahir said.

"Look at the rock outcropping ahead," Celine added. "This beach is beautiful."

"You said there are other sites with water further down the beach," Paul said to Kim. "Sounds like we should go for it."

"Great!" Kim replied. "See how the beach slopes down to the sandstone shelf at the mid-tide level? The shelf will be a great walking surface until the tide moves in over it."

"Let's do it!" Zahir said.

They helped each other on with packs and moved down to the hard stone that tilted like a great washboard into the water. Walking on the driest portion of the plate, they spotted what looked like a big drum. As they approached the cylinder, they could see it was a large metal boiler about the size of a tanker car, lying with parts of a massive propeller and shaft.

"This must be the wreck of the *Michigan*," Tomo said as he reached into his breast pocket. He pulled out a little book titled *A Guide to Shipwrecks Along the West Coast Trail* by R. E. Wells, folded back to the page headed *Michigan,* and handed it to Celine.

Celine read the first sentence. "'Steam schooner, 695 tons, official number 92023, built in Skamokawa, Washington Territory, 1888, dimensions 158' x 34', lost January 21, 1893, one mile east of Pachena Point.'"

Celine looked at the accompanying drawing showing the *Michigan* on the rocks, with her long sweeping bow pointed up the beach as though she had navigated there intentionally.

"She was one of the first wooden steam schooners built in the Northwest," Kim said. "Like a lot of other vessels, she became disoriented in bad weather and, with the strong northerly current, overran her position."

The waves broke and gurgled up the shelf they stood on, reminding them they were there at the pleasure of an incoming tide.

"Same thing happened to the *Valencia* in 1906, about halfway down the trail," Zahir said, as they moved on. "Back at the lighthouse, June was telling me the *Valencia* was an iron steamship with 108 passengers and a crew of 65. Only 37 survived, no women or children."

"Was there no way of saving them?" Celine asked.

"They ran aground at night in bad weather and could not make shore due to sheer rock cliffs." Zahir said. "Rescue parties arrived by land and sea two days later, but the wreck was unapproachable. People who remained clinging to the rigging were eventually thrown to the sea as the ship was smashed apart."

A shudder seemed to move through the group as the ocean silently invaded the sandstone shelf.

"When the *Valencia* went down, the only light station was at a place called Cape Beale," Zahir said.

"That's on a point of land just north of the Bamfield area where we started the trail," Kim offered.

Zahir nodded. "When word of the *Valencia* wreck got to the station, the keeper's wife, Minnie, sat by her telegraph key for 72 hours trying to get word of the wreck to the outside world, and then she cared for survivors as they arrived.

"In December of that year, she gave birth to her fifth child. One morning soon after her son was born, they awoke to see the vessel *Colma* drifting toward the rocks. The storm that took the *Colma's* rigging also took out the telegraph line, so Minnie ran seven miles to the lighthouse tender in Bamfield Creek while her husband prepared to rescue people off the rocks.

"Wading through the water and knee-deep muck on the trail, it took Minnie four hours to reach the rescue boat and only an hour for them to reach the *Colma* and take the crew off. She insisted on returning that evening, and nearly perished doing so."

"Proving there are few rewards to caretaking," Tomo taunted.

"That's not how Minnie saw it," Zahir said. "Later that year, around Christmastime, the lighthouse was inundated with gifts and testimonials from seamen's societies, shipping companies and women all along this coast who had heard of her ordeal."

"Minnie was remembered to have said, 'If going over the trail in bad weather is worth all this, I had better do it every time it storms, so we can retire and go away from here.'"

Zahir paused at the sound of a few chuckles. "She didn't live to retirement. Within a few years, Minnie died, they say as a result of her ordeal on the trail."

The tidal water reached up the broad, finger-like stratifications in the rock, sending the hikers through various routes over the corrugated stone.

Soon they were all forced into the soft sand that was intersected by another creek that Tomo identified on his map as Darling River. The water was low and the creek passable in several spots where the channel curved deeply and narrowly in the sand.

Realizing it could not be jumped without getting boots wet, Tomo and Zahir detoured up the beach and retrieved a couple of log butt ends to use as stepping stones. Tossing them into place, Tomo hopped on one and then the other, rocking them until they were lodged firmly in the wet sand.

Zahir followed to the other side where the two men walked upstream, dropped their packs and scooped a drink from the crystal clear water. The others followed, resting on a hillock of sand near the creek, adjusting boots and straps on packs that had traveled awkwardly over the soft sand.

Tomo sat motionless, staring back in the direction they had come. "It's strange how some people fulfill their quest for meaning," he said, in apparent reference to Zahir's story about Minnie.

Paul smiled over at Tomo. "Before I met you, I thought 'Chief' referred to an native leader."

Tomo joined everyone in a laugh at himself as Kim took advantage of the moment. "The quality of choice continually deepens our quest for meaning," she said.

"People have always sought meaning in their lives," Tomo responded.

"In a simpler time, or with simpler issues, the relationship between things was less complicated," Kim said. "Take Minnie's act of courage, for example. The relationship between acting and not acting was painfully clear."

"Now, none of the relationships are clear," Tomo stated in a defeated tone, as he rose and hoisted his pack onto his back.

As Kim followed, Tomo moved to help with her gear. "I think we're learning to see ourselves as capable of making decisions in the context of a new reality that fulfills our quest for meaning," she said, as if to jolly him out of his mood.

"I wish I could share your ideal. I fear the old reality is gone and nothing is replacing it," Tomo said as he nodded to the head of this beach.

Kim followed Tomo's eyes to a jumble of timber and wire at the edge of the forest. "There must have been a bridge over this stream. I can't remember," Kim offered, knowing Tomo had made his point metaphorically.

"Want to check it out?" Zahir said to Tomo.

"Sure," came Tomo's response, directed more to Kim than Zahir.

"We'll wait for you at that sandy point down the beach," Paul said, as if calculating his next rest stop.

As Tomo and Zahir headed up the beach, Kim helped Celine, and they walked together to where Paul stood with stick in hand at the damp intertidal sand.

"I thought it might be good to leave Tomo a little message," Paul said, grinning with his stick resting on the last letter of the words he had written. *Old Reality/New Reality.*

Kim smiled, took the stick and wrote an example that described each of these categories. They moved down the beach, taking turns writing phrases in the sand. They taunted and quipped, scratching out words and replacing them with others. The laughter and debate moved down the beach in a quick first draft. Reaching the point of sand where they had agreed to wait, they watched Tomo and Zahir move toward them. Zahir was pointing his long arm to inscriptions in the sand, starting at the heading:

Old Reality/New Reality

Abundance/Limits
Simplicity/Complexity
Authoritative/Collaborative
Uniformity/Diversity
Repetitive/Innovative
Quantitative/Qualitative
Mechanistic/Humanistic
Parts/Patterns
Static/Dynamic
The hierarchy/The network
Evolutionary change/Spontaneous change
Man-made linear systems/Natural cyclical systems
Unsophisticated public/Knowledgeable stakeholders
Monetary consumptive economy/Social restorative economy
Institutional desensitized values/Personal caring values
Individual equity/Social equity
Material goals/Spiritual goals
Local vision/Global vision
Chaos/Transcendent order
Semantics/Meaning

As the two men approached the others, it was clear Tomo knew the lesson was for his benefit. "If I choose the *New Reality*, will I find meaning?" he challenged Kim.

Kim shrugged. "I suppose the quest for meaning begins by breaking down the habits of the old reality and establishing the habits of the new reality."

Tomo slowed to a stop, took a shot from the water bottle and passed it to Kim. "As dysfunctional as it might be, it's suicide to tear down a structure that supports you."

Kim held the nozzle away from her lips and squeezed. "Not if it's about to collapse," she said, as they started walking again.

"How can we expect to live the New Reality when it points us to some unknown vision of the future?" Tomo asked.

"Tomo," Kim responded, "we were raised, educated and hired to fit into the system. Now we feel an urgency to fix the thing we have been taught all our life to accept."

"Perhaps we should start by resorting our educational priorities," Tomo added doggedly.

"Education can teach new reality, but for fundamental change to happen, society must embrace a new global vision." Kim replied.

"So, Kim" — the challenge had now fallen from Tomo's voice — what makes you think the pursuit of that vision is something that we are moving toward?"

"The quest for meaning has become universal because we know the old reality is delivering us to an uncertain future. As we find the language to express a new world vision, a new system of belief will prevail," Kim replied.

Tomo stopped so abruptly that Kim almost walked into him. "Sorry, Kim," he said. "I could swear I saw a gray whale jum—Look!" Tomo shouted, pointing to a rock outcropping in the water ahead.

"I saw it," Zahir said.

"Me too," Celine added, as two more gray whales jumped out of the ocean almost at the same time.

The group hurried their pace, hoping the whales would remain until they got to the beach adjacent to the rocks. By the time they reached the point, they decided they were watching a pod of five, now less than a swimming pool away.

"Their bodies look enormous to be jumping out of the water like that," Zahir said.

"Those are actually small whales," Kim said. "Grays can get up to 46 feet and weigh 37 tons."

"I still wouldn't want to be sharing this swimming hole," Zahir quipped.

"They're harmless," Kim replied. "They don't eat anything larger than an organism. On the other hand, fishermen in these waters have found dozens of porpoises and seals in the stomach of a single killer whale."

As Kim spoke, the animals retreated to the open ocean. Zahir looked over at Kim, his eyes still wide with excitement. "You know, I think I believe you," he said.

"Well, it's true."

"No, not about the whales," Zahir said. "The notion that through our quest for meaning, we are moving toward a new system of belief—a new reality. But, given where we stand today, you have to agree a new global vision is a pretty tough sell."

Kim smiled at Zahir's sincerity. "No tougher than it will be for you to convince your buddies in San Jose that you saw whales dancing."

Part 3: *Modeling*

Patron Saint of Sailors: *Humanizing systems*

As if working to the precise schedule of a marine show, the whales disappeared under the smooth blue swells of ocean. The group turned and walked to the crest of the sandy point where a new vista opened up before them.

The beach curved to a rocky reef nearly submerged by high tide. Above the reef, jagged bluffs rose 200 feet, topped with tall spruce trees that tilted off the cliffs like giant gates about to close the passage.

"Looks like we're coming to a dead end," Zahir said.

As they walked along, straining to see if the beach around the point was passable, the sound of water falling on the land side overcame the sound of water breaking on the sea side.

Walking up the beach, they could see a tumbling waterfall that emerged halfway down the rock face as though slicing the rock headland open. Above the falls was a large, scourged bowl with mist rising from its hidden belly. Above the damp cave, at either edge of the cliff face, a suspension bridge spanned the 100-foot gap marking the trail through the woods above.

"This looks like home to me," Tomo said as he scanned the empty white sand beach that surrounded the pool at the base of the waterfall.

"This is Tsocowis Creek," Kim said, recognizing the suspension bridge.

"It's the perfect spot for tonight," she added, happy that the group had been rewarded for their perseverance.

They walked up to one of the large logs that lay in random patterns around the pool and sat against it to lower their packs.

Amidst the euphoria of arrival, the Garwood group quickly divided the task of setting up camp. Tomo, Paul and Celine erected the four-man tents Tomo and Kim had been carrying. Zahir collected wood and started a fire while Kim prepared the extra meal she had brought in light of James not being there to do one of the day's cooking.

Within half an hour, they were congregated around the fire, sharing a cup of tea as the last rays of sun filtered through the low branches that draped toward the beach.

Kim served fresh pasta in herb and vegetable sauce, and everyone savored the last fresh vegetables they would taste for a while. They spoke of the day and how surprised they were with the sights they had seen. Kim said little, knowing the most dramatic parts of the hike were ahead. As they finished their praise of the inland waterways, the forest and the coastal headland, they reflected on the discussion that had moved them across the territory.

Like the trail itself, those discussions, reflected Kim, left impressions behind and anticipation ahead. The camp was set for bedding down, but there were other bearings that needed to be established before calling it a day.

Zahir served those who wanted second helpings. Returning to his indentation in the sand, he leaned against a log and stretched his long legs out past the fire. "Paul, when we were talking back on the trail, you said that we would cling to old habits in the face of expanded knowledge."

Paul stared at the fire as if sorting the implication of his response. "The new reality we scribbled in the sand today is in collision with habits of the old reality." He looked up to Zahir's changing expression. "More than anything that new reality speaks of an increased understanding about our basic equality."

"You're saying that much of what we support in the caste system of the old reality is held together by convention—by habit," Zahir clarified.

Paul nodded his head slowly. "The old reality is like a wall of habit that blocks the humanizing of systems. But when you consider the aggregate of human knowledge is doubling every 15 years, it's hard to believe the habits of hierarchy survive."

"Tell the people trapped in the middle of a huge organizational chart that," Tomo rebutted.

"Big business is a dinosaur," Celine interjected. "In 1920, the Fortune 500 companies accounted for 70% of the US economy. Today they represent less than 10%."

"So much for the old reality," Tomo said dismissively.

"Unfortunately not," Celine said. "It may seem that commerce is being humanized by the million new businesses that start yearly, but the economic system in which they operate is still locked into the habits of the old reality."

"That's a big habit to change," Tomo taunted.

"By changing the way we measure progress, we can promote a new economic system," Celine said as though oblivious to Tomo's skepticism. "We record our economic well-being through the Gross Domestic Product, which is simply a total of all monies that have changed hands. It makes no distinction between desirable and undesirable economic activity."

Paul was quick to pick up on the example. "As we report the GDP going up, we count the cost of crime prevention, treatment of pollution, out of control population increases and high-consumption lifestyles as economic gains."

"It's like one big adding machine," Celine confirmed. "It not only can't subtract, but it fails to count any activity performed without the exchange of money."

"Back in 1961, Robert Kennedy said, 'The GDP measures everything except that which makes life worthwhile,'" Paul added.

"So," Tomo said. "The whole economic system reports growth when what we see happening socially and environmentally is entirely different."

"New measures that distinguish between the costs and benefits of growth are being defined that show Genuine Progress Indicators, or GPIs," Celine replied. "By adding the value of homemaking and community work, and subtracting costs associated with the problems Paul mentioned, the GPI shows a different picture.

"The GDP would have us believe life has gotten consistently better since the 1950s, but the GPI shows a decline in the quality of life since 1970."

"People are just going to argue that those qualitative measures are nonscientific and value-laden," Tomo posed.

"Not counting social or environmental decay is making a value judgment," Celine responded. "It values these issues at zero—which is the most inaccurate judgment possible."

"You will never see institutions shift from maintaining the illusion of positive growth," Tomo replied.

Celine flashed her disarming smile at Tomo. "Who said anything about institutions?"

"So who will?"

"Women," Paul interjected, pausing as though the word on its own addressed the topic. "What Celine didn't mention is that, of those million businesses being created each year, two-thirds of them are being created by women. Soon women will own more than half of all companies. As this marginalized population becomes mainstream, you've got structural change."

"Are you saying the source of change today centers on feminism?" Tomo asked.

"No," Paul replied. "The source of change centers on humanism. It's not a quality unique to women; it's just that men have a lot more historical deprogramming to work though. From kingship, through to our paternal institutions, man has sought control over his environment."

Paul paused, as if waiting for his comment to be challenged, then continued. "When women move into institutions that are counted in the economy, they don't see dominating the structure as the objective. As they import caring values into the economy, we will redefine our measurements of progress."

The silence was spanned by the peaceful rumble of Tsocowis Falls. Kim thought of women she knew who expressed their insecurity by trying to duplicate the aggression-based style of institutional life.

Tomo, obviously responding to Paul's comment, spoke first. "You sound like my wife, but she seriously thinks these are the tools she will use to change the organization. I'm just concerned they're going to give her the chance."

"What do you mean by that, Tomo?" Kim asked.

"The word is she is going to be asked to be president of the Western Region, and I think they are going to eat her alive," Tomo said.

"Why eaten alive? They obviously recognize her abilities," Celine said.

"I've watched a lot of the guys that have pushed their way to the top of the ladder throughout the international brokerage house she is with. They are insecure about their position, and they don't want to disclose what they don't know, so they keep their cards to their chests and run around in little packs like dogs."

"Barb, my wife, is an open book," he continued on a calmer tone.

"She wears her heart on her sleeve, she admits she doesn't have all the answers, and she is embarrassingly open."

"And she is the archetype of the change that is happening throughout the professional world," Kim said.

Tomo looked bewildered by her response; at the same time, Paul started laughing. "Tomo, you're pretty hard on the male model, but basically accurate. We were taught that we should have all the answers, play only on the winning team, and never give the other side the advantage by admitting what we don't know. It may have been effective training for an adversarial system, but it doesn't work any more."

Tomo looked at Celine questioningly. "And how were women trained?"

"Women learned to care for those aspects of society, like child care and home care, that are not counted in our economic system," Celine responded. "Because many tasks that center on caring values have not been acknowledged with pay, many concerns of women are invisible until they enter work, which is within our economic measure of value."

"But that doesn't change the basic structure that excludes qualitative concerns from the economy," Tomo said.

"Change is happening on several fronts," Celine replied. "As more emotionally intelligent values are adopted, I think Paul is right; we will move to humanizing systems."

"I'm just concerned that too much of that change will be carried out on my wife's back," Tomo said. He turned to Kim. "What do you think?"

As Tomo had spoken of his wife Barbara, Kim had been watching different shapes emerge from the fire. "Did you know that the name Barbara was first given to the patron saint of sailors?"

Their eyes met as Tomo shook his head passively.

"You'll have to ask your Barbara if she trusts her mates are ready for the voyage."

Patterns of Understanding: *Spontaneous change*

The sun had set behind the large buttress of stone on the west-side of Tsocowis Creek, leaving a halo of light on the western horizon. Tomo reached over to the pile of wood beside him and tossed two large pieces on the weaning fire sending burning embers aloft like fireflies in the indigo sky. He watched the embers die out and disappear.

"I can tell you exactly what her mates will say about the voyage— 'You're on your own'," Tomo finally replied, sounding totally defeated.

Making a slight involuntary shake of his head, Zahir looked over at Tomo. "I don't think people need to be forced to abandon the old reality. In a world of open information no one can build a fortress to keep out ideas or knowledge. We are connected— we share an expanding consciousness. This pattern naturally changes how we relate to one another."

Tomo frowned as though resisting a counter. "Global access through computer networks does not ensure a global perspective."

Zahir's expression refocused to one of concentration. "Global access through a technological network is only one example of how network thinking affects all of us. As we come to see networks as being less a tool, and more a way of life, we adopt other connective patterns."

"No matter how you cut it, technology that enhances the exchange of information does not guarantee a better society," Tomo concluded. "Integrated communication is not integrated living!"

Zahir swung his legs away from the growing blaze. "I can't tell you what the post-technological world will evolve to, but I can tell you that every time society has an increase in its ability to communicate, you get massive surges in innovation. To communicate globally is to engage a global consciousness. This will create unpredictable levels of social feedback and the resulting explosion of communication will transform our ability to act."

Kim thought back to their discussion near the trail head. "Didn't you say that unstable systems experiencing a high degree of feedback can move to dramatic new forms?"

"Transformational," Zahir responded, as though clear only of that fact.

"Transformational, no doubt. But to what ends?" Tomo replied. "Nothing that has happened in the information age has demonstrated a greater benevolence than the age that preceded it."

Zahir squared himself against the log to face Tomo directly. "Processes that allow the knowledge gathered on any subject to be transferred into your hands instantaneously mean that you can avoid being falsely medicated, educated, informed, organized or governed."

"Tomo, your concern about the self-serving nature of the commodity-based system evaporates when inequities in the structure are exposed."

"We're just replacing self-serving commodity based mega-structures with self-serving information based mega-structures," Tomo rebuked.

Zahir stopped dead and his face contorted into the expression of one who has gone over the handlebars. "You might be right, Tomo," he replied unenthusiastically. "That's something I really don't have an answer for."

Kim had gone to her pack to retrieve some date squares. Hearing what Zahir had said, she walked to him and knelt down as though he were the obvious one to be served first. "You do have your answer," she said, looking compassionately into Zahir's eyes. "Tomo isn't aware that you created the program which brought order to the chaos of the Internet."

Kim turned to Tomo. "When the, 'Net was first created, there was no organizing structure to catalogue and access the rapidly expanding database. Zahir worked on the team that developed the original shareware. The only way he was able to make that available was to release it as an open system free for everyone to use."

"Sorry, Zahir," Tomo responded. "It's just that the new breed of high-tech developers seem frantic about capitalizing on their intellectual property rights." He paused. "I should know—I'm one of them."

"Don't feel bad, Tomo," Zahir said. "I'm afraid that I'm caught in the same dilemma."

Kim looked to Zahir again and thought of James' description of him having kind eyes.

"I just can't help feeling that we've split up or consumed the value of the physical world," Tomo rationalized. "Now, we're trying to put a fence around every square inch of intellectual property. As we move from ownership of physical assets to ownership of processes, we're putting up the same kind of barriers."

"Open systems are an example of what we can do at our best," Zahir responded, "but even cyberspace runs the risk of being commercialized or regulated away from its inspired beginnings. As we work in these totally new mediums, we are compelled by their transformational capacity."

"Then issues of control, absolute ownership and ego defeat the inspiration that created the innovation." Tomo had finished Zahir's thought.

As Zahir stared down at the nearly extinguished fire, he shook his head as though he was struggling with some inner conflict. "The pace of innovation is so rapid, there is no fixed standard for technology. This means we come to see technology as a fluid and constantly expanding capacity."

"A capacity to transform?" Tomo challenged him.

"By focusing on processes that go the next stage deeper in the physical world, new patterns emerge," Zahir replied. "Microbiology, molecular science, subatomic research—they are all pathways to high-yield, low-energy processes."

"And on a practical level," Tomo persisted.

"It absolutely practical, take energy itself," Zahir replied. "Meters in homes throughout North America are running backward as people sell clean solar power back into the grid. Wind, solar and micro power plants are decentralizing energy creation and distribution just the way computing did 20 years ago. What's compelling is that transformation arises from a focus on mental processes that leapfrog our earlier energy-intensive/high pollution processes."

"So we're going to think our way out of pollution," Tomo asserted.

Kim spoke to Tomo's unchanged expression. "Maybe we do think our way out of pollution. There's a company in Vancouver that is developing zero-pollution hydrogen-powered motors. They've been able to reduce the size of fuel cells that NASA uses in space, down to prototype commercial applications."

"Hammond Power Systems," Paul said, in an encyclopedic fashion. "Zahir is right. Technology has moved to a deeper leverage point with the natural world. Harnessing the power of hydrogen is just one area where the blending of several technologies is creating new patterns of understanding."

Kim could sense a new, unspoken awareness occurring. "Not only technological change, but the nature of change itself has moved from incremental to transformational, to something even more dynamic," she said. "We know man-made systems are at a tremendous state of imbalance. Like living systems at the point of transformation, there seems to be a maximum flow of energy brought on by a high degree of feedback in the system, and we sense a new order has to emerge from this chaotic state."

"Very subtle influences can trigger the system to massive forms of self-organization," Zahir observed. "Self-organization that advances living systems extended to a theory of spontaneous change in man-made systems."

As Kim poked the waning fire with a stick, several embers glowed to life. "The positive changes that many desire, but no one person can achieve, must transform to that desired state," she said in the same propositional tone in which Zahir had spoken.

"That kind of spontaneous change took place when the Iron Curtain fell between East and West Germany," Paul said. "They say there were no orders, no agreements; just one night, a mass of East Germans walked to the Checkpoint Charlie border crossing because they felt something would happen—it was time—and the Wall began to crumble."

"The change looks to be spontaneous, but it's really a critical mass of expanded knowledge that several people act on at the same point in time," Kim said. "People do not see an event or an object, but a new pattern of understanding that offers a sense of improvement over the existing state."

"After it happens, we look back and say—'I wonder why things carried on in the old way for so long,'" Paul added.

"This is what breaks old habits to a new dynamic," Zahir observed, pulling their earlier conversation into line. "It's not the linear decision of one; it's the networked influence of many."

"This is the process that took place in Czechoslovakia." Paul paused as his voice lowered in concern. "But there's often a struggle for the higher forms of self-organization to emerge from the chaotic state."

Kim watched Paul's eyes move from the dying fire up to the heavens, and she realized he still had deep feelings for his homeland.

"If the four elements are there, change will follow," Kim said. "Oppressive conditions, chaotic unrest marked by a maximum amount of energy and feedback in the system, a self-organization to a higher form marked by the emergence of a new pattern and, finally, group insight that a better state is replacing the convention marked by self-organization appearing as spontaneous change."

Then, as though having heard her own thoughts clearly, Kim added, "This is the enhanced pattern James spoke of. Feedback in human affairs has caused an explosion of relationships resulting in new patterns of understanding."

"But what brings the pattern into focus?" Tomo asked engagingly.

"Under the right conditions, the enhanced pattern will emerge," Paul said as he pointed up. They all looked overhead where the sky exploded in a mass of starlight. It was not the arrangement of discreet points of light that they were used to when looking up at the heavens. It was a dense, connected pattern of light.

An involuntary hush intensified the impact of the light as everyone stared overhead. "I never would have believed so many stars could be seen from earth," Zahir finally said.

As if in reply, Tomo said, "I suspect, if the conditions are right, the enhanced pattern will emerge." As he spoke, Kim saw that Tomo and Zahir had locked eyes, smiling.

Inspiring Organic Growth: *Building the Natural Economy*

Kim awoke from a deep, peaceful sleep. The dark green branches overhead layered her vision upward to the tree tops glistening in the morning light. It was exactly how Kim had awoken on summer mornings as a child, and for several moments, she held only that consciousness.

Space and time drifted back to order. She remembered the beauty of the previous night, how they had pulled their sleeping bags out of the tents to sleep under the stars, Tsocowis Creek rumbling down the rocks, setting up a natural white noise of tranquility.

"Good morning, Kim." Celine's voice held an inflection that confirmed the day.

Kim stretched her arms up out of the bag into a dewless morning. "Good morning. Wow! What a sleep!"

Celine was brushing her thick, dark hair. "We are traveling with some real gentlemen. Paul has brought us over coffee, and he's got porridge on." She bent over, taking a cup from the log and handing it to Kim.

"Thanks, Celine." Kim raised herself on one arm and took a sip. "Have I been holding things up?"

"No one's been up long. It's just after seven. Tomo and Zahir have gone to check out where the tide is falling on the beach ahead." Celine rose to put her brush away in her pack.

"That coffee tastes great, Celine," Kim said, putting her cup down and looking over at the falls. "What a way to go. Not only that, I hear my bath running."

"I got a quick dip before the boys got up," Celine replied. "I recommend it—the place is magic."

Kim smiled. "I admire how you are so incredibly feminine and trail-ready at the same time."

"It's a curse," Celine replied with a mock curtsy. "When you're built like this, there are a million assumptions made about your character or lack of it. I used to pray for an athletic build like yours, but—hey—you learn to work around your handicaps."

They laughed, knowing that only a woman could understand how stunning good looks could be a handicap.

"I guess we shouldn't expect any spontaneous social change in that regard," Celine added.

"No, but it's a wonderful time in the history of man to be a woman. And I'm going to get in that pool before some guy beats me to it." Kim laughed as she sprang out of her sleeping bag, grabbed a towel and headed to the water in a canter, her blond hair and men's flannel pajamas billowing behind her.

The basin of the falls was the size of a large swimming pool. Kim noticed there was no exiting stream from the lagoon and concluded that the water flowed through the sand to the water table and out to the sea. Two truck-sized boulders that had sheared from the wall above were lodged in the sand at each end of the pool.

Kim stripped behind the privacy of the boulder closest to their tent and willed herself into the icy cold water. As the creek pushed a gentle current against her, she resisted the impulse to get out of the cold, and let a deeper feeling of relaxation take hold.

Soon she felt like she was meant to be there, suspended in the flow before it disappeared into the earth again. She closed her eyes so she could see all the beauty at once, floating in a connected pattern. It was not a pattern that resolved life to her, but that resolved her to life. A growing warmth expanded in her chest as she submitted to the source.

Time held still in such a way that Kim was not really sure how much had passed. Surfacing from the connection she had learned to find in nature, she dressed hurriedly, called the hospital on her cell phone, and then joined the others.

Enthusiastic greetings were exchanged as Kim approached the ring of logs the group had occupied the previous night.

"Paul, thanks for the coffee," Kim said. "Do you spoil your wife like that at home?"

"My wife is like a great calm lake," Paul replied as he dug a ladle into the steaming pot. "No matter how I serve her, she always refreshes me."

Kim smiled, taking the porridge with thanks and savoring it. The cool breeze ventilated from the forest, making the hot cereal feel that much better going down.

"Any word from home yourself?" Paul asked.

"No change," she replied simply, not wanting to dwell on the implications. "So how does the hiking down the beach look?"

"The tide is low enough to get around this point," Tomo said, gesturing to the rock bluffs immediately beyond them. "But a quarter-mile down the beach, the cliffs drop straight into the water."

"It's beautiful over there," Zahir said. "There's another waterfall at Billy Goat Creek that comes directly off a saddle of rock onto the beach. Tomo climbed up it to see if there was access to the trail."

"There are solid rock walls that curve down from the forest and form a massive half-pipe. It's impassable," Tomo confirmed.

"Is there no access back up to the trail?" Kim looked at the suspension bridge overhead.

"I don't think we'll get up anywhere near Billy Goat Creek, but there's a rough trail back down the beach we should be able to use," Tomo replied, pointing in the direction from which they had come from the previous night.

"I've never been on this part of the beach, but I know the trail is nice through this area for a couple of miles, and then we hit the beach again at Trestle Creek," Kim said.

"Sounds great. Let's do it," said Zahir, finishing his coffee.

The eager anticipation to get underway was evident, and within 20 minutes, the Garwood group had packed camp.

As the men headed over the logs towards the trail, the women paused for one last look at the falls. Celine studied the white sand where they had camped. "Last night our little domed community looked so perfect. Now we leave without a trace of having been here," she said.

"That's why it's even more perfect this morning," Kim responded as the women smiled at their quiet understanding.

A voice shouted from down the beach, "This is it!" They looked up to see Tomo waving a knotted rope. "We should be able to get up here," he said.

Paul and Zahir were only steps behind him and, by the time the women caught up, Zahir had already disappeared behind the large tree trunks and rock slabs. The party helped one another up the broken face, using a network of tree roots as the principal climbing aid. Kim noticed that Tomo stayed at the back of the pack and made sure everyone made it to the trail elevation safely.

They spilled out of the forest that rimmed the cliff and onto a boardwalk that ran in a dog-legged fashion through the green undergrowth teeming with life.

The thick forest folded down to a rich tangle of salal at ground level. A carpet of moss rolled up both sides of the narrow boardwalk in a way that even what was man-made seemed organic. The group sat in the wild as if transported to a reality of its own unique order.

"This is civilized," Paul said, bending over to catch his breath.

Kim was thinking the same thing and then realized that Paul was referring to the boardwalk. "There are many wooden walkways through forest areas," she replied. "The earth is so soft it would turn into a bog if people walked on it. Boardwalks make for quick hiking, but you have to be very careful. If the boards are wet, they're like sheet ice."

The group set off, and within a few hundred feet crossed the wooden suspension bridge over Tsocowis Creek. The dark and gloomy, scourged bowl formed by the creek stood in contrast to the glistening pool and bright white beach at which they had camped. Within a few minutes, they approached another suspension bridge over Billy Goat Creek.

"That really is a 'half-pipe'," Paul said as they stopped to view the 60-foot-wide channel carved into the rock.

"I'm glad we didn't try this as an approach to the trail," Zahir said. "We would never have scaled the rock walls, let alone gotten through the tangle of underbrush to this bridge."

They stood on the swaying suspension bridge absorbing a heightened sense of presence as light filtered through the forest veil to the endless ocean. The group was silent, as though attempting neither to deny nor define some palpable connection with the surrounding.

As they moved single file off the bridge and down the wandering path of wooden slats, only the odd murmur of wonder was spoken. Kim recognized the phenomena. The excitement of being imbued with nature's beauty was being replaced by the quiet contemplation of spiritual rejuvenation.

At one point, the trail veered nearer to the cliffs, and Kim stepped towards the edge. "This is the site of the *Valencia* wreck," she said. As they grouped around looking at the cavernous rocks below, Zahir spoke.

"Nature—we used to try and conquer it; now we're just trying to save it."

Kim stepped back from the edge of the cliff, still staring at the turbulent water below. "Somehow I don't think moving from consumption to preservation is the end of our continuum with nature," she said as she turned toward the main trail.

Traveling quietly through the rich coastal rain forest, they encountered a large piece of machinery, its rusting mass of gears and levers clustered around a 10-foot-high boiler.

"What's this?" Tomo wondered, as he jumped up on its frame and inspected the derelict equipment.

"It's an old steam grader," Kim replied. "Probably used in the early days of the trail."

"It's amazing they could even get that thing out here," Zahir said.

"It sounds corny," Celine added, "but I already feel less association with the man-made and more a part of something else."

"Welcome to the second day on the trail," Kim said, smiling. "Now you know the reason we're here."

—·—

They pushed through the coastal forest without speaking, as though each was enjoying a private connection to it. Descending to a rocky beach, they crossed the trickle of Trestle Creek, where another world opened up. A vast sandstone shelf stretched out before them, forming a gray-green plain that ended with the blue band of the Pacific Ocean.

They walked along, stopping to inspect the rich plant and animal life that flourished on the foreshore. Bathtub-sized basins hollowed out of the sandstone created natural inter-tidal aquariums. Soft pink coral, vibrant green seaweed, purple starfish, steel-blue mussels and green sea urchins were magnified in the shallow turquoise ponds.

Paul waded into a thick, slippery field of kelp to inspect a large boulder where the root system of the whip-like plants had anchored themselves. "Zahir, you're into networks. Look at this," he said as the others followed.

Reaching Paul, they looked down at the gnarled pattern of roots, which smothered the boulder in a fractal of flat brown veins. Paul folded back a flap of the net-like surface that had been ripped loose by some passing tidal drift. "See how this chunk has been torn away, but the network of roots still function."

"Networks serve the whole of the community they belong to," Zahir offered. "They represent a mass of relationships with endless feedback loops that result in pure cooperation and interdependence."

Kim watched this serious systems thinker emerge from Zahir's carefree personality.

"You make it sound like a series of human behaviors," she asserted.

"Our mental organizing patterns—outlines and formal hierarchies— offer a limited number of static parts in linear format," Zahir replied. "As we adopt the pattern of the network, we achieve cyclical, restorative and self-administering ways of thinking and being."

"It's holistic," Paul added, still holding the flap of woven seaweed in his hand. "This kind of pattern adopted in a business environment opens new realms of opportunity because its outcome is not consumptive growth, its organic growth—in a word—is sustainable."

"That organic growth theory wouldn't have found a testing ground in your company, would it, Paul?" Kim asked, having intuited the origin of his conviction.

Paul smiled broadly as he glanced up. "To me, the network of relations on this rock is Beerman at its best."

Kim noticed that Paul never referred to Beerman & Associates as his own company. "How is that, Paul?"

"The way it is evolving is organic also. The structure of the organization does not dictate its function. The function creates a pattern of relationships that enhances what we call sustainable growth." Paul ran his hand over the textured sphere of the rock. "By avoiding linear relationships, we see people grow precisely because they have freedom to move where they feel the greatest utility."

"Paul, what exactly is your business?" Zahir asked.

"That gets more difficult for me to answer every year," Paul replied as they all turned to head down the beach. "Part of the outcome of our associates' growth is that we keep getting into new businesses.

"When I graduated in the late 70s with a degree in chemical engineering, 'plastics' was a booming field. I started there and then moved into polymers. Before long we were making special application coatings on all sorts of commercial and industrial products. Everything we make or coat prolongs the life of products used before our products were introduced."

They walked along with the breeze at their backs. The broad shelf of sandstone made for easy walking, and they remained clustered around Paul as he continued. "It was around that time I met James. The company was growing, and I was trying to be a good manager, directing all my new employees. James pointed out to me that, if I expected to hire people who would build on what I had started, I'd better offer them the freedom of initiative that attracted me."

"Sounds a lot like what organizations are trying to accomplish today," Celine said.

"Yes, but back then, when we set up self-governing administration and teams around the actual work projects, people thought we were trying to avoid management. We kept plant sizes down to 200 so people could develop knowledge and trust with those they worked with, and we ensured that everyone got paid in proportion to his or her contribution."

"Doesn't it get into the same old politics when the boss sets the salary?" Celine asked.

"There are no bosses," Paul replied. "A new associate will have a sponsor when starting out, but eventually each will work on several teams. The team assesses the newcomer's contribution and ranks it with other associates making similar contributions."

"Doesn't that just get to be a popularity contest?" Celine asked.

"When people are compensated based on the success of the group, the most popular person is the one that makes the group function well," Paul replied.

"You must have people pulling every trick in the book to show a profitable bottom line," Celine pressed.

"I think that's where true organic growth comes in," Paul said. "When you give people an environment in which they can thrive, they do things naturally to make things work at optimum."

This was fresh ground for Tomo. "So you're saying profit optimization is not the primary goal?"

"When people are constantly making commitments to internal and external sources, their work environment is like a community," Paul answered. "Technical knowledge that may lead to short-run profits is not enough. They know that, if they are going to hold community support over the long run, other aspects of judgment and integrity play a much larger role."

"'Community' is a nice word, but the business still stands separate," Tomo asserted.

"In many towns we operate in, they are inseparable," Paul replied. "On a larger scale, business is the engine that has to drive social reform."

"'Reform' is typically a long list of casualties on the road to 'efficiency,'" Tomo replied.

"That's not how I see it," Paul replied.

"When shareholder return is the only guiding principle, transnational corporations are free to move around the world with the ethic one-dollar-one-vote," Tomo retorted. "Where's the social reform?"

"The challenge is not to fight globalized thinking—it's to import community values into that thinking," Paul stated. "We do not differentiate corporate work from community work; we use processes that link the two structurally."

"I'd like to see that as a transnational ethic," Tomo asserted.

"It's happening," Paul replied. "You can't ask someone doing sophisticated work to suspend judgment in or out of the workplace."

"In the financial services market, we are asking staff to integrate a complex range of products," Celine offered. "But for the most part, the enlightened employee is still meant to be seen and not heard."

"I can sure second that in education," Kim said as they moved off the sandstone table that had been invaded by rising tide and stepped onto the pebble-infested sand.

"Banking and education are two industries that give their people all the responsibility but not the commensurate authority to take charge," Paul replied. "They are patriarchal hierarchies, based on a lack of trust as it relates to the judgment or competency of subordinates. If those organizations were designed around the self-administering form of the network, there would be more equality and capacity in the system."

Kim noticed Zahir had been listening attentively but had said little. "Zahir, you run a software development firm. What goes on there?"

"We just do it," Zahir replied. "We rank our potential projects on the degree to which they will empower the user. It creates an energy that attracts a team—from there, it just happens."

"Who do you report to?" Celine asked.

"We report to each other," Zahir replied. "The project compels us to find the right balance of skills; then we work to encourage each others' best."

The group was now walking five abreast. Raising both her eyebrows, Celine looked past the other three to Paul. "That sounds like a place of respect."

"We are respected in the sense that everyone knows or is brought to understand the big picture. There's no big boss who pretends he's the only one in the know," Zahir said. "Ours is a complex industry, so we don't pretend anyone holds absolute truths—we strive to form coherent interpretations together. If there are 'firsts,' they are firsts among equals."

"Sounds very communal," Celine said.

"It's difficult for me to understand how an enterprise can create if it doesn't come together as a community that's bonded by a compelling sense of purpose," Zahir said.

"Your organization, like ours, has leveraged equality through respect," Paul said. "It is proof that we can operate at a new level of human interdependence." Paul eyes brightened as he looked almost directly in the sun to focus on Zahir's face. "All we need to do is stop resisting the nature *of* things."

"Another step in Kim's continuum," Zahir acknowledged. "Consumption of nature, preservation of nature, function of nature."

—·—

They walked quietly on in the soft sand, conserving energy. As they approached a peninsula, Kim could see the forest on the foreshore was broken to show a faint transition in color. The others, who had become accustomed to reading the beach topography, began to speculate that the physical transition marked the outflow of Klanawa River. But reaching the peninsula and turning from the vast expanse of the blue sea and sky, they were surprised by the unexpected sight before them.

The mouth of the Klanawa River was dammed off by the windswept beach and formed a broad turquoise lagoon surrounded by a rich green mosaic of forest. As they adjusted to the sudden change of scenery, a point of focus stood out.

"What is that?" Tomo exclaimed, pointing to what looked like a box suspended over the 300-foot expanse of contained river.

"It's a cable car," Kim replied. "There's a number of them ahead that cross impassable rivers."

Anything that hung on a cable interested Tomo. "Let's go for it," he said, and without any further reflection on the beauty that surrounded them, they set off up the beach in search of a path to the cable car.

Passing through a grove of giant trees along the edge of the broad lagoon, they reached the man-made conveyor. At each side of the river was a 30-foot-tall wooden tower, with ladders to a platform at the top of each. A giant clothes-line rig was suspended from large pulleys on top of each tower. At the center of the river, a simple metal box frame hung where the support cable reached the lowest point of its arc.

Tomo was already hauling in the cable car before the last of the group reached the tower. As the square frame clanked against the landing platform, Tomo and Zahir jumped into the two metal seats that faced one another and, with all the preparation of fledgling birds, pushed off.

As the flying frame whizzed over the aqua plain, those left on the tower laughed at the apprehensive shouts that echoed back across the water. When the hauling rope, rigged like a clothes-line between the towers, came to a stop, Paul started pulling the car to the far side. Within minutes, Tomo and Zahir had vacated the tram and helped convey it back to where Kim and Celine got in. Their free-fall to the center of the space brought a new round of laughter.

Kim tilted her head back and let the cool rush of air flow around the back of her neck. The effortless travel, so unlike the heavy plodding with a pack, seemed like free flight itself. Breaking out of the shadows and over the bright green water brought an involuntary sense of euphoria. As the men at both towers hauled on the line, the women absorbed the feeling, too quickly reaching the other side.

At last, Paul took the ride that would be the dream of small boys, arriving with a smile that made him look like one. Celine and Kim pulled Paul into the station and helped him out of the cage. Kim let the tram go and they watched the metal frame travel to its natural resting point over the middle of the aqua lagoon. As the tram coasted to a stop the group perched on the platform, rested their packs on the railing and soaked in the sun.

Tomo broke out a bag of trail mix and passed it around as the group shared the views and the elevated sense of energy.

Celine seemed determined to make this a comfortable stop, and slid her pack awkwardly onto the decking of the tower. "Paul, I'm still wrestling with the nature of things," she said. "I can see you have been able to tap the common values of your associates, as you call them, but what has given them such a great sense of purpose in creating industrial products?"

"We took the next step in the continuum," Paul said, turning to Zahir. "It's as Zahir said; we moved to the function of nature." Paul looked out to the tram bouncing gently in response to their movement on the tower.

"Several years back when I was bragging away to James about all our community service plans, I can remember him saying to me: 'When planning for the future, your first concern should be to make sure there is one.'"

"'What are you talking about?' I replied.

"'The base for a majority of your products is poly vinyl chloride," James said. "That stuff lasts 20,000 years in a landfill; even worse, when incinerated it becomes a dioxin. Paul', he said, 'your motives are admirable, but your molecules will kill us.'"

"He put me in touch the work of Dr. Karl-Henrik Robert of Sweden. Robert, a former cancer research scientist, founded The Natural Step. They showed me that taking the raw material through the manufacturing process resulted in 94% waste and 6% product. On top of that, 80% of the products we produced were eventually discarded as waste."

"So you cut back industrial waste," Celine posed.

"More than that," Paul responded. "The Natural Step demonstrated how utilizing waste could represent energy savings if we developed cyclical rather than lineal processes for production."

"What kind of cyclical processes?" Celine asked, clearly engaged.

"At the heart of Natural Step is a framework of four-system conditions," Paul replied. "The first two conditions are to not take substances from the earth or produce man-made substances at a greater rate than they can be regenerated or reabsorbed by nature. The third is to ensure that the physical basis for the productivity and diversity of nature is not systematically diminished. And the last is to be fair and efficient in meeting human needs."

Kim knew of the work Paul and James had pursued in this area and that Paul had just blurted out some weighty concepts. "Stated simply," she said, "it means a commitment not to create waste faster than the earth can deal with it, not to harvest more from nature than she can create and to distribute Nature's bounty in a socially equitable manner."

Paul was nodding. "It was very easy for our associates who had expressed strong values of operational interdependence to expand their goals to reflect these system conditions," he added. "It offered a framework that deepened the purposes of what we wanted to achieve. We set our vision to operate as close to a natural system as possible."

"Which is?" Celine asked.

"Building the Natural Economy," Paul responded with a smile as broad as the emerald lagoon behind him.

"So when you said that Beerman would function at its best if it emulated the kelp on the rock back there, you meant it." Tomo asserted.

"Absolutely," Paul replied. "We estimate that with our current levels of production on a linear basis, we would be creating 300 millions pounds of waste a year. Through our own efficiencies we are getting very close to closing the loop, in that little finds its way back to the landfill, air or any part of the natural system. Like the kelp back there, we are self-sustaining but do little to compromise the broader system in which we operate."

"How did you do actually alter such a huge environmental impact?" Tomo asked in disbelief.

"Over seven years ago we began system mapping," Paul replied. "We totally redesigned our processes. It was extremely difficult, but resulted in massive product innovation, created lower costs with higher efficiencies, and deepened our commitment as a knowledge-based industry."

"What about the products your clients purchase from you? Surely they are part of the waste stream?" Tomo asked.

"We have instituted a lease and repurchase program. Whatever the lifecycle of our products, we will in some form pay to take them back, because we have developed processes to use their residual value."

"Teach that to the transnationals," Tomo said as he transferred the weight of his pack back onto his shoulders.

"We do," Paul replied mater-of-factly. "The community reach our associates are into is the global community. They understand the science of cyclical processes in industry, but quite frankly, for most of them building The Natural Economy has become a religion."

As they moved to take turns descending the tower, Tomo looked out at the tram with his eyebrows furrowed. "Religion and business," he said. "Seems like someday you'll run into a separation of church and state."

"As more people find their religion in the natural world, it will be impossible to separate church and state," Paul replied.

Kim looked up from the ladder where she was starting her descent and smiled back at the men. "Now we're really talking about the nature of things."

Back on the trail, the boardwalk moved through an array of ferns, salal, wild flowers and salmonberry in bloom. Moving up from beach to cliff-top elevation, the trail skirted past overhangs of thick growth brimming with life. As the path led in and out from the edge of the bluff, long stretches of beach punctuated by massive rock outcroppings could be seen ahead. The incoming sea was littered with reefs slanting up towards the beach as though they had been washed ashore in some forgotten Pacific storm.

Knowing they were approaching Tsusiat Falls, Kim had spotted quick glances of mist through the trees but said nothing, aware of the impact gained arriving by surprise. As they moved down the gentle sloping boardwalk through a stand of small cedar, the sunshine played with the shapes ahead. The wooden walkway dividing the green forest floor appeared to rise into the shadowy timbers and beyond to the persistent light.

Kim noticed their pace had quickened, and speculated to herself which set of instincts had triggered the mood of anticipation. They were silent as they walked out over a newly constructed wooden bridge that spanned the 50-foot-wide sandstone plate of Tsusiat River.

Standing at the railing and looking towards sea, they could see the river flowing some 200 feet before dropping off the edge to the beach below. The light reflecting off the currents of the river mirrored that reflected in the waves of the sea beyond, and it was impossible to actually see the transition line between the two.

"Do you get the feeling Nature is trying to tell us something here?" Celine said.

"She certainly is," Zahir responded.

"What's more important," Paul said, "I think we are starting to listen."

Kim smiled out at the ocean, knowing that some unseen order was falling into place.

Hole in the Wall: *Freeing stakeholder activism*

Moving along the wooded headland, the Garwood group came upon a ravine that offered a beach access by way of long, steep ladders. Climbing awkwardly down this new medium, they descended 200 feet, pausing at platforms that anchored the labyrinth to the steep cliff. Leaving the vertical shadow of woods, they crossed a tangle of driftwood and flotsam into an expanse of sand and sea.

Tsusiat Falls, now in clear view, draped like sheets of satin from the sandstone ledge above. The group gathered and moved back along the beach to the large pool at the base of the falls. Stopping on a peninsula of sand that curved towards the white falls, they stood there mesmerized by the grand scale of its beauty.

"I have to be in that," Tomo said, as if feeling a tangible calling. "Who's up for a swim?"

"I am," Zahir said.

"Me too," Kim added.

Celine helped Paul prepare a late lunch while the others found relative privacy to change for a swim.

Paul was completing the construction of sandwiches made out of thick grained bread, cheese and smoked meat as the others returned in bathing suits. The heat of the day moved in waves down the beach, catching the mist rising from the falls where it settled on the hikers' warm skin. The earthy textures were consumed as the cool spray massaged its way to weary muscles.

They had barely finished lunch when Tomo said, "Come on, you guys! Let's go cool off." Within moments, Tomo, Zahir and Kim headed down the beach as Tomo directed them to the west end of the falls.

Paul and Celine watched the three wade across the wide lagoon—Tomo's powerful legs pushing the water like a bear, Zahir stepping over the surface like a great blue heron, and Kim moving with the light sure-footedness of a deer. "One spirit—three body types."

Celine spoke as if lost in thought: "I wish I could say that about my board."

"You're having trouble with the directors at the bank?" Paul asked as he settled against the log, watching Tomo point out some game plan against the stone cliff.

"We seem to have trouble identifying any common spirit," Celine said. Then, as though she didn't want to get into it, she asked, "Are you serving on any boards, Paul?"

"I have served ineffectively on several boards."

"What do you mean?" Celine chuckled.

"Most boards don't know or are unable to agree on what their real role is." Paul paused, looking over at the falls. "For the most part, corporate governance becomes an exercise in protecting privileged positions."

"Self-interested governance, the big oxymoron," Celine said, shaking her head. "Everyone is bought into position and afraid to go out on a ledge."

"Not everyone," Paul said, pointing to Tsusiat Falls, where Tomo and Kim stepped gingerly along a rock shelf that ran 20 feet high across the entire width of the waterfall. From 80 feet above, the water cascaded in an almost perfect plane, landing in a spray at their feet. Kim's yellow Speedo made her look delicate compared with Tomo's solid build and black boxer shorts. They moved tentatively across the slippery ledge, the force of the water pushing from behind.

Zahir, clearly not impressed with this stunt, followed below Kim as she moved along the upper ledge. Within a few steps, Zahir sank to his chest, and stopped as if in cold shock, then turned, realizing a fall in the deeper water would be safe.

Paul watched Tomo move 40 feet out to the center of the falls where a rock buttress broke the cascading water; he then turned and reached out for Kim. Once he had taken her hand, they both gave a mighty shout and jumped to the churning water below.

"When there ain't no audience, there ain't no show," Paul said to Celine as their companions disappeared under the frothy spray.

"A standing ovation," Celine proposed, rising to her feet. Zahir turned and raised his arms as if to say, 'What do you do with people like this?'

From Kim and Tomo's reaction surfacing, it was obvious that the water was cold. Within moments, the cliff jumpers had taken their bows and were headed back for dry towels and clothing. Celine and Paul had just finished packing up as the others returned.

"Great show, you guys," Celine said. "Are you sure you want to leave this playground?"

"Too crowded here," Tomo said, looking at the four or five domed campsites set up on the beach away from the noise of the falls.

"That would be crazy if I didn't know you meant it," Kim said, looking at the vast expanse of beach to his back. "Given how far we can go this afternoon, water is a little scarce. These beaches eventually end in rock cliffs about three miles from here. Just before that point, there's a stream which we can go for if you like."

It was clear that everyone wanted to press on, so they substituted staying by taking some pictures. Zahir set up his camera and got Celine and Kim to form a pyramid on Tomo and Paul, then he somehow mounted the group until the camera clicked and the structure tumbled. Laughing as they brushed the sand from hair and clothes, they helped each other with packs, took one last mental picture of the falls, and were gone.

As they moved through the fine white sand, Kim reflected on how unique the group was. They were definitely driven, the pace they were setting alone proved that, but they also had a uncanny ability to take in the trail. No, she thought, it was more than that—they weren't accepting life at some comfortable threshold. Each of them was on a mission, drawn into some personal unknown.

Kim wondered if part of the mission pulling them down the trail was a race to discover the unknown about James. They had spoken of James only a few times, but the theme of their discussions invariably moved to those interests expressed in his paper. It was as though they had constructively refocused their concern for James by having him present through his ideas. The more she thought of this, the more she longed to be with him.

"Hey, Kim, if you keep up that pace, you'll run us into the ground," Paul shouted. She turned and found the others smiling, perhaps aware she was walking in the depths of her feelings. She flashed a huge grin, grateful to be called back to her emotional surface.

"Sorry—I got a little lost in thought," Kim said, as they approached. Deflecting the next question, she said to Celine, "So you two looked like you were having a business lunch back there. Any stock positions you're going to let us in on?"

"Public stocks are riskier than cliff jumping," Paul said.

"We were talking about the privilege of corporate board rooms," Celine explained.

"Celine is worried the elite will hold the status quo together forever," Paul added.

"I see it everywhere," Celine admitted. "We finance organizations and the great ideas about the role of today's corporate entities yields to the pressure to conform."

"The public is getting wise to the fortress mentality," Tomo said.

"Institutions used to operate independently from the publics that supported them," Paul offered. "Customers, employees and stockholders were accustomed to accepting what the institution wanted to supply. From health care to hamburgers, you got what was served."

"You're saying stakeholders are redefining the role of these corporate elite," Kim suggested.

Paul was nodding. "As both consumers and owners we insist on investment criteria beyond the single plane of financial return which they know intuitively, if not historically, has upside limits."

"It's all a house of cards," Tomo broke in. "I tell my wife that public corporations are the greatest evil on earth. Stocks used to be valued on a multiple of earnings—now it's all just blue sky."

Tomo adjusted his pack as though the subject were causing the discomfort. "We are not building The Natural Economy; we're losing grip on the old one. As we celebrate a global economy, most are just exporting jobs and our responsibility to the environment, while importing low margins and ever more consumptive habits."

"As free markets sweep the globe, there are massive false economies," Paul offered. "But for the first time in history, real activism can mobilize the new reality to The Natural Economy."

"Paul, you're mobilizing on your own!" Tomo retorted, clearly agitated. "How can you imply that the economic machine that drives consumption is on the cusp of change to a better state?"

"As power moves out to a connected network of stakeholders, we question the traditional premises of growth." Paul spoke in the same measured steps they took down the beach. "We see cheap products have hidden social and environmental costs. We see the goal of profit is made in the absence of distinctions as to what or who was exploited, depleted, abused or stressed. We see that corporations are granted natural resources owned by 'the common', with little accountability to the care for them. We see that growth must answer to conservation, production to cyclical systems, and economic standards to moral principles." He paused, as though looking for some reference point down the beach. "Don't underestimate the broad movement in stakeholder awareness that leads to activism."

"I see a broad movement in North America better called stakeholder complacency," Tomo responded.

Paul laughed softly. "If you believe that change will come about through the insights of many, then you watch for new levels of awareness. The awareness expands at an organic level until it connects across many, and the resulting network of action overcomes the previous structure."

"Paul, are you suggesting that stakeholder awareness is growing organically towards some kind of spontaneous change in the marketplace?" Kim asked, thinking back to what Paul had said earlier.

Paul's smile showed he was aware of her reference, and he, too, returned to their earlier conversation. "Ultimately we can't resist the nature of things."

"So, if stakeholders are to redefine the marketplace through universal access, where is this new dynamic order?" Tomo asked as they closed the gap to another rock outcropping.

Paul looked over at Tomo as they walked slowly around the point. "The thing that precedes the new dynamic is a universal expectation that the new reality must happen. We have seen that expectation spread like wildfire through our work in The Natural Economy. Eventually, this network must connect. The new pattern must emerge."

"That's the Hole in the Wall," Kim said, as they rounded the wedge of stone.

"Exactly!" Paul replied. Then, looking up, he understood Kim's different meaning.

Operation Nightingale: *Executing the mission*

"Oh! *That* 'Hole in the Wall,'" Paul said, gazing at the clear span of sandstone in front of him.

Since leaving Tsusiat Falls, they had traversed the beach that widened as the bluffs turned inland. Now, at the end of its sweep, they walked past the point of rock that revealed the famous landmark. A 200-foot bridge of rock, spanned from the headland and arched over the beach before submerging its mass in the water. The hole had been carved in the peninsula of rock by the endless pounding of the sea.

"Let's see if the tide is low enough for us to walk under it," Tomo said.

"Sounds good," Paul replied. Approaching the great gap, they could see the mid-tide was exposing a beach passage underneath. "How about a water break in the shade?"

Entering the cave-like coolness, they dropped their packs and flopped into the bean-bag texture of loose pebbles. The moist stones massaged the back of Kim's legs and the waves hugged the headland as she reflected on the other hole in the wall.

"Paul, what kind of universal expectations do you think will free stakeholder activism?" she asked, with a sense that some secret would be shared in this intimate space.

"Expectations of how the tools of commerce are meant to serve us," Paul replied.

"A revolt outside the walls of industry," Tomo interjected.

"Industry is training itself to revolt from within," Paul replied.

"How so?"

"Through participative strategic planning, most companies have documented their vision, mission and values. That's a statement of group awareness."

"'Document' is the perfect word," Tomo said. "They just sit on the shelf."

"But you can't tell people their values and goals are strategic one day and forgotten the next," Paul said. "The implementation of those values is difficult because acting on group values goes beyond the traditional structure of the organization."

"So, practically?" Tomo pressed.

"In practical ways, we are all stakeholders in executing the mission," Paul mused, "because by mobilizing emerging values we can change the most entrenched path of any enterprise."

"Fits into the story about you and James running drugs, doesn't it, Zahir?" Kim asked, smiling over at his stretched-out figure in the bed of pebbles near the water's edge.

"Yeah, what is that all about?" Paul asked.

Zahir propped himself, lodging one elbow in the pebbles. "A few years ago, James was approached by a pharmaceutical company. They asked him to address their problem in finding 'suitable acquisitions.' Their legal people suggested purchasing companies that held losses on their books so they could use the tax write-off.

"Turns out that customers were switching brands because they were learning about enormous profits this company had and all the shady techniques they were using to tax-shelter them," Zahir continued. "James did a study of their stakeholders and proved his intuition that the course they were on would lead to wide-spread boycotting of the brand."

"So how do you fit into all this, Zahir?" Celine asked.

"James heard that I was working on a graphical web browser, and he approached me about using the technology on an applied. His idea was to set up a worldwide relief program to countries that needed generic drugs. We used the 'Net to post the offering and locate distribution points at the most depressed regions throughout the world."

"And the drug company?" Celine asked.

"Last time I spoke with James, he said they are benchmarking the best practices needed in the industry," Zahir replied. "He said they called the first exercise 'Operation Nightingale,' and they are now setting up medical centers to train and supervise locals in depressed areas."

"Seems everyone has jumped on the bandwagon," Kim offered, obviously knowing of the plan. "The industry at large has seized upon this enlightened capitalism as an opportunity to dump inappropriate or out-of-date medicines on people they believe will not know the difference. For most of the pharmaceutical companies it has become an opportunity to gain a tax break, save itself the cost of warehousing or destroying old stock, and in the process looks like a saint."

"So the plan failed," Paul suggested.

"That's where Operation Nightingale truly comes in," Zahir replied. "We just used the network to pit the power of the pharmaceuticals against themselves. The network allows us to monitor pharmaceutical activity in foreign countries. We also worm into the local area networks of the pharmaceuticals to let employees know our findings. Our best information regarding the dark side of these corporate giants comes from within through the anonymous voice of internet cafés. When reports of corporate skullduggery are confirmed, we blanket all the stock-watch sites."

"The same sort of thinking is starting to impact the financial world," Celine said. "Several organizations are utilizing performance screens to help investors identify ethical investment opportunities. These funds have consistently proven to generate better returns."

"NASDEX has the Sustainability Group Index," Paul added. "It's comprised of 250 public companies that are rated on everything from their environmental record to how broadly their ownership is distributed."

"How do they stack up against private companies?" Celine asked.

"That's difficult to answer, but I can say our non-traditional practices have led to some of the best business opportunities."

"Such as?"

"I guess it was my understanding of how under-tooled the former East

Block was that led us to recycle machinery to several countries," Paul said. "It started out with gifting modest bits of equipment, but as we grew, the program became a central part of our planning."

"Most business people would not be willing to bear that cost," Celine observed.

"Ironically, the program encouraged us to be developing the most advanced technology, which is what really secured our reputation in the marketplace. Meanwhile, when things started opening up in eastern Europe, they were eager to tool up and turned to us as a trusted partner. Looking back, it seems hard to believe we questioned what we were doing, but believe me, at times we did."

"So these emerging economies are hobbling along with your old equipment," Tomo asserted.

"The waste equals energy equation is not missed by industries starting from scratch," Paul replied. "It has taken our associated companies very little time before they leapfrog us technologically to more sustainable practices."

Tomo threw a stone in the water and the sound reverberated on the ceiling of the cave. "Your experience is convincing, Paul," he said with less aggression in his voice, "maybe industry can clean up its act. But the minute we step off this trail, we all jump right back into our old gas burners."

"Maybe that's where Hammond will come in," Kim said.

"Hammond Power Systems. How so?" Tomo inquired.

"I don't know much about their planning, but James is working with them on ways to realize the optimum social impact of their technology. It appears they are willing to view their mission in its broadest terms."

"And what's their stated mission?"

"'Power to change the world,'" Kim replied.

"It will need to be more than the greatest technology on the planet to live up to that promise," Paul cut in.

"You're right, Paul," Celine agreed. As she rose to put on her pack, the others followed suit. "We're great at the vision thing, but one has to wonder if society as a whole will ever find the courage to execute the mission."

As they stepped out from under the cool enclosure, the gravel rolled like ball bearings under foot and the warm sun encouraged everyone to conserve energy. The group walked in silence, except for the murmurs they shared about the beauty that surrounded them.

They watched the eagles soar on updrafts and eventually take roost in the tallest trees that rimmed the beachfront. They stared back at the sea lions' curious inspection of their progress from off shore.

Passing the dramatic rock outcropping of Tsuquadra Point, Kim observed that it would not be long before they arrived at Tsuquadra Creek.

As they walked along the carpet of sand that hugged the base of the rocks, Paul fell into stride with Celine. "You seem a little down," he said. "Is it that vision thing?"

"It's an execution problem," she replied. "Were our bank measured against the wealth of countries, it would be the 15th-largest in the world, yet as a contributing entity in society, it takes a relatively neutral position."

"Depositor's assets, fiscal accountability, return on investment," Paul offered.

"Sure. But, as the bank's corporate assets continue to increase, their contribution in terms of social accountability languishes. The public knows this, and the armies of people that work for us are ready to revolt from within. They don't want to be riding a global juggernaut that finances the rationalization of everything in its path."

"So what are you going to do about it?"

Celine boosted her pack on her back as though acknowledging some additional load. "Over the last few years, I have been working on the concept of a Social Capital Network."

"Is that in conjunction with other banks?" Paul asked.

"Yes, it's a federation of financial institutions that would both fund and channel funds to social causes worldwide. When we present the program to the Boards of the big banks they are glowing with enthusiasm, because they know the lack of social equity is a global time bomb—but in the end they are afraid to act."

"Maybe you're trying to effect a pattern that doesn't fit the establishment structure," Paul proposed.

"Institutionally, perhaps," Celine said. "But talk about an untapped market. Do you know that the 350 billionaires in the world have a combined net worth of almost half the population on the globe? Working with investors, I've witnessed a growing redistribution of wealth to social purposes."

"Maybe you should be appealing to those investors directly."

Celine did not respond immediately as they watched a great swarm of sea birds take flight from the beach directly ahead of them.

Then, tentatively she replied, "Connect the Nightingales to the needy."

Part 4: *Insight*

A Projected Wellness: *The good world view*

The late afternoon sun and southwest breeze were directly at their backs. Kim was aware that, if they had been walking the other way, these natural elements would be working against them. She contemplated how the trail was unfolding their thoughts, and wondered where the territory ahead would lead them.

Approaching a peninsula of white sand, they came upon a small creek that carved sweeping 'S' turns at its base. On the other side of the stream, the small peninsula stood like a natural building site with an open view of the Pacific.

"Here's a great spot to spend the night," Tomo said, having hopped over the stream and mounted the top of the natural levee.

As the others caught up and dropped their packs, they entered the quiet appreciatively. The rock headlands they had traveled around in the afternoon were acting as a natural breakwater to the broad bay they were in. The stream, unlike the tumbling falls, flowed silently below them.

"This is a very peaceful place," Celine observed, peering up at the towering trees on the foreshore.

The low sun pulled the apricot and lavender colors out of the surrounding woods as they worked together setting up camp.

They went about their tasks as they had before, but Kim realized everything was different now. They were not just known to one another, not even just friends; they were connected in how they were experiencing this journey. Conversations during the last two days had affected all of them in a similar way. The world as they viewed it was not on the edge of the abyss, but on the edge of its socially creative capacity. In this small community, they were exercising that same capacity.

Kim's thoughts evoked a strong connection to James, and she decided to try her luck phoning the hospital. Moments later, having established there was no change in his condition, she was thankful she had not drawn attention to the call. As she turned off the phone, the "low battery" light flashed on heightening her concern.

The others decided to try their luck digging for clams, while Tomo found a large slab of plywood worn smooth on the edges by sand and water and fashioned a table using a stubby round of tree as the base. This find encouraged him to construct a complete dining room suite. Collecting sun-bleached curved branches, logs and various bits of driftwood, he assembled a remarkably formal set of bent wood chairs with long sweeping backs that curved down to random supporting arm rests.

As Tomo neared completion of his project, the others returned with every cooking container they had brimming with clams.

"Will your dining room view onto a fireplace?" Zahir asked, noticing that Tomo had placed the benches in a 'V'-shape looking out to the view of the western sky.

"Sure, why not?" Tomo replied, as Zahir and Kim turned to collect firewood while Celine dug a clean cotton cloth from her pack and spread it out across Tomo's table.

Soon they were seated with the fire started and a greatly anticipated meal of pasta and clams before them. They took full advantage of the creature comforts and shared the easy conversation of friends who might have met at a favorite restaurant.

Paul excused himself and went to the creek, pulling from it a container he had lodged earlier. "I can't think of a better place to enjoy this," he said, pouring a round of white wine from a plastic flask into small paper cups.

"Would it be premature to say 'Here's to 'The More?'" Celine asked.

"If not now, when?" Paul responded, raising his cup.

As their private thoughts lingered with the rich taste, Kim sensed they were all thinking of James.

During the dinner, they spoke of their pasts, finding similarities of thought through a diversity of backgrounds. Celine was the first of 10 French Canadian generations that spoke both French and English. Zahir was a first-generation American whose parents were Ugandan refugees. Kim's family included the first settlers in British Columbia from England. Paul and Tomo were new Americans who had arrived from different ends of the world. Those differences of history were marked by a similar present that seemed ultimately to embrace a positive world view.

As the exchange took place, Kim thought of James' purposes in bringing this group together. She knew these were the kind of people that interested James, not because he saw himself as the greater spirit, but because he saw the greater spirit in others. At the very heart of James, she thought, was a man who had always believed human qualities would transform institutions from dispassionate to compassionate.

Kim thought of the initiatives in which James was involved, where new approaches to governance and stewardship were being embraced. Approaches that were caring, inclusive and focused on sharing values, not institutional norms of the past. Then she realized that the members of the group each held goals that were broader than those institutional norms; they were trying to push the sectors they worked in toward positive social change.

James had brought this group together because he saw each of these people as capable of acting on an awareness that had surfaced in their social sphere. She understood now that, for James, the spheres had begun to overlap, and the overlap had formed a connected pattern that represented a positive world view. But the vision wasn't formed by James, or any individual; it was an emergent world view of concepts and models they had unwittingly explored on the trail.

Kim felt her internal temperature change, as if a warm breeze had swept down the beach through the night air. She flashed upon an image of James as a prospector of precious metal. The value was in the metal. James was merely exposing the richness inherently there. He mined goodness. He looked for ways to exploit it, process it, and blend it into other processes. James was reading the landscape of change, sensing a big strike when the collective consciousness would expose a new world view. A view that embraces the welfare of the whole before the critical part is gone. A view that sees human beings as stewards of the natural world not as its competitors. A view that says our path is meant to be one of prevalent donor, not dominant predator. It was as though for the first time, she realized his true purposes. For all these years he had been preoccupied with this search. Her mind focused to establish their relationship in this broader context.

"Hey Kim, what do you see at the edge of the Pacific?" Paul's voice pulled her out of thought.

Realizing she had been absent for some time, Kim looked back to the horizon, trying to find an honest response.

"It's more like the edge of the world," she replied as though still referring to the geography. "I was thinking of how our experiences seem to promote a good world view. Somewhere in that view is a unifying force."

"James said a unifying force results when widely-held knowledge converts to judgment," Tomo said.

Kim recognized the statement from James' manuscript, but was more interested in the fact that Tomo was forming a proposition instead of questioning others.

"And what do you make of that, Tomo?" she inquired.

"I'm fighting a losing war against crime, just as you are in educational reform. Paul is at the leading edge of business that few are following. Zahir has made sacrifices which the marketplace simply moves to capitalize on, and Celine can't get her project approved at the bank—proving just how exceptional Nightingale Operations are." Tomo paused as though resisting his own conclusions. "I don't see a unifying force that can deliver the good world view."

"The judgment that is held by many is evolving to a new level of thinking that unifies," Paul replied.

"As many minds enter the decision-making process, there is no assurance that judgments will unify," Tomo said. "If you look at the chaos the world is in today, it seems we are simply transferring bad decision-making from a few individuals to many." Tomo's statement hung on the waves of heat rising from the white ashes.

"Or maybe the pattern just hasn't emerged," Zahir said as he looked up from the glowing shapes in the fire. "Didn't we say disequilibrium, maximum flow of energy into the system, chaotic unrest, and the emergence of a new pattern will result in spontaneous change?"

"Sounds like we agree on the part about chaos," Tomo said.

"And the part about energy," Kim said. "As decision-making moves from the few to the many, there are maximum flows of energy and feedback into the system."

"If you are speculating on spontaneous social change, I fail to see a pattern," Tomo muttered.

"Are you not the one who reminded us that, when widely held knowledge converts to judgment, there will be a unifying force?" Paul needled. "That force is a convergence of many wills that sense a new pattern of life supporting actions that must come into play."

Kim dug her feet into the cool sand and looked at the faces framed in the firelight. "What widely-held patterns of judgment are we seeing today?"

"A belief that we must stop consuming the natural world at a pace that is non-sustainable," Tomo replied.

"A belief that we must alter an economic system to serve the basic needs of people equitably," Celine added.

"A belief that we must develop clearer visions to a good world view," Paul concluded.

"If society is in the process of self-organizing around these beliefs, the pattern that will arise represents a very different set of actions," Kim proposed as the setting sun cast an orange light across the beach.

"A unifying force based on the judgment of many," Paul suggested.

"A convergence of our wellness of spirit," Kim concluded.

Only nature spoke now as the sea and sky blended to the same milky color and the sun glowing orange on the horizon became a singular point of focus.

Then Celine's melodic voice moved out into the night air. "That unifying force must hold within it a great capacity for wellness, so for tonight, let's just project that wellness to James."

The Garwood group sat in silence as the setting sun grew to a large red sphere on the horizon. All the colors, noises and patterns disappeared, and in its place there was nothing but an endless field of light.

The Spiritual Quest: *An endowed morality*

Tomo studied the massive rock wall that curved around the beachhead and straight out to sea. Half a mile behind him, the Garwood group was just stirring from sleep.

Exploding towards the wall, he snagged a firm grip and hung over the broad expanse of sand that laid out for miles behind him. He held himself in suspension for several minutes. Then, as if having reached some personally defined summit, he spun off the face and walked in his lone footsteps toward camp.

The sun crept higher in the eastern sky as the ragged cliffs cast dancing shadows on the rolling blue Pacific—one man's entertainment.

Returning to camp, Tomo found Celine cooking crepes and the others studying the trail map.

"Good morning, Tomo. How does it look ahead?" Paul asked.

"Great until you run into cliffs," he replied. "Not too far from here, we'll have to hit the trail again."

"The trail ahead is beautiful. About a mile from here we reach a place called Nitinat Narrows," Kim explained as they peered over her shoulder at the map. "Through this narrow passage, a massive lake system drains and fills with the changing tides. There are only a few minutes each day that the tide is not surging through, but the First Nations run a motor-boat service that can power us across."

"The 'First what'?" Zahir said.

"First Nations people were those native to Canada before European settlers," Kim replied.

"We call them Indians," Zahir said innocently.

"Not if you want to get across Nitinat Narrows," Kim joked.

"I should be the last person you have to correct," Zahir replied, waving his large hands in front of his own dark skinned body. "Do all hikers use this First Nations water taxi?"

"Yes, but a lot of people hiking from the north turn back, as the trail ahead is more challenging."

"These are my kinds of challenges," Zahir said as Celine arrived with a huge plate of apple crepes. Each person held up a plate as Celine dished out the sweet, steamy pancakes that quickly disappeared amidst gulps of appreciation.

"Those crepes are great, Celine," Zahir said. "I just feel badly that James has to have hospital food this morning."

"So you think our projection of wellness last night awoke James' consciousness?" Kim said, happy to entertain the thought.

"Absolutely. He could not possibly have missed our cosmic healing energy," Zahir replied in a self-mocking manner.

"Don't be too cynical, Zahir," Celine said. "A lot of people have come to believe that energy directed positively can have miraculous effects."

"Actually, I'm one of them," Zahir replied. "I'm convinced that our subconscious minds are connected in a super-conscious knowing—*that* to me is spiritual."

"If you want to know spiritual," Tomo said, "take a walk down that beach."

"I don't think any of us would argue with you there, Tomo," Paul said as the first rays of sun filtered into their campsite.

"Interesting that times like last night transcend to the realm of spiritual," Kim offered.

"We would all like to make that kind of connection," Tomo replied as though he knew they were speaking of James. "But, as people turn to new spiritualism, it leaves a great deal in this world devalued."

"I think that's why people are so taken by the new spiritualism," Kim said. "Because the insight of a spiritual potential is viewed as arriving through the individual, not a removed deity or authority."

"This may be so," Tomo replied, "but as we pursue new expressions of spiritualism, there's a huge gap between our aspirations and our actions."

"You're saying that, by taking a mystic approach, we are missing the opportunity for fulfillment on a secular level," Kim said.

"How can we aspire to a higher self outside time when we fail to aspire during our time here?" Tomo replied. "I think it is fraudulent to profess a goal of higher consciousness without first striving for a higher humanness."

"Are they mutually exclusive?" Kim posed.

"Perhaps not, but often people speak of a higher state of being with no connection to positive change on the ground. We are big on theoretical spirituality, but in terms of a practiced morality that demonstrates some spiritual quest, we are nowhere."

Kim had come to appreciate that Tomo's thoughts were connected to insights that were easily missed if one didn't slow down and drag the content out of him. "To connect with our desire for spirituality is to connect with our deepest humanness, which is achieved through a 'practiced morality'?" she said, attempting to restate his comments as a question.

"In the circles I travel, I'm lucky if there's any practice of morality," Tomo said, furrowing his brow. "We didn't talk about this on our climb last week, at least not specifically, but I know James believes that many of the changes we have been speaking of bring us to a time of great opportunity."

"What kind of opportunity?" Celine asked.

"He sees this as the first time in the history of man that we are called to apply special human qualities to our everyday lives."

"What do you think, Tomo?" Kim asked.

"I think he is right. If we don't start to set our spiritual goals closer to where we live, all the mystic speculation of a spiritual being will be set in an increasingly nightmarish reality."

Tomo's comments stood like a challenge to the understandings they had reached the previous days.

"Who knows when humankind developed its spiritual sense," Paul mused. "What we do know is that the spirit quest of early thinkers of our culture had no reason to question the limits of the earth or its inhabitants. As we institutionalized and focused on an external God, we were able to reason that our compassion need not be focused here on earth. By externalizing our worship, we lost sight of the sacredness of life. But a new vision of our spiritual quest is arising from an endowed morality."

Kim could sense that Paul was reaching to put to words the same ideas that had consumed her that morning. "That endowment is a collective consciousness that is redefining our role on earth," she added. "Before thoughts converge in the actions of many, they start as an awareness, as one small voice from within."

"We only have to look within ourselves to know the voice exists, but we're not listening," Tomo rebuked.

Paul seemed unwilling to give his ground. "Our authentic voice speaks of our untapped depth, value and meaning. Understanding that we are keepers of one world is an endowed morality which defines our spiritual quest."

"We are defining spirituality based on how we will actually respect all living things," Tomo said thoughtfully. "Our endowed morality is our spiritual quest because our goal as humans converges with the needs of the natural world."

Paul smiled as he rose from the log he was sitting on and reached to pull Tomo to his feet. "You're stubborn, but you can be persuaded," Paul concluded. "Let's see where the voice leads us."

—·—

It occurred to Kim how good it felt to walk along the hard-packed sand, following in Tomo's earlier footsteps. The fresh morning brought observations about the increasing ruggedness of the terrain around them and about a sense of approaching new ground.

They traversed a quiet bay between two rock out-croppings. Spotting a fluorescent orange marker hanging in the trees, they moved away from Tomo's earlier footsteps toward the trail.

Stopping at the forest edge, they looked out at the breathtaking beauty of the rugged sand-and-stone-framed seascape. Tomo grinned at Paul, then scurried up the steep bank at the edge of the forest, pulling the others up behind him. As he helped Kim last, he held her hand a moment longer than he needed to, and in his eyes she sensed a new closeness.

They entered the path to the steepest climb they had encountered on the hike. Deep breaths substituted for discussion as they reached the cliff-top trail that dipped through narrow ravines and between groves of twisted shore pine.

At times, the trail broke out to the cliff edge, revealing pockets of white sand between the towering rock headlands. As they traveled through the constantly changing landscape, it was difficult to discern whether the scenery had improved or they were simply more capable of taking it all in at once.

The trail moved inland, dropping off the higher bluffs. Climbing through a rugged ravine, they caught their first glance of Nitinat Narrows, the undulating current moving heavily against the direction they were traveling.

As they continued to forge against the swirling narrows, Kim couldn't help equating the natural turbulence to the one she was feeling internally. Their discussion about an endowed morality seemed perfectly obvious on the one hand, and completely nebulous on the other. Like a half-assembled puzzle, several pieces were in place, but the big picture had not yet emerged. If our endowed morality moves us to worship all living things, what prevents us from taking that spiritual sense to practice? What causes us to act, or fail to act, on the voice from within?

Her thoughts were interrupted as the path stepped down to a rock beach where a small dock was pulled up on the shore of a protected levee. Less than 500 feet across the channel, they could see an aluminum boat just leaving shore, loaded with hikers and packs.

"That must be the shuttle headed this way," Zahir said. "Look at how the current is dragging them down-stream as they're crossing."

"Actually, the tide is still going out, so the lake is draining to the ocean, making the channel look like a river," Kim said, as she pulled her hair back into a bun to bring relief from the heat of the day. "People have made the mistake of trying to swim across and been carried out to sea in the back-eddies and currents."

"It looks like that's where those guys are going to end up." As Zahir said this, the boatman turned several degrees into the current and increased the throttle of the outboard engine. The frenzied water slapped against the metal hull like a hollow drum. Slowly, the craft churned its way across the channel to the dock where the Garwood group was waiting.

Four women looked relieved as Kim and Tomo fended the boat off the dock. A First Nations man in his late twenties remained sitting in the stern. He held casually onto a rope that had been tied from one side of the dock to the other.

"What's it like ahead?" one of the women asked Kim, as if Kim's answer would determine if their party got out of the boat.

"It's paradise," Kim replied.

"Good, because it's Hades back there, so I figured we were either headed for heaven or hell."

The Garwood party helped the women with their packs. Just as Celine started to ask the woman who had spoken about her meaning, the boatman barked, "Are you guys coming or not?" After three days of collaborative decision-making, this implied order made them jump to. Gear and bodies toppled into the boat, and without another word they were off.

Kim shouted back over the whine of the motor to the forlorn group of women left on the dock, "You'll love it!" She cast a broad wave and smile as her hair blew to one side of her face. Turning back to the helmsman, she said, "Service is just like I remember it."

"What do you mean?" he asked, cavalierly.

"Prompt," she replied evasively.

As they crossed, they could see up the mile-long length of the narrows to the outflow of Nitinat Lake. Kim thought of the Garwood group as the swirling currents tugged the boat towards the vast Pacific. She knew crossing Nitinat was a psychological mid-point of the hike and, scanning the excited faces, could only imagine what the rest of the journey would bring.

Realizing there would be no discussion with the pilot on the other side, when the boat slowed in its approach to the far dock, Kim asked, "Hikers used to be able to purchase fish or crab here. Is that still possible?"

Tucking his shoulder-length hair behind his ear, the pilot turned his head and studied her for the first time. "It's been a while since you've been on the trail."

Kim was willing to accept his response as a "No," but then, as if this brief knowledge of history separated her from other tourists, he said, "My uncle is fishing up towards the lake." Pointing up the narrows, he said, "You can go and ask him."

"Thanks," Kim said as the boat bumped into the dock. They threw their gear out and pulled some money together to pay the pilot as he casually tied the bow of his boat up to a big ring at the corner of the dock. Paul confirmed the price of five dollars a head. It appeared that the pilot was going to take it without a word, but then he turned to Kim and said, "The spirit is with you."

Kim looked into his eyes, and he held hers as if he were bestowing a special confidence.

Before she could respond, the pilot turned and walked up the beach towards a small settlement where some rusting corrugated tin roofs could be seen scattered amongst the second-growth trees.

Reversing the Tide: *A new relation with man*

Having emerged from the cool shadows of the forest, they now stood in the comfortable mid-morning sunlight. The group agreed it would be nice if they could get some fresh seafood for lunch. Seeing that the beach ended at a rock headland, they walked to the base of the bluff and found a trail leading up and around, eventually returning to traverse the narrows. After they had walked beside the waterway for several minutes, the trail opened to a white sand beach at the end of which was a single figure. As they approached, they could see it was an older First Nations man mending a fishing net.

"Hello," Zahir called out as they approached. The older man lowered the nylon twine into his lap and turned his shoulders to face them. It was a totally different kind of body language than the younger man, Kim thought to herself.

"Hello," he replied.

"The fellow who brought us across the narrows said we might be able to purchase some fish from you," Zahir said.

"Yes. My nephew," the old man replied. "The tide will be slack soon. I will put this net out for fish. I have some crab."

To the general chorus of "yes," the old man pulled a metal-framed trap up from the water's edge. Fishing out two large Dungeness crabs, he made a gesture towards Tomo and Kim that they should take them from him. Kim knew the way to hold a crab, when alive, was behind its legs at the back of the body. When she moved to position herself beside the old man, he acknowledged her awareness by bending his arm so she could approach the crab from the back.

Tomo, missing the more subtle movements of this exchange, moved forward to take the other crab. As he reached out, the crab reciprocated by taking his right hand with both its front claws. Jumping back with the crab firmly attached, Tomo looked over at Kim, who had just taken control of her crab. Tomo quickly duplicated Kim's grip and turned to Zahir. "Pull this thing off me," he pleaded.

Zahir backed up and said, "I have a deal with meat—I won't eat it if it doesn't eat me."

The old man reached forward and opened one claw. Then, closing it in his palm, he used his index finger and thumb with the other hand to release the other claw. He held the claws closed in both hands and looked at Tomo's face to see if he still had his grip.

"He will taste extra good to you," the old man said. "You are blood brothers."

"How much will those be?" Paul asked.

"Because this one is so poorly behaved, he is no charge," the old man said, gesturing to the crab suspended between him and Tomo. "The other one is ten dollars." Paul handed him the money, with a smirk.

"How will you kill these crabs?" the old man asked.

"We usually throw them in a pot of boiling water," Kim said.

The old man winced. "We believe that when an animal is killed with respect, its spirit is free until it finds another body to inhabit, so it can wander into the world again." As he said this, he released the claws and reached above the crab Tomo was holding. Grouping the side legs in both hands, he bent down beside a sharp rock and swung the crab down towards it.

From where Kim was standing, she could see the small bump at the front of the shell crush against the rock, and the crab go totally limp. She duplicated the old man's actions, her crab now lying still in her hand.

"He did not struggle in death. The meat will be very tender," the old man said. Then, pointing to the head of the beach, he added, "There is a large pot boiling on the fire. You may use it."

"That would be fantastic. Those crabs would never fit into our pots," Celine said.

As the Garwood group turned to walk up the beach, Paul asked Kim softly, "Do you get the feeling that he's known all along that we would be buying him lunch?"

Kim smiled back as they approached the top of the beach where the steam rose from a large black iron pot suspended over smokeless white coals. Tomo and Kim placed the crabs in the dark water while Zahir fumbled in his pack, searching out some "boil-in-the-bag" pasta he tossed in the pot.

The old man cast his net into the perfectly still narrows and watched the floats that suspended the net at right angles to the shore. When he was confident that the weights at the base of the net would hold its 25-foot length in place, he slowly turned and walked up the beach.

Kim had just finished helping Tomo bandage his hand as the elder took a place near the fire. "They will be ready now," he said, reaching behind his back where some chopped wood lay. He handed Tomo two slender cedar sticks. Tomo took them with his bandaged right hand, accepting the implied challenge of getting the crab out of the pot without burning himself.

Lifting out the crab with the familiar pincher claw, Tomo suspended the now-pinkish crustacean above the pot. The old man, anticipating this further lack of preparation, held forward a large flat slat of split cedar, the size of a large roofing shake. Tomo placed the crab on the wooden slab, and the two men repeated the procedure with the second crab.

Whether hungry or impatient, the old man decided not to prolong the next step. He placed the cedar plate on the white sand, and picked up a smooth round stone and cracked the hard shell with a few solid blows. He passed the first plate to Kim, repeated the procedure with the second crab, took a large leg for himself, and passed the second plate to Tomo. Zahir fished his pasta out of the water, and everyone concentrated on the nourishment of an early lunch.

The sweet fresh meat awoke a sense of taste that had become accustomed to trail food, and they agreed that nothing had ever tasted better. Zahir, less preoccupied with his lunch, spoke to the old man who seemed equally unimpressed with his bill of fare.

"Do you live back there?" Zahir asked, pointing towards the small settlement they had passed after crossing the narrows.

"My people come here to fish and hunt in the summer season," the old man replied.

"So the village has not been here long?" Zahir speculated.

"It is the oldest of our people's places," the old man replied.

Kim interjected, "Whyac is speculated to be the first settlement on the coast of North America. First Nations people were drawn here because of the salmon runs through the narrows."

"You mean the first inhabitants on the coast ever—here?" Zahir asked in surprise.

"Yes, we are the Ditidaht," the old man added, as if their tribal name would clarify what Kim had said.

"That's amazing," Zahir said.

"We had much to speak of in the past and little to say in the present," the old man said.

"Why is that?" Zahir questioned.

"We lost our way of life," the old man replied. "Now we have lost our purpose."

"There are few men your age who could do the things you are doing today," Kim said.

"The future of my people is not with elders like me. It is with young men like my nephew. He has grown to see that the white man has also lost purpose. He is like the crab." The old man placed the cracked shell of the vacant body in front of him. "His spirit wanders—but it looks for another world to occupy."

"Can he return to the ways of your people?" Paul asked in a conciliatory tone.

"The ways of our people are gone," the old man said without a vestige of drama. "The Great Spirit spoke to us through the earth—her forests and great oceans. For thousands of years, our people have fished and hunted here. Now a narrow strip of trees is all that's left. People move through it like a white man's shopping place."

"Your nephew feels, like many of us do, that we have lost some special relationship with nature," Kim said.

"White man has never found his way with nature."

"And what is your way?" Tomo asked.

"There is only one sky, one ocean, one great land, one man," the elder said. "To live by the earth you smell the weather change, listen for the birds to tell you fish have arrived, and leave the land as though you had never been there. To live by nature, man must read the signs."

"Signs of nature?" Kim responded.

"Signs within himself," the elder said.

"What are the signs within man that lead to a new relationship?" Kim asked.

"The earth is crowded. Now we must learn to listen to the one voice," the older man replied.

The elder seemed to anticipate Kim's next question, although he paused a long time before he spoke. "The voice," he repeated. "Our people have said that man is not separate from the web of earth. The web is hurt. The cry, man will hear. The cry of children, the web will not support."

Kim looked over at Paul and back to the elder. "We are hopeful that a New Reality for man is upon us, where he both respects and patterns his ways after nature."

The elder seemed unmoved, although he shifted his focus to Kim's eyes. "What man has done to the web, he has done to himself. It is only nature in man that mends the web."

Kim watched this man whose life order had been imposed by nature, saying that man facing natural limits to his species was part of a new order.

"Man anchors the web," Kim said as she turned purposefully to look at Paul.

The look in his eyes confirmed that the big picture had emerged for him also, Kim realized as he nodded his head in agreement.

The old man seemed to sense they had understood his deepest meaning. "Our people have a legend that speaks of a Great Awakening. It is to happen seven families after the ships came."

He rose to retrieve his net from the current that had just started to reverse towards the inland lake. As he stood above them, his ancient features appeared divined by wisdom.

"Nature will now cleanse the body of the lake," he said, pointing to the altered current. "She accepts the natural flow of life man resists."

A Great Awakening: *The voice from within*

As though some personal confirmation had taken place, Paul stared at the old man approaching the water. "Because their way of life has been extinguished, they see there's only one reality left for us," he said.

"More importantly, they see our way of life is extinguished," Kim responded.

Zahir was about to speak, but saw the old man waving them down to the water. He and Celine stayed to pack up their belongings while the others went down to the water's edge.

The old man had drawn his net in halfway and pulled from it a large, humped-back salmon with beautiful blue/green markings. Stepping aside, he pulled a large knife from the sheath at his waist and with a single blow of the handle on the forehead of the fish, he ended its struggle. In almost the same movement, he slit the fish its entire length and, holding onto the gill at the side of its head, submerged it in the water. After a few sweeping movements that seemed like gestures in prayer, he rose and walked to where the three hikers stood watching.

"This is a sockeye," the old man said, holding the fish forward as though a prize. "This is the wisest of all salmon. It proves this by being the most difficult to catch and the most flavorful to eat. It is for your journey. To move your beliefs to actions."

Kim reached out and cradled the cleaned and gutted salmon, knowing this was a gesture of understanding between them. "We will carry the wisdom to better purposes," she said, sensing the elder would trust her words.

The old man walked over to the stack of wood from which he had pulled the cedar slats. He returned with two large, flat shakes. He held one up and Kim laid the fish down on it. The elder cradled the fish in the two boards, then ran the knife down its inner spine, almost cutting through to its outer top layer of armored skin. He then flipped the salmon open so both its exterior flanks lay flat on the board.

"Soak this board, and cook like this over hot coals," the old man said, as he put the other wooden slab over the exposed flesh of the fish and handed it to Paul with the formal gesture of a gift.

"Will it last until this evening?" Tomo questioned.

"The cedar keeps the fish, the fish keeps you," the old man said while holding his focus on Tomo.

"Could we...," Paul started to say.

But the old man anticipated his offer and said, "Your promise is your payment."

To their chorus of "thank-you," the elder held up his hand and echoed his nephew. "The spirit is with you," he said, his eyes still on Tomo. "You will follow him," he added in a clear tone of respect, pointing to Tomo. "He is your warrior." Then, as if to explain himself, he added, "We will need fearless people to arrive at the new ways."

Tomo looked at the elder in a manner that showed the respect was mutual.

"We will need a generation of fearless people," Kim confirmed as she cast a broad smile at Tomo, which they all shared with the old man as he turned to tend his nets.

Kim walked with her arm around Tomo's shoulder as Paul carried the cedar-wrapped fish to where the others were preparing to put on their packs.

Celine was delighted to have fresh salmon to cook for dinner, while Zahir acknowledged it meant another meal of packaged food. Paul used the broad cinching straps across his pack to fasten the splinted salmon, and within moments they were underway. They waved good-bye to the old man still busy at the water's edge, and retraced their steps along the narrows and then inland around the rock bluff.

Returning to the beach, they came upon the main trail and entered the woods on a long boardwalk that stretched through a second-growth forest. The sun was reflecting on the split cedar walkway, converting it to a silver ribbon rolled out through a sea of green.

The dry boards and solid footing sent a hollow beat of footsteps through the silence of the inland forest. Soon the terrain started to rise, and the boardwalk gave way to a path through shallow rock bluffs.

As they came upon a side trail that headed towards the ocean, Kim said, "This leads down to stone carvings that they say are the oldest petroglyphs on the coast." The sound of the waves signaled they were not far from the water, and they decided to take the detour.

Within a few hundred feet, the forest opened to a small, circular-shaped bay of sandstone that resembled a large ceramic bowl. The smooth surface of the rock sloped into the mid-tide ocean. They dropped their packs at the trailhead and moved onto the smooth sloping rock.

The porous sandstone felt secure underfoot as the Garwood party wandered at the high-tide line looking for the carvings of which Kim had spoken.

Kim had just located an ancient inscription of what looked like a man hunting an animal when Tomo shouted, "Look here."

The group gathered around where he and Paul were crouched. There in the rock was the clear inscription of a three-masted sailing vessel showing the full square rig in a primitive box-like rendering.

"Can you imagine seeing something like that when all you've known is hand-paddled canoes?" Celine asked.

"They must have believed it was the arrival of some god," Paul added.

Tomo looked up from where he was bent down rubbing his hand over the stone etching. "Unfortunately, one that forced them to surrender their gods."

"What gods?" Zahir asked.

"First Nations, like every indigenous culture before ours, worshiped the gods of the earth that provided their bounty. Our culture worshiped a transcendent God that praised the ascension to heaven, but was unclear of how this applied to the human relationship with Mother Earth. First Nations left in their culture a warning to abide by their relationship with nature until the seventh generation finally speaks in one voice," Tomo said.

"You saw it too!" Kim exclaimed, grinning as though she was talking about the scenery. "They had a prophecy about our generation. That nature in man can mend the web."

Paul turned to Zahir's confused look. "Their culture was based on an understanding of their place in a natural system. Ours has been based on an understanding of our place in a man-made system. His nephew is despondent because he expected the white man's reality to be the one of meaning. But, as we worship at the altar of consumption, professing our adherence to God's laws, they have been asked to abandon the gods that sustained them for millennium. The old man believes the prophecy that we are destined by nature to arrive at the Great Awakening because only we can make the conscious choice to re-anchor the web."

"Man is the anchor of the web because he can assimilate the many impacts of his species with all aspects of nature," Kim said. "We are nature's deepest accomplishment, its highest form of consciousness, its greatest threat and its only hope."

"How does nature in man bring us to define this new relationship?" Zahir asked, clearly still perplexed.

They looked down as Tomo continued to rub his hand over the rough stone etching. "We are the seventh generation since the arrival of the Europeans. There's a vast awakening that must arise as one voice from within."

The Preordained Unity: *Spiritual determinism*

They moved up and over the headland to a bay that held the deserted town site of Clo-oose. It was less a place than an idea, with a few reminders of a dream that never materialized. As they walked through the rich mix of wild and domestic growth, Kim spoke of the early pioneer plans to develop the area at the turn of the century.

Broad-leafed maples grew where the clearing for a luxury resort lost its manpower to the First World War. Domestic flowers of blue bell, foxglove, periwinkle and hydrangea lined the trail as if in tribute to the settlement of 250 people, who suffered the highest per capita war casualty of any community in Canada.

They walked past the traces of civilization as the trail established itself back in virgin forest, moving beside a tidal estuary and eventually to the river that formed it. Following upstream several hundred yards, they came upon a majestic suspension bridge slung low over a still river. Walking two abreast out into the midday sun, they stopped, resting their packs on the rough timber railings. The water was murky, but the white sand flood planes and tilting trees on either side made the stop most compelling.

"I'm up for a swim," Tomo said, wiping his brow with his handkerchief.

Quick agreement found them changed and in the water within minutes. The still water was warmer than they were used to, providing excellent bathing. One by one, they stretched out on the ebony smooth surface of long-fallen trees to absorb the warmth of the day.

Tomo lay draped across one of the larger logs, speaking up to the sky. "This must be the Cheewhat River," he said. "I wonder what that means."

"I was hoping you wouldn't ask until after your swim," Kim said. "It means river of urine. A name given by the natives because of its color."

"Hope the analogy ends there," Zahir said as he finished drying himself off.

Celine seemed keen to change the subject. "It's hard to believe that anyone could conceive of turning this wilderness into a kind of Coney Island resort."

"I suppose when the first settlers came to the new world, it was all pretty wild," Paul replied.

"It would be interesting to see how today's frontiers appear in the next century," Celine said.

Kim watched a river otter slink down to the water and swim purposefully to the other side of the stream. "A Canadian author, Margaret Atwood, once wrote a poem called 'Progressive Insanities of a Pioneer,'" she said. "It spoke of a homesteader who was given a deed in the northern plains. When he traveled into the vast wild lands, he realized there were no reference points on which to establish the tangible bounds of his deed.

"The lack of order in the physical world reflected his internal state and signaled his impending insanity," Kim continued. "But, at the last moment, an 'ordered absence' occurred. He willed himself to set his bounds and establish a new reality."

Stretched out on a huge log staring up at the sky, Paul recited the poem for her:

> This is not order, but the absence of order.
> He was wrong, the unanswering
> forest implied:
> It was an ordered absence
>
> He dug the soil in rows,
> imposed himself with shovels.
> He asserted
> into the furrows, I
> am not random.

"Paul, how much stuff do you have in that head of yours?" Zahir quipped.

Kim chuckled at Zahir's back-handed compliment. "The pioneer knew what had to be done, but it took an act of will to establish his reality in the midst of ambiguity."

"Is that the point you think society is at today—an ordered absence?" Celine inquired.

It was only then that Kim saw the connection to their earlier discussion. "An ordered absence," she repeated, trying to catch up to Celine's question. "That's not an absence of order. It's a sense that a new order is struggling to establish itself."

"And, if we were talking about society, what would that act of will be?" Celine asked.

"It would be the statement, 'I am not random,'" Zahir said. "I will listen to the voice from within."

His comment was met with casual affirmation, and Kim smiled, confident the Garwood group was traveling to the new order together.

Throwing their clothes over dried bathing suits, they were soon moving along a wide trail through a wispy second-growth forest, cleared 80 years earlier as part of the town site of Clo-oose. Nearing the beaches of Clo-oose Bay, they left the last remnants of the speculators' promise for an "unparalleled investment opportunity" buried by a century of shifting sand.

As the trail moved up and skirted a long bluffed headland, the wide path became a deer trail. It cut through deep salal and krumholtz that formed long green archways over the narrow trail. As the hikers moved in and out of the sun and shadows, the trail wandered to cliff-edge views and over streams that intersected the thick tangle of growth.

The mood was ethereal; Kim felt they were not just viewing, but were part of the surroundings. The terrain that had once provided them a psychological connection to nature now seemed to be offering some consistent spiritual connection to their destination.

"Look at that," Zahir exclaimed as the group finished a long descent towards the beach.

Viewed over the ground cover and through a frame of trees was a half-mile-long blade of rock running straight ahead, shielding the broad white sand sweep of Dare Beach.

"Those are the 'Cribs,'" Kim instructed. "They are the tail end of the sandstone shelf on which we have been walking."

"That must be Carmanah Point off in the distance," Tomo said, looking at the forested headland a mile away. "I'd like to make it to Carmanah Creek today."

"There's a beach much like this one on the other side of the point, called Carmanah Beach. The creek is at the end," Kim said.

"Well, let's do it," Zahir asserted, to no one's surprise, as he took long steps down the shallow bluff to the beach.

They climbed onto the blade of sandstone, its leading edge cutting into the sea, and moved quickly along its flat surface. The tide was rising around the natural breakwater, and the ocean gurgled under its surface like a massive shipwreck half buried in the sand. Crossing breaks in the rock at the far end, they stepped down onto the compacted sand.

Tomo kicked his toes childlike into the beach. "Listen—it squeaks," he said as the others duplicated the bird-like sound with their feet.

"This beach was once known as Whispering Sand Beach," Kim said. "Last time I walked here, someone said it was the whispering souls of the hundreds who have been shipwrecked on this coast."

The Garwood party looked several hundred yards up the beach, noticing for the first time the endless field of sun-bleached logs stretching off in both directions. Staying low on the beach, they walked towards Carmanah Point with the sands whispering beneath their feet.

The contrast between the expansive shore and the intimate covered trail seemed to shrink the group as they moved on in a tight pack.

"I am not random," Celine philosophized. "Those mariners, like the pioneer in the poem, were searching for meaning by asserting themselves into an unknown order."

"It was the next frontier," Kim offered.

"I was thinking of what you said about establishing a new order and how it requires an act of will towards what we know has to be done," Celine said. "It reminds me of the breakthroughs that people in crisis make—when ordinary people are moved to do extraordinary things."

"I see what you mean," Kim said. "It's not a leap of faith. It's a determination to access the deeper capacities within ourselves."

"Yes, but what does it mean when a whole society makes this move?" Celine asked.

"It means they have acted on the unifying force. They have exercised the judgment to listen to the voice from within," Paul said without hesitation. Then he added slowly, "The question remains—will the force that unifies come about through acting on insight or reacting to crisis?"

No one spoke as they walked together around the point. Looking up at the ragged cliff top, they could see the Carmanah light beacon above the towering trees.

They moved to the metal stairs at the base of the cliff and started the long vertical ascent. Reaching the top, the hikers caught their breath and surveyed the grounds. As they moved along a cement walkway, the first structure they passed was a raised helicopter pad, behind it a small house, then a towering white lighthouse.

"Hello," a voice said from behind.

The group turned to the doorway of the house where a dark-haired man stood.

"Hello," several voices echoed.

"I hope we are not trespassing," Celine added.

"No, not at all," the man replied hospitably. "There's fresh water in the large tanks if you need some. Feel free to walk around. The view is the best from the heli-pad."

The group lowered their packs and headed over to the water tanks, gawking at the panoramic view.

"It's nice and cool," Celine said, taking a drink from the cup Paul offered her.

"Don't have to boil it either," he replied.

"Why not grab the best seat in the house," Zahir said, and they all moved back to the heli-pad perched on the edge of the cliff.

They sat in the center of the big "H", as if on some great saucer in flight over the Pacific. Long stretches of white sand beach moved out on either side far below them.

For some time they relaxed in silence, peering out at the great expanse of the Pacific. As if moved by the forces of the ocean below him, Paul repeated the First Nations elder's words, "She accepts the natural flow that man resists."

Kim raised her cup as if celebrating some unconscious connection. "Here's to the natural unifying force."

The relaxed response confirmed her toast.

"That's it!" Tomo's voice broke the peaceful silence. "That's what he meant by 'Spiritual Determinism.'"

"Who meant?" Paul said, spinning around like an inbound chopper.

"James," Tomo replied as if his name explained the statement. "Our spiritual quest is the attainment of the natural order within man. Our movement toward unity is pre-ordained by nature."

Kim couldn't tell if people were more surprised at what Tomo said or that he was the one to say it.

Tomo continued speaking as though the silence arose from the former. "We have always questioned the essence of human nature. Seeing man as a creature of free will missed the broader reality that we are spiritually evolving to a higher order. Free will evolves within a naturally predetermined capacity for unity."

Paul spoke with the caution of fingers turning the last number of a combination. "Our evolving relationship has moved from Nature being the provider within her limits to man being the consumer beyond her limits. Our taming of nature meant that only species that assisted human expansion were encouraged. The result is a crisis in growth of our species and a crisis in the elimination of other species."

Paul turned his attention to Celine. "The unifying force is brought on by both a crisis and an insight. Humankind had to dominate nature to realize its fragile codependence. It is at the edge of the abyss that we realize nature has endowed us with the insight to see these errors and correct them. We had to learn these lessons before we could see the preservation of all species is the only way we are preserved. Preservation of the whole is our spiritual quest. We were meant to evolve to understand and unite in that quest."

"Human nature is destined to redefine its spiritual goals around the unity and caring for all living things," Kim concluded. "Spiritual determinism says we can't resist, we have to act!"

"I am *not* random. I *will* listen to the voice from within," Zahir said with confidence.

"That is nature in man," Tomo said. "The natural flow we can't resist."

The Garwood group turned to Zahir, as his familiar chant rang out with new meaning. "Let's do it!"

Part 5: *Transformation*

The N-gen: *An awakening character*

The mile walk along Carmanah Beach was the last push for that day, but Kim couldn't help feeling it was their first. As they moved along the postcard-perfect scallop of sand, there was a silence of new discovery. The waves rolled up the beach filling footprints as the Garwood group moved without a mark into the future.

As they approached Carmanah Creek, they could see the long sweeping beach was interrupted by the creek that formed a sandy peninsula.

Paul, who was the first up the rise, turned and said, "That which you can't imagine has come true, Celine."

"How's that?" she inquired as she mounted the dune.

"Coney Island has come to the wilderness," he replied as they stood watching a game of volleyball being played at the end of the sandy point.

"I think I'm just jealous that someone has the energy to pack a net and ball in here," Paul added.

As they approached, they watched a group of about a dozen young people jump and dive in the pure white sand. The blue Pacific was now high at the edge of their endless court.

The Garwood group cut across the point, waving to a few of the young people watching the game. Moving up along the river past the large camp, they found a clearing in the logs near the cable-car crossing.

They set up camp quickly, making a fire so they could bake the salmon.

"It will take awhile before we get the hot coals for cooking," Celine said.

Zahir responded in a goofy voice, "Mom, is it okay if I go play for awhile?"

Seeing him look towards the volleyball game, Celine played along. "Yes, dear, just make sure you come when I call you!"

"You up for it?" Zahir said, turning to Tomo, who was already on his feet.

"Someone has to keep you from hurting yourself," Tomo replied, and the two men set off back down the beach.

Paul looked up from his book and said to Celine, "I'm so happy with how our boys are developing." They shared a smile over their increasingly familial group.

As Tomo and Zahir approached the game, the teams had dropped down to four a side, some members having retreated to prepare dinner. Witnessing the arrival of new recruits, one of the first players to see Zahir claimed him for their team. Within moments, casual introductions had been made, and Tomo and Zahir were in the game.

What Zahir accomplished in height above the ground, Tomo more than made up for in speed and agility on the ground. The game was re-energized, and soon the shouts and catcalls had brought back all but core kitchen staff to watch body language span two generations.

A "show-no-mercy" set had just concluded when Celine's voice could be heard.

"That's our mom calling us for dinner," Zahir told the twenty-something crowd, leaving curious onlookers to puzzle over how old and of what nationality this mother to him and Tomo must be.

Among the quick handshakes and warm smiles, there were questions about getting together again. Tomo said, "If you really want to party, we will probably crack open a pot of Earl Grey later this evening."

The fellow who had introduced himself as Jonathan replied, "If you guys get into tea the way you do volleyball, it might be a new experience."

They all laughed and said goodbye. Tomo and Zahir ran down the beach, stopping long enough to refresh themselves in the clear cold Pacific swells.

They arrived back at camp just as Celine pulled a perfectly cooked salmon from above the white-hot coals.

"That's a big group," Paul observed.

"They are not in any hurry," Tomo said idly. "They have been here for two days already."

"I'm sure most of us were not in much of a hurry when we were in our 20s either," Celine said as she dished up the salmon. Everyone savored the cedar-tinged sweet flaked meat while Zahir looked over longingly from his bowl of rice.

They reminisced about a time when anything seemed possible. As the conversation moved on and the sun shone low on the giants bordering the edge of Carmanah Creek, Kim couldn't help but feel that ironically they were moving back to an attitude that saw all things as possible.

Dinner was finished, and the last rays of light left the highest tree-tops.

"Here comes your fan club," Paul said as he finished pouring second cups of coffee for those who wanted it.

Tomo and Zahir looked down the beach and recognized Jonathan, Cam, Laurie and another woman, who hadn't been in the volleyball game, heading towards them. They both waved, and the gaggle of young people waved back.

Kim had just put the cedar cooking slabs on the fire, the fish oil filling the air with a burst of light and fragrance.

"Wow! It smells great over here. What did you guys have for dinner?" Cam asked.

"Same old stuff," Tomo replied. "Baked salmon with wild blueberry sauce."

Kim thought the smaller girl looked physically weakened as Jonathan said, "We wouldn't want to interrupt our steady diet of Kraft dinner, anyway."

"We've got some good homemade cookies and coffee on if that will help," Kim said, noting the smaller girl's pallor.

"I'm Michelle," she said, responding to Kim's offer. "That sounds great."

Introductions were exchanged as Kim located some spare Styrofoam cups and poured four piping hot coffees. Everyone settled in with one of Celine's massive "everything-but-the-kitchen-sink" cookies.

"You guys sure know how to live," Jonathan said as he held up the cookie, boyishly inspecting it like a fine wine.

"We've just had more practice," Tomo replied truthfully.

"Yours is a big group to be hiking the trail at once," Kim observed.

"Some of us just walked in from Carmanah Valley," Michelle clarified.

"I heard there is a fine for entering the park off the logging roads," Kim responded.

"Yeah, 700 bucks," Michelle replied. "But we haven't seen a ranger the whole time we've been here."

"There is concern that a lot of people moving through the lower Carmanah Valley could endanger the ecosystem," Kim pressed.

"Our little footsteps could never amount to the vicious assault the forest companies have committed further up the valley," Michelle scoffed.

"I heard the lower 10,000 acres of the Carmanah Valley was reserved as a park a few years back," Tomo interjected, "and that it is the home of the largest tree in Canada."

"Yeah, the 'Carmanah Giant,'" Michelle said. "It's only 15 minutes up the creek. What a mother of a tree—over 315 feet tall."

"I think the trail should be accessed by people who make the commitment to experience the full trek," said Laurie, obviously part of the group that had hiked the whole trail.

"Oh, Laurie, you're such a purist," Michelle retorted.

"How do you guys come to be on the trail?" Kim asked Laurie.

"Some of us know one another from university or work stints. Others have met online and are getting together in person for the first time," Laurie offered.

"Yeah, you could say we are kind of a virtual community of the over-educated/underemployed," Jonathan shot back.

"If I did say that, it would fit nicely with most older folks' perceptions," Kim replied.

Cam, who had been aloof up to this point, turned his deep-set blue eyes to Kim. He was about to say something when Michelle's voice rose from the opposite side of the fire. "I hate that. We are unique," she said, her small body framed by the large hemlock log against which she was leaning.

"Our lives have been ones of seeing both families and institutions fall apart," she continued. "In the process, our generation saw that adults were less caring than we like to believe."

"That may be what makes you angry, but it's not what makes you unique," Kim said.

"Actually, you're right," Cam said. "It did make us angry that we felt vulnerable in our own homes, our schools and ultimately the places of work. The worst part is we've joined an older generation in selling ourselves short."

"How do you mean?" Celine asked.

"My friend Jonathan here introduces us as 'over-educated and under-employed'," Cam replied. "The fact is, few of us would thank you for a 9-to-5 routine. Because for most of us, it would mean doing some brain-deadening process job with no way out."

"We seek out episodic periods of highly involved work." Laurie spoke with a confidence that betrayed her late-20s looks. "Taking on projects allows us to focus on stimulating work and leave the politics for people putting up with staff positions."

Kim detected the look of surprise in Celine's eyes. However, this was the generation Kim had worked with for the last decade. She knew they were quick, pragmatic and able to step outside themselves to see how the world really works.

"Do you think sometimes that you miss out by not being a constant part of the organization?" Celine baited them.

"The same way you miss a dysfunctional family if you're part of one," Jonathan replied. "We've developed our own networks of people who thrive on meaningful projects, and when work happens, we pull a team together."

"That's right," Laurie said. "Jonathan, myself and two other people at our camp just finished developing a human-resources plan at the Royal Bank. It was a ton of work and we had a blast."

"Sounds like you wish you were still there," Celine persisted.

"Oh please!" Laurie groaned. "The fact that we were working on some progressive planning doesn't mean it will happen for another decade. The way we play it is a blend of contemplation and action. It's a reasonable way of living on the fringe until the center shifts."

"Where do you see the center shifting to?" Celine responded.

"To work performed in an environment of emotional competency," Laurie replied with clear resolution. "One that sets standards that converge rather than consume resources."

"Human resources?" Celine asked.

"We are just part of the earth's resources that are not being respected. Corporations need to be transformed so that their central purpose is service to all resources, not the other way around. But we need to build structures that support this new center."

"Tell me more about the 'new center,'" Kim posed.

"The new center is an awareness that a shift is about to take place," Laurie replied. "An awakening character is amassing."

"Shift?" Kim pressed.

Laurie looked to Cam in an engaging way.

He responded, breaking the intensity of his gaze. "At the center of these organizations is a mass of intelligence. The center knows they are getting drawn into the doctrine of consumption and meaningless jobs. They see this trajectory has brought us to unsustainable ways and they feel empowered to change the system from within."

"Empowerment of the center is broader than the corporate application," Laurie added. "Throughout the economic system there is an amassing of character that looks to transform society."

Kim looked over at Michelle and wondered if she shared this view of reality. "Now, that's unique," Kim concluded.

"How about you, Kim?" Cam said. "What do you do?"

"I'm in education," Kim said. "I grew up here but have been living in Boston for the last several years."

"Teaching?" Cam responded.

"Well, it's become more administration."

"Ah, a bureaucrat," Jonathan piped up.

"Well, not exactly," Kim replied, deciding she would get her story out before her visitors drew their own conclusions. "I founded a program called Teach America. We target underprivileged schools and put the best and the brightest teachers in them."

"I bet you get them lining up at the door," Cam said.

"Underprivileged schools?" Kim asked.

"No, qualified teachers looking for a real challenge."

"You're right," Kim said. "I think the first surprise I had in the program was that people were looking for relevance and were willing to do dirty jobs to find it."

"That's really cool," Laurie said, with the same idolized eyes Kim had seen often before. "You must be very proud of what you've accomplished there."

"Thanks, Laurie," Kim said, graciously. "Sure, for what it is, I'm very happy, but it's just the tip of the iceberg in educational reform."

"Where do you go from here?" Cam asked.

Kim let it hang as a personal question. "I have applied for a job in public administration. I'm not sure the system's ready for it, but education has to find a way to support the new center, as you call it."

"Is this going to be another one of those big social problems that will be left for the repair generation to straighten around?" Jonathan asked with an air of invincibility.

"That's great." Michelle interrupted angrily. "The same generation that describes us as the country's janitors and carpenters is expecting that we'll clean up the mess the world is in and build a new one."

"Speak for yourself," Jonathan said to Michelle. "That sounds like Generation X whining. We're the N-gen. We have all the tools and opportunities of the Net-generation."

Laurie smiled at his enthusiasm. "What is more exciting is that as we work in network environments of co-dependence, collaboration and mutual aid, these skills become values—that's the kind of awakening character we see transforming society."

Kim glanced at her traveling companions, aware that Laurie had captured the essence of transformation. "Boomers really do have a lot to learn," she replied.

"As boomers took control from their elders, they did not make the world a better place to live in," Michelle asserted. "Our generation is looking for something better, but our voice is not heard. Our complaints about not having the opportunity to make better choices are being misinterpreted as jealousy for being deprived of those things earlier generations had."

"When you speak of choices, I see it from a business person's point of view," Paul said. "To me, it seems the generation ahead of us—the old guard—sees us breaking down control structures in a manner that opens up opportunity for others in a much more democratic way."

"Is that happening because your generation has to, or wants to?" Cam interjected.

"I suspect it's both," Paul said. "In our company, we have an educated workforce that takes full responsibility and is rewarded for it."

Laurie's alert brown eyes had been watching the exchange. "Let's say you created this democratic company because you thought it was right and wanted to, and now the rest of the world is changing because it has to. What do you do next?"

Paul looked really stumped, as though he couldn't say he was satisfied with where he was because he knew there was more he would like to do. But in terms of going beyond the framework he was in, he had no answer.

"I'm afraid you've got me in a double-bind, Laurie," he said.

"That just proves there is a 'beyond' for you," she said with a broad smile. "I think it will be a very interesting world when the boomers confront their own awakening character."

"How is that?" Kim questioned.

"I think they will finally do what they wanted to do in the 60s," Laurie said, turning back to Paul. "Change the world."

"You're speaking almost as though you liked us," Paul said.

"Boomers are a generation of spoiled brats," Laurie said with a disarming smile. "But deeper they are humanistic, so there has to be a discovery of caring values in their lives."

"Maybe that's what we've been exploring over the last 30 years," Kim said.

"The increasing chaos of those years has only proven to them that their early ideals of equality, ecology and love were right," Laurie said.

"Do you see that happening in today's world?" Kim asked.

"I see it as a longing in my generation that our capacity to care surfaces as a way of being," Laurie replied. "But the awakening character of the N-gen can't move to the light unless the boomers take the lid off."

"I think you're right." Paul spoke directly to Laurie. "Our generation started out believing we could create an ideal existence, but we took a material rather than spiritual-centered approach."

"Do you believe the boomers will now adopt a spiritual approach?" Laurie asked.

"We have been speaking of this ourselves," Kim confessed glancing at Paul. "We have concluded that society is moving toward seeing the earth in a spiritual context and that when this happens, we will hold sacred all of nature's resources."

Laurie's large eyes narrowed in understanding. "It's the awakening character," she said, as if to herself.

"The character of many that connects in a pattern of caring," Kim concluded.

"Exactly," Laurie whispered, averting her eyes towards the fire.

Kim watched her, thinking there was only one way to describe her look: the future.

A peaceful silence lingered, and then Cam said, "We should be getting back to our tepees."

"Yeah," Tomo added in agreement, "we'll be heading out early."

"Of course," Cam replied. "Otherwise, you guys are not at all like boomers."

They laughed at his inference, and Paul said, "We'll take that as the highest compliment."

"Exactly," the chorus of four young voices broke out. The loudest one amongst them was Michelle.

Among Giants: *A commitment to The More*

Through the mosquito mesh of the tent fly, Paul could see the sky was gray and assumed it was the pre-dawn sky. He was about to roll over when he noticed Tomo was gone. Within a few moments, his curiosity aroused him and, crawling out of bed, he pulled on his second and last set of clean clothes.

Finding his watch in the outside pocket of his pack, he saw it was 6:15, which confirmed the change in weather prior to stepping out of the tent. Standing in the gray morning, he marveled at how different everything looked. The white sand, stones and sun-bleached logs cast against the blue river, sea and sky now all blended into shades of gray. The great towering trunks of the Sitka spruce offered little relief. Only the brightest new green growth overcame the misty monochrome landscape.

Paul spotted Kim at the meal site and walked over.

"Good morning, Kim."

"Oh, good morning, Paul. Just pouring myself a cup of coffee. I'll get you one," she said.

"Thanks. Kind of a gray day." He sat down on the log beside her.

"I think that's all it is. Probably just sea fog. It may burn off later."

"Yes it seems calmer now, but man, was the wind ever blowing last night. I just hope our luck continues." Paul noticed Kim had the cell phone in her hand. "Were you able to reach the hospital?"

"No, my battery is shot," Kim said as she snapped the two wafers of technology together.

Paul looked to Kim emphatically. "I miss my wife so badly. I woke this morning to give her a hug and no one was there."

"It's a good thing Tomo got up earlier," Kim said, trying to lighten both their moods.

Paul smiled at her resilience. "I don't know where he is."

"He can't have been gone long," Kim replied. "Tomo's the one who brought the food pack down and made the coffee. It was still warm when I got here a few minutes ago."

Paul drank his coffee as fragments of conversation came to mind. "I remember when we started this trip, I asked Tomo about a metal hook thing he had in his pack. He said it was something he'd use to climb an old-growth Sitka spruce."

"And last night the kids were telling us that the largest tree in the Canada is only 15 minutes up the river," Kim said as they both downed their coffee.

They walked quickly up the beach until it narrowed to the boulders of the creek bed; then, picking up a small path, they disappeared into the towering forest. More in touch with the earth than movement with packs had allowed them to feel, they moved quickly over the ridges and gullies at the riverside. In the gray light, the trees seemed to consume all of the overhead space. Deeper in the valley, thick green mosses and ferns covered the tree trunks, branches and forest floor, converting all the grays to shades of green.

They came to a point where a buttress of rock hung out over the river. Among the giant first growth on the far bank, a single towering spire ascended sharply above the others. Kim and Paul stopped in their tracks.

"That's got to be it," Kim said.

"Yes, I can see a rope barrier at its base," Paul said.

Looking up the tree, Kim said, "Tomo has to be around here somewhere."

"You're right; he is," a voice said from behind.

They turned to see Tomo nestled among the giants. He was reclined in a natural high-backed chair of root, with a thick cushion of moss extending beyond him in all directions. His climbing hook and rope lay coiled beside him.

"Sorry to disturb you, Tomo," Kim noted a difference in his expression.

"I got what I was supposed to come here for," Tomo replied, rising to his feet.

"Did you scale the tree?" Paul asked tentatively.

"No, I didn't have to."

Kim looked away at the grove across the river. "It's a marvelous place," she said, avoiding further invasion of Tomo's thoughts. "I think we should head back and check on the others."

"I'll join you," Tomo said, apparently ready to leave this place of private epiphany.

They walked through the forest, sharing observations about the dense vegetation and soon breaking out to the open beach valley. It was shortly after 7 a.m. when they approached the campsite. Celine and Zahir were cooking up a batch of pancakes.

"Did you conquer the big one?" Zahir called out.

"In a manner of speaking," Tomo responded with a broad smile.

Kim knew Tomo was referring to something other than a tree and was happy they had given him some space. "Thanks for pulling breakfast together while we were off playing in the woods," she said.

"Thank Zahir. He did it all," Celine said. "He tells me he will restore our health after yesterday's carnivorous binge."

"Yep, it's my day to cook, and I figure three square meals of bird seed and you'll be just fine," Zahir warned, as he dished out thick whole wheat wild berry pancakes, margarine and syrup.

"If this is bird food, we'll fly down the trail today," Kim said, accepting a serving and sitting with the others.

As they enjoyed the hearty breakfast, they speculated on the weather, spoke of their morning adventure and discussed the plan for that day's hike.

Finishing his breakfast, Paul pulled out the map and studied it. "Looks like about three miles of beach walking. Then the trail starts up again for about a mile to Walbran Creek."

"They told us at the ranger station that the Walbran cable car is washed out," Celine replied.

"It's easy enough to wade across at the mouth of the creek," Kim said. "With these low tides, we can stick to the beach all the way."

"Some of the kids were saying last night that the trail between Walbran and Logan Creeks is kind of a bore," Zahir said.

"I've heard the sea-side ledge from Walbran is beautiful, but there's a dangerous surge channel that has to be crossed," Kim said.

"Yes. 'Adrenaline Surge: Passable only during dry weather and at tides below 5.5 feet'," Paul quoted a note on the map.

"Maybe by the time we get there, the weather won't be dry," Celine said, peering at the gray sky.

"We should be there before early afternoon, which is when the tide is at its lowest," Kim said. "Why don't we leave the decision until we get to Walbran?"

"It's nice, cool walking weather, so let's get going," Tomo said.

Without the temptation to linger, the group was quick to pack, and soon they were heading up the beach to the cable car that crossed Carmanah Creek. As they left, Paul looked back and could see Laurie sitting outside her tent.

"You guys go ahead. I'll catch up with you," Paul said as he moved back down the beach towards the large camp.

The others reached the wooden tower, helped each other to the top with their gear and took turns crossing in a substantially-worn cable car.

Tomo and Kim were the first to cross, hanging for a moment in the middle of the gorge, maintaining a purposeful silence. Watching Tomo's expression, Kim couldn't help looking up the Carmanah Valley with the hope that she would somehow see what he was seeing.

By the time Zahir and Celine had crossed, Paul was waiting at the far side. Soon Paul had made the crossing, and he and Tomo moved off the tower to join the others at the beach.

"Doing a little recruiting?" Kim asked, smiling at Paul.

"Something like that." Paul looked over at the far shore where a half-dozen young people had now emerged from their tents.

When the Garwood group waved over at them, hands and bodies immediately shot up from the other side.

"Lots of raw potential on that beach," Paul said as they moved south.

"Standing in the shadow of our generation, one has to wonder if that potential will ever be recognized," Kim said.

"You don't hear them say it outright because I don't think they believe it can happen, but they deeply desire what we have come to see as 'The More,'" Tomo said.

Kim was walking on a log slightly behind the others. Tomo's comment caught her so off guard that she slipped, catching herself with one hand. "I thought you were having trouble believing that yourself."

"As the desired way of being, I've never questioned it. I've only had difficulty believing we would evolve to that better way."

"And now?" Kim queried.

"And now I see an N-gen that's looking for us to lay the tracks."

"And the 'better way'?" Kim asked.

"I saw last night that with each generation the voice gets louder," Tomo said. "But when they look to us to confirm that voice—we are not listening."

Kim felt like asking, "And what did you see at the Carmanah Giant," but resisted the urge.

They carried on, the soft sand mirroring the difficult passage of the issue Tomo had raised.

As they approached the rock headland of Bonilla Point, they saw several solitary rock towers in the distant ocean. As they neared, bunches of forest clinging to the top of the slender columns came into view. The geography acted like a focal point accentuated by the gray sky and horizon.

As they approached the stacks of rock, they stopped, resting their packs on table-like stones that littered the foreshore.

Tomo slipped his off and walked to the base of the tower rock nearest to the group. He looked up as if addressing some giant personality.

"They look like figures walking out to sea," Celine said.

"I don't know the story, but the First Nations have a fable that the sea stacks symbolize people," Kim replied as she sat next to Celine on the flat rock.

They looked at the distant rock towers scattered in the ocean.

"Maybe the legend was about the white man, and that's our generation leading the others into deep water," Paul said.

"Maybe you have the legend backwards." Tomo said. "They are all moving this way, and our generation is here." He pointed to the proud monolith at the shoreline.

"Sounds like you agree with Laurie, that Boomers will return to an earlier idealism," Paul said. Tomo stood in front of the others as though he were leading the stone figures out of the ocean that spread endlessly beyond him.

"The voice from within is the awakening character. We can't help but listen," Tomo said. "When we can't help but act, that's when we've made a commitment to The More."

Destiny & Decision: *Choosing a new path*

The Garwood group walked for almost two hours, but the sandstone shelf they had stepped onto just after Bonilla Point changed little. Its entire length appeared as though some great machine, curving aimlessly in and out of the ocean, had plowed furrows in the rock. Pig-sized boulders littered the stone shelf, and the gray sky challenged a deeper sense of optimism.

The group zig-zagged down the beach, taking different paths to avoid water trapped in rows of rock or the harvest of slippery green seaweed. They alerted each other when they came upon particularly good or bad footing but otherwise concentrated on setting their own directions.

Fragments of conversation that arose, where clean slabs of stone would permit, confirmed to Kim that they were focused on identifying their commitment to The More. Celine was asking Zahir about communication over the World Wide Web. Paul sought Celine's opinion on issues of governance. Zahir approached Tomo, testing his thoughts about a high-tech invention.

Kim pondered some transition in her own life, knowing that a new dynamic of destiny and decision-making had been activated. In this community of five, an act of will had been initiated as though they were each choosing a path to their own deeper purpose.

Kim watched Tomo move sure-footedly across the fractured ground. He, more than any, was a person that relied on his own determination to set the course of his life. She realized he had resisted seeing some external deity represent all that is good because it left the perception that human nature is evil by default. His insight that saw man naturally evolving to a spiritual regard for all of life seemed to resolve not only his own struggle but enabled him to see humankind is destined for unity.

Her mind reached to draw connections that converged on the term "spiritual determinism." Could it be that a society so out of equilibrium is in some dynamic movement to the higher-order values by which it professes to want to live? If it is in a process of self-organizing to a caring culture, what new pattern emerges? What marks the spontaneous change to the higher order? What new form of determinism transforms to spiritual ascension?

Her thoughts were interrupted as the rock headland funneled inland to the forest, bringing them quickly upon Walbran Creek. As the broad stream came into view, they could see sweeping curves of water move up the beach, forming lagoons at each of the bends. Nearby, two young men were trying to build a makeshift log bridge across the 30-foot stream.

"We'll meet you halfway," Tomo shouted to them, seeing they were having trouble bridging the current on their side of the river.

The Garwood group dropped their packs and helped pull logs down the beach, quickly constructing a half-floating platform to the jumble of stones at the center of the creek. Tomo walked out on it and attempted to secure some of the larger logs the boys had felled.

He turned to the others and shouted over the noise of the creek. "Take your boots off and wade across. This is never going to be stable enough to cross with packs."

As he said this, the logs behind him dislodged, and he turned to see the two boys laugh as their labor surged down the creek.

When Tomo returned, they all had their boots off. "It's not deep," he said. "As long as nobody slips, we should be able to keep our shorts dry."

"Considering the length of your legs, that's good news," Zahir said.

"You'll wish your center of gravity were at your knees when you're out in the middle of that creek," Tomo responded good-naturedly.

"Keep the waist strap of your pack undone, so you can get out of it if need be," Kim said.

"Need be?" Zahir replied. Alerted that Kim shared Tomo's concern, he unclipped his waist strap.

They stepped to the water's edge, and Tomo moved across first. He kept his body low and moved with his feet spread wide apart. The others followed mimicking his movements. The water was numbingly cold, and the slimy surface of the boulders turned underfoot while the current pushed hard against their thighs.

Tomo got to the other side. Dropping his pack, he waded back in and braced himself at the deepest part of the creek. As Celine neared where the current raced past both sides of Tomo, she lost her balance and grasped Tomo's hand as he pushed her twisting pack back upstream with his other hand. They all quickly reached the other side amidst gasps of relief to be out of the cold water.

"Thanks, Tomo," Celine said. "I was going swimming there for sure."

"I probably broke your concentration," Tomo said modestly as they sat down, happy to put on dry socks and boots.

"Look at that!" Paul exclaimed, pointing up the beach.

The two hikers were returning with a disproportionately large log over their shoulders. They struggled, dropping it over the river, and then the taller man tested it, wobbling to the center of the stream.

The smaller man walked over to the group. "I think you guys had the right idea," he said.

"We have to give you two full marks for determination," Paul said to him.

"Yeah, my buddy is a little single-minded," the young man replied. "After coming across that trail, he wants to stay far away from anything wet."

"Is the trail in bad shape?" Paul asked.

"It's a mud hole from here to Logan Creek," the young man replied.

"We were thinking of staying on the beach and trying our luck at Adrenaline Surge," Paul offered.

"That's what we should have done," the young man said, "but we came this far yesterday afternoon when the tide was too high to go the beach route."

"Low tide in an hour and the surge is a mile down the beach," Paul informed the group.

"What do you think, Tomo?" Kim asked.

"It's a group decision," Tomo replied. "I don't feel good about it, but I'm willing to go because we have lots of rope."

"We're a group that believes in destiny," Zahir said, as he reached over and scooped a sand-dollar shell off the beach. "We'll flip this coin."

"So much for the voice from within," Tomo said, in an unsuccessful attempt to draw attention to his concern about proceeding.

"Okay, the flat side is tails and we go the beach; the round side is heads and we go the trail," Zahir said as he flicked the crustacean with his thumb. It waffled a few times in the air and landed in the sand. "Tails!" he shouted, obviously happy with the results.

"Looks like your partner is going for it, too," Tomo said to the young man, who had now taken his boots off.

He looked up the creek just in time to see his heavily-loaded friend slip, feet plunging in the water either side of the large log.

"Oh!" the group gasped involuntarily.

Straddling the log as though riding a wild horse, his long legs obviously touching the bottom, the young hiker raised one hand and let out a loud "Yee-haw."

"We'll have to give him full marks for attitude, also," Paul said.

"It's wet slogging down the shelf, anyway," Kim said to the young man. "There's a great campsite at Bonilla Point where you can dry him out."

"Thanks," the young man replied. "I'd better get going before he insists the log is the only adventurous way to cross that creek."

They all said goodbye as the young man waded into the creek.

"Any one care to top-up on some journey cakes?" Zahir asked, as he opened a plastic container containing wild rice and carrot-based squares. Although it was still only late morning, each of the hikers accepted, enjoying the sweet spicy flavor.

"I'm offering dessert to anyone who makes it through Adrenaline Surge," Zahir added as though testing the decision they had made.

Kim gently lifted the sand dollar off the beach. "Zahir, haven't we learned more about destiny than the flip of a coin?"

Zahir cracked his inherently disarming smile. "At least that's natural currency."

Adrenaline Surge: *The invincible spirit*

Moving across the broad sandy peninsula formed by Walbran Creek, they came immediately upon a rock shelf. It was different from the one they had crossed earlier. This was a dry plate of sandstone with absolutely no beach. The flat stone surface curved up at the base of the cliff rising to 75-foot vertical walls that wove down the distant shoreline like an endless skateboard ramp.

They walked quickly across the solid terrain, aware that the cliffs offered no escape if they were caught by an incoming tide. Their anxiety heightened as they approached a deep slash in the stone shelf that cut a jagged trough from the ocean to the cliff edge.

The water in the trough surged and sucked with the ebb and flow of waves. As the ocean drew out, 15-foot rock walls appeared; then, pulsing to the top, a chain reaction of spray would surge up the channel, soaking the immediate foreshore.

They stood at the narrowest point, where there was only a four-foot gap between the two rock walls. The heavy packs on their backs made the thought of jumping across the channel seem twice its actual distance.

"Is this Adrenaline Surge?" Celine asked.

"Somehow, I don't think so," Tomo said, as he slipped off his pack, untying the rope fastened to the outside.

"Are you going to transport the packs over a traveling line?" Kim asked.

"Yes. I don't think it's wise to free-jump the channel with this weight on our backs." Tomo tied the rope around his waist, handed the coil to Zahir, and said, "Pull on it only if I fall in."

Tomo made a careful hop across the gap, his foot landing solidly on the other side. Untying the rope from his waist, he tossed it back to Kim, who tied it to Paul's waist. Zahir fed out some line as Paul jumped across without incident.

Ensuring that Paul and Zahir were braced against footholds in the rock, Kim and Tomo used the two men as anchors for the traveling line. They showed both men how to hold the line taut around their waists with a release knot if they had to let the load go. Kim then clipped the first pack onto the traveling line and tied the loose end of the line to the pack, tossing the balance of the coil back across the surge channel. Tomo pulled on the hauling line, and the pack slid along the traveling line suspended between Paul and Zahir.

They performed this maneuver five times until all the packs had been transported. Paul then braced himself with the lifeline as Celine, Zahir and Kim took turns crossing the surge channel. Finally, Paul tied the rope firmly around his own waist, Tomo managed the line from the far side, and he jumped across.

Little was said as they helped each other on with packs and moved on quickly, apprehensive about what was ahead.

As Kim walked with Tomo, who was tying a knot around the coiled line, she said, "A cleverly disguised dry run."

"At least now everybody has an idea of what to do when we hit the real thing," Tomo replied.

"Tomo, what makes you think that wasn't Adrenaline Surge?" Zahir shouted back over the waves crashing against the rock foreshore.

"No adrenaline," Tomo shouted back.

Kim wondered if the others silently disagreed.

They walked single file along the curved base of the cliff where the rock was smooth and dry. Within a few minutes, they came around a bulge in the headland and Tomo said, "There it is."

"How do you know?" Celine asked.

"See the cliff ahead has a big rock outcropping that looks like an elephant's trunk?" Tomo said. "It looks like water flowing down this side of it, which must be Adrenaline Creek."

By the time Tomo had finished this observation, they had moved close enough to see the surge channel in the rock shelf.

The long gash started at the ocean and cut through the shelf they were walking on to the base of the cliff. From the cliff top, Adrenaline Creek spilled a constant veil of water over the protruding trunk of rock into the channel below.

Reaching the edge of the channel, they could see the only conceivable crossing was over two large boulders that lay like beached gray whales in the thirty-foot-wide channel. The group stood in silence, studying the intimidating terrain. Every third or fourth wave submerged the barnacled boulders and then retreated, leaving the stones standing proud in the dark water of the surge channel.

"It's going to be tricky jumping onto those boulders," Paul said.

"It's going to be tricky getting up that slime on the other side," Tomo replied, studying the greasy ridge of rock that lay like a giant slug near the base of the falls.

Kim watched as another instinct triggered in Tomo. She could see there was no question about turning back, because he was already fully concentrated on going forward. The gray sea, sky and landscape blended into one plane. Tomo studied the passage across the surging channel as though he were choosing a route on a big wall.

"This is Adrenaline Surge," Tomo said, as if forcing his heightened awareness into a visual plan. "We will follow the procedure we used at the last channel exactly." He tied Kim's spare rope around his waist. Handing the line to Zahir, he took his long rope with the rappelling hook over his shoulder and watched the ocean as he looked for a break in the waves.

The first boulder was three feet beyond and below the edge of the wall on which Tomo stood. He took two half-steps down the wall and then stepped, totally centered on the head of the first rock. He shifted his feet around and shouted back, "This is very stable underfoot."

Looking up, he could see a large wave coming and decided to take the ebb while he had it. He ran down the 10-foot length of stone and jumped over to the larger rock that lay at a right angle facing down the channel. As he ran up the long slope of rock, the wave chased him almost to the top.

Arriving at that point, Tomo paused, and Kim sensed that the scene confirmed his worst suspicions. Standing at an elevation lower than the wall from which he had started, he found himself unable to see over the wall in front of him. The wall rose straight out of the channel, then tilted on a 45-degree angle for a few feet, where it ended at a crease in the rock. From the crease, the wall moved upward again over a long greasy belly before flattening out. Tomo searched the rock shore ahead but could not see over the immediate foreshore.

"Do you see a place I could hook a line?" he shouted back to Zahir.

As Zahir strained to see a ridge in the rock shelf ahead of Tomo, Kim had Paul bend over so she could get on his shoulders. "Tomo, there's a pool 30 feet in front of you, at 11 o'clock, that looks like it may have a rock ledge on this side," she shouted.

Tomo squared himself to the wall and threw his hook blindly ahead of him.

"Perfect!" Kim shouted. "It's in the pond. Pull it back slowly towards you."

As Tomo followed her instructions, the line grew taut.

"It looks good," she called.

Tomo gave it a couple of test pulls and then jumped for the crease in the rock ahead. Using the rope, he landed with a calculated lean outward, jamming his foot in the crease. It held, but as soon as he pulled himself vertical with the rope, his footing gave way and he slammed hard against the greasy rocks. He instinctively knew not to search for footholds, and used his immediate strength to drag himself over the rocks, hand over hand, using only the rope.

The others cheered as Tomo stood up on the other side, turning to show his entire front covered with green slime. With fists clenched over his head he shouted back, "*This* is Adrenaline Surge!"

"Do we all have to come out looking like reptiles?" Zahir hollered.

"No, I've got a plan for that last step," Tomo shouted back as he untied the waist line so Kim could pull it back.

"You're the one with the lucky sand dollar," Kim said to Zahir. "You're up next."

"Does anybody believe in destiny?" Zahir pleaded as he tied the line around his waist.

Tomo found a firm ledge near the edge of the channel. Jamming his hook in the rock ledge, he tied his rope so there were two long leads running from the hook. He let one drape into the surge and, with the other, lowered himself back over the ledge and to the crease again. He tied the rope off at his waist and, with hands free, grabbed the other line, holding it up, waiting for Zahir.

Following Tomo's lead, Zahir crossed smoothly and agilely. He jumped onto the first boulder and, without hesitation, moved down it and then up the big rock directly across from Tomo.

"Step across onto my foot and pull yourself up with the rope," Tomo said, holding the free line out to him.

Zahir did exactly as told, and, as he started to step away from Tomo's foot, he got a powerful push up the bank. Tomo scaled up the slope behind Zahir, using only the rope in his hands for forward traction.

Establishing Paul and Zahir as anchors, they conveyed each of the packs across the gorge as they had at the smaller channel, and then readied for the remainder of the group to cross.

Kim was next. Waiting too long on the small rock, she got her feet wet, but then moved quickly across the boulders and, with help from Tomo in the crease and Zahir above, hardly touched the slippery wall on the far side.

Celine followed, appearing more comfortable about the odds of a safe crossing. Tomo, watching the water, was waiting to suggest a starting time. He saw a big wave moving up the channel and, just as he turned to warn Celine, she stepped over to the first rock. His warning sent her scurrying down the boulder just in time to meet the full force of the incoming wave. She was swept over with such force that the lifeline was jerked violently from Paul's hands.

Celine disappeared in the cauldron of black water and then reappeared as the wave pumped her further up the ragged channel. She flailed her arms as the surge crested in the rock fissure; then, as the water receded, she was flushed back down towards the whale-like boulders from which she had fallen.

Tomo instinctively released rope at his waist, jumped over to the large boulder with the free line in his hand and positioned himself, facing up the channel.

Suspended in the ebbing surge, Celine was heading for the gap between the large rock on which Tomo stood on and the greasy headwall. Her body slid helplessly toward the narrow slice in the rocks, the current drawing her out as if intent on taking its captive.

As Celine approached the narrow channel, Tomo wrapped the rope around his arm and jumped in, falling immediately in front of her. She clung to his shoulders as he locked one arm around her and the other around the rope. As the wave drew further out, they were left suspended just below the crease that Tomo had used as a foothold.

Kim guided the line Tomo had discarded from his waist to Celine, shouting from above for her to take it. Celine, clawing at the line, finally took firm hold. As Tomo pushed from below, Zahir and Kim hauled on the line, delivering Celine out of danger.

Still running on some primal drive, Tomo pulled himself up the rock slope, where Zahir's firm grip took hold.

Tomo moved to the flat shelf where Celine stood dazed, dripping and gasping for breath. He reached out and took her trembling hand, as his eyes scanned her entire body. With his free hand Tomo pulled a handkerchief from his pocket, squeezed out the water and dabbed the blood on Celine's right shoulder, thigh and knee. It was clear they were surface abrasions, and she moved each joint as if to silently confirm this was so.

Within seconds, Tomo positioned himself squarely in front of Celine and took firm hold of both her hands in his. "Are you okay?" he gasped, still taking gulps of air.

"Yes, I think so. Are you okay?" Celine replied, equally winded.

"Yes," Tomo repeated, a fact that seemed so funny at the time that they both burst out laughing. The relief was instant for the others, and they joined in while Paul shouted from the other side, "Is everybody okay?"

"YES!" they all shouted back, laughing even harder.

"We'd better pull him over," Tomo finally said to Kim.

Tomo and Zahir threw the ends of both ropes over to Paul, and he tied them to his waist.

"If you go in, we're going to haul you right over the rocks," Tomo hollered.

"That's reassuring," Paul shouted back. He waited for the right moment, then jumped onto the first boulder, ran down it and quickly up the larger one.

Tomo and Zahir managed their lines until Paul stood on the crest of the rock directly across from them. Tomo said to Paul, "You get ready to jump, and lock your body at the waist, because we are going to give you a mighty tug and you're going to fly up here."

"Right," Paul said. "On three—one, two, three."

Tomo and Zahir cranked on their lines and delivered Paul right into the arms of Celine and Kim.

"I don't deserve such a reception after dropping you like that," Paul said to Celine.

They all laughed, sharing a massive bear hug.

"Do you believe it?" Paul said, looking up at the top of the falls where the sun had just broken through the sea fog. The Garwood group watched as the light washed down the edge of the cliff and across the rock slab, bathing them in a field of warmth.

"Oh, that feels good," Celine said. "But that surely doesn't," she added, taking Tomo's right hand and elbow gently in her hands and inspecting the rope burns on his forearm.

"No risks, no rewards," Tomo said, brushing it off.

"You deserve a reward, Tomo," Celine replied, looking deeply into his eyes. "But not this," she added, looking down again at his arm.

"How did you feel before crossing Adrenaline Surge?" Tomo asked.

"Insecure," Celine replied.

"What do you feel when you look down that beach?" Tomo asked, pointing in the direction they would be traveling.

Celine paused as if searching for her true feelings. The sea fog had now retreated to the water's edge. It formed a wall of cloud that mirrored the cliffs at the head of the beach. Between the two, the rock shelf lay like an open passage to the blue sky above. "Invincible," Celine finally said.

"No risks, no rewards," Tomo said again as they smiled, sharing his full meaning.

Kim could feel herself being carried vicariously from the commitment they had made that morning as a group, to a new level of determination as an individual. She felt certain that the silence that followed was that same private journey being taken by each of them.

Finally, Zahir broke the silence. "Kim, why don't you help Celine and we'll see if we can clean up this guy?" he said, cupping his hand at the back of Tomo's neck.

Kim and Celine walked to the base of the protruding cliff that flanked the surge channel. A veil of white water slid down the elephant's-trunk protrusion of rock into the channel below. Celine peeled off wet clothes as Kim dug a towel and first aid kit from her pack. Soon Celine was in dry clothes, and they both put on runners, then tied their wet boots to their packs.

They sat on the dry bench of rock in the sun while Celine folded her damp hair into a loose French braid, ignoring the large bandage Kim placed on her shoulder.

"Only you could get thrown into nature's washing machine on spin cycle and come out looking like royalty," Kim joked.

"I'm just glad that a prince was around," Celine replied, looking down the foreshore as Tomo, accompanied by Paul and Zahir, approached in dry clothes.

"If I'm not mistaken, that prince became a king today," Kim said, thinking back to Carmanah.

As the men approached, Kim asked, "Who wants to have that dessert Zahir promised us on the soft sand of Logan Creek? It should only be 20 minutes or so around that corner," she added pointing down the shelf.

"Yeah, let's get off this slab of rock," Zahir said. "I am beginning to feel like a reptile."

As Zahir spoke, the incoming tide delivered a large rogue wave that spilled over the edge of the channel and onto the shelf. The others could see it would be a film of water by the time it reached over the table to them. But Zahir, with his back to the surge, was so startled when he saw the water at his feet that he ran up the curved wall at the base of the cliff, clinging with his toes near the top of its arch.

As the waters receded, Tomo looked up at Zahir and said, "You know, you do kind of look like a reptile up there."

Zahir looked down from his compromised position and was the first one to enjoy Tomo getting the last laugh.

A Calling: *Seeing The More*

It had been a quick walk off the rock plain and up the long draw to the sands of Logan Creek. They sat on a 10-foot-wide log that had probably been on the shore before the first hiker crossed the beach in the 1960s.

Kim watched Zahir fuss over Celine, and detected a deeper look of caring in those kind eyes. He pulled out home-made fruit rolls and dehydrated sliced bananas while Paul went upstream for water. The water was very clear, but the shore quite rocky for camping.

When he returned, they were all talking about their adventure. The danger was an aspect that had been pushed to the back of their minds like the passing of the sea fog. It was three in the afternoon, and their desire to push on was tempered with concern for Celine and Tomo.

Celine said she would like to walk further, and everybody seemed to understand that she did not want Adrenaline Surge to be her last physical memory of the day.

"There's a steep ravine we have to climb to get above this creek bed," Kim warned.

"Do we have to pull ourselves out using Tomo and a rope?" Celine joked.

Kim smiled. "No. We're getting into big ladder country. A chain of ladders out of here and another set down into Cullite Creek a little over a mile from here."

"Let's do it!" Celine mimicked Zahir.

Kim smiled back at her gutsy friend and said, "You will be rewarded by the bathing ponds of Cullite Creek."

"Say no more," Celine added, and they all stood, closed up their packs and headed up the creek.

Within minutes, they found themselves staring up in wonder. A network of rough timber ladders moved up the precipitous cliff to where it met a narrow suspension bridge that spanned the canyon. Above the bridge, on the other side of the canyon, several platforms poked out of the thick carpet of green ferns and wild shrubs. Bridging to each were ladders that ran up the ravine almost as far as the eye could see.

After a morning on the bare sandstone shelf without a human trace, they were all affected by being back where the abundance of nature had reached some tentative agreement with man's presence.

They moved up through the underbrush, climbing with the aid of exposed tree roots to get to the formal trail. The exertion eliminated the energy of full sentences. Single words of exclamation described the feeling of being immersed in the dense coastal rainforest wilderness.

Helping each other onto the small platform, they stopped to catch their breath. The long ribbon of the suspension bridge ended its sweep across the wide expanse by disappearing in the thick woods on the far side. The vertical wall they were about to travel was now in clear view on the opposite face of the canyon. Far below, the waters of Logan Creek wandered gently through the thick undergrowth.

The cables supporting a single board width of the bridge swayed in the onshore breeze. It occurred to Kim that they should have left this challenge until nerves, muscles and wounds were more settled.

"No risks, no rewards," she heard Celine say as she stepped forward. Holding onto the support cables at shoulder height, Celine stepped tentatively out onto the narrow catwalk.

Tomo moved gently on behind her as the structure bounced deceptively under their weight. The group gently encouraged their passage and, as they reached the other side, gave a loud cheer.

When all had crossed, they continued rising through the shaded canyon, their attention increasingly absorbed by the task. Moving up past the trunks of twisted shore pines and beyond through planes of spreading branches, they finally reached the top.

As they rested on the highest platform in the bright sun, they looked back at a world that had changed so incredibly fast. "I'm glad we did this," Celine said, her meaning clearly going beyond the ascent of the ladders.

Celine leaned over and gave Tomo a kiss on the cheek, from which he blushed like a schoolboy. They all laughed at Tomo's embarrassment and turned back into the forest and higher ground.

Almost immediately they came upon a bleached boardwalk that ran through an open bog covered with a tapestry of flora and fauna. Pink salmonberries, flowers and white strawberry blooms were replaced in damper areas by long spiky broom, lily-of-the-valley and pond lilies. Walking was a breeze, and the group willfully absorbed the heat of the day while bounding down the boardwalk.

When they submerged once again into the woods, the light through the trees on the horizon indicated that they would soon be dropping down to Cullite Creek. Approaching the ladders, Kim was surprised to see erosion of the canyon wall on both sides of the creek since she had last been there. The far set of ladders and landings were now pinned to solid rock from top to bottom. They made their way down the ragged landscape as Kim wondered if the trail itself had contributed to the devastation.

Reaching the bottom of the deep gorge, they crossed in a cable car slung low over the broad stream. Then, moving towards the ocean on an access trail, they arrived at the setting exactly as Kim had remembered it.

Wooded campsites nestled beside the creek where large pools had formed. The water was so clear and still that the reflection of the cliffs on the far side of the river blended with the collage of stones deep in the bottom of the pools.

They stood in the towering first growth overlooking the inland waterway. "It's so peaceful here," Celine murmured.

"You deserve a little peace tonight," Paul said.

"Starting with a bath," Celine responded.

"Why don't you two go for it while the sun is still getting down here?" Zahir suggested. "We'll set up camp." The other men quickly agreed, and Kim and Celine allowed the indulgence.

The women moved back upstream where the sandy foreshore narrowed before opening to a large sculpted pond. The cliffs at the opposite side reflected the warmth of the sun as the playful motion of two dragonflies left a delicate wake on the mirrored surface of the water.

They lingered as they bathed, letting the compress of cool water reach into their heated cores. Emerging refreshed, they sat on two large flat stones, and Kim once again helped Celine tend to her wounds. The women toweldried their hair and brushed it, as the last shards of sunlight reached through the first growth at the top of the canyon.

Celine was quiet, and Kim surmised she was thinking about the surge channel. "Do you want to talk about it?"

"You mean my fall today?"

"Yes."

"The danger I was in hasn't really gotten to me," Celine said as she stared at the still water, the pupils of her eyes almost masking their brown color.

"Why do you think that is?"

"I have been thinking all afternoon about Tomo's statement about 'risk and rewards,'" Celine replied.

"Tomo asked you how you felt, but I wondered what you saw when you looked down the beach through the clearing sea fog."

Celine looked at Kim as though Kim had read her mind. "You're right. I felt invincible, but what I saw was a different approach to things ahead."

Kim knew she wasn't talking about geography, and pressed her further. "What do you mean by approach?"

"Risk has always been something I measured on a financial statement, and rewards were some external incentive or benchmark." Celine's eyes focused back on the water as if searching for some personal answer beneath the surface.

"And the different approach to things ahead?"

"I saw pursuing things that really mattered to me. I saw rewards that were far more meaningful to me internally. I saw the courage to take the risks to step outside the conventions that keep me from these things."

"You saw The More," Kim insisted.

Celine was silent for some time. Kim watched as a softness grew around Celine's eyes and her facial muscles relaxed as though some internal sorting were taking shape under this new classification.

"Now the question remains—will I pursue it?" Celine said, looking back at Kim.

"When we see what we can be at our most inspired it converts to a calling that we cannot ignore," Kim said, her clear blue eyes locked with Celine's.

Celine reached out her hand, and Kim clenched it in a silent pact.

Part 6: *Testing*

Dark Side: *The enemy within*

Celine and Kim returned to the campsite to find the tents pitched among the tall trees and their boots drying upside-down on alder sticks lodged in the sand by the fire. Zahir and Paul were assembling dinner around a makeshift table of logs.

"Hi, you guys," Kim called out. "Thanks for draining our footwear."

"Yes," Celine added. "Love your new place. Plan to stay here long?"

"No," Zahir replied. "The women we are traveling with are on some sort of mission. They're driving us down this trail at record speed."

Celine and Kim laughed, then Kim asked, "Where's Tomo?"

"He was a little green around the edges also, so we sent him away to clean up," Zahir replied. "We've got enough dinner to serve ten as soon as he's back."

Tomo returned as Celine and Kim were putting their things away in the tent. They congregated around the fire, grateful for the fellowship and the food put before them.

"Man, this is good!" Tomo exclaimed as he dug into curried rice and a heated zucchini loaf with tomato sauce.

"That's one advantage to being vegetarian. We can really survive in the bush," Zahir commented. "Most of this stuff doesn't need the kind of refrigeration that meat products do."

"I've heard that for every acre it takes to feed a person on a vegetarian diet, it takes 20 acres to support the animals consumed by the same person on a meat diet," Paul said.

"Some day we'll wake up and stop eating animals," Tomo offered.

"Maybe, if that spontaneous change doesn't take place, you'll be pushed to being vegans by default," Zahir said.

"I think we'd all go happily if we could figure out how to make it taste like this," Celine said.

As she spoke, the noise of footsteps on the stones near the river sounded. The group turned just as a man and woman pulled themselves up the side of the bank and into the campsite.

It was so obvious that this couple was physically exhausted that the entire group moved to help them.

"Are you two okay?" Kim inquired, stepping toward the woman who was struggling to take off her pack.

"I don't know how I let him talk me into this," the woman said as Kim relieved her of her weight. "We've been lost since we started two days ago, and we've just spent four hours trying to find our way through the worst devastation I've ever seen."

"Devastation?" Kim repeated, looking curiously over at the other hiker.

"It's a mess up there," he said, obviously in no better mood than his companion. "There's been a blow- down of forest, trees are piled-up like matchsticks, and it's nearly impossible to find your way."

"This is the first time we've seen the water since we started," the woman barked in a blaming tone.

"What about Camper Bay?" Kim replied, knowing that the creek there flowed out with beautiful access to the ocean.

The man was quick to answer in a defensive tone. "When we left Port Renfrew by boat, we were hoping they'd take us to Thrasher Cove, but they dropped us at Gordon River. It's has turned out to be sort of difficult hiking."

Kim knew the starting point of which he spoke added four hours onto the inland trail, and they had obviously missed any of the subsequent beach-access options. She was thinking it was probably just as well, because careful planning to work around the tides was essential.

"What he is saying is that I've been so slow that when we got to Camper Bay he insisted that we keep going." Now some internal struggle this woman was feeling seemed to be coming to the surface. "We've broken our camp stove, my feet have been eaten alive by these boots—I don't know why we can't just turn back."

"We're not turning back," the man snapped.

Zahir, broke in hospitably: "Sounds like you two need a warm meal. We've got lots. Just drop your stuff and relax here for a while."

The two hikers seemed so shocked by an intervention of kindness that they shuffled over to the fire like truant children.

Before introductions were completed, Zahir had put beautiful plates of hot food in front of the couple, now known as Frank and Sheila from Detroit. Everyone concentrated on eating warm food while Frank and Sheila cooled off.

The Garwood group spoke of the highlights they had encountered, careful to avoid dwelling on any of the dangers they had overcome. Sheila appeared to rationalize her earlier behavior saying, "I guess our attempt at escaping the crazy world out there hasn't gone so well." She pointed to some unidentified civilization in the darkness.

"It's early in the game yet. You'll have a great time," Zahir replied.

Kim was questioning if there was a deeper attitude problem these two would have to overcome. Paul seemed to have come to the same conclusion and looked to redirect the conversation. "We haven't heard of the outside world for several days. What's the news?"

"It's all bad. The world's gone to hell," Frank said.

"What do you mean?" Paul responded.

"Ah, everything's gotten so corrupt. We're all just getting sucked down the gutter."

"That may be a point of view, but it's not the news," Paul said evenly.

"If you're looking for something better in the news, you won't find it," Frank said, as though the reasons for his attitude were self-evident. "The day we left, they finally shut down the whole system."

"Who shut down what system?" Paul responded.

"Who knows?" Frank said between his teeth. "Probably the rich bas-tards that call themselves 'good Americans.'"

"What are you talking about?" Celine asked, clearly perplexed.

Frank looked up, now more despondent than angry. "No one seems to know why, but at the beginning of this week, there was a massive sell-off on the stock market."

"Black Monday all over again," Paul suggested.

"Yeah, but this time it didn't correct."

"What's happened to the banking system?" Celine asked.

"The dollar bottomed out," Frank replied. "People got scared about their savings, and there was a run on the banks. The government had to freeze all accounts."

"And now it has moved to a global situation," Paul suggested.

Frank looked at him suspiciously. "They say there is no reason why it should have. A few high-tech stocks soared, and then were pulled off the market. After that, sell orders started flooding into international brokerage houses. The panic seemed to cause a chain reaction in all the financial markets."

"So the international monetary system really is at a standstill," Celine added reflectively.

When Frank spoke, he could barely mask his own panic. "It's the eeriest thing I've ever seen. No one knows who's behind it all. The whole world is just hanging out there in limbo. It's like we can't find the enemy."

Everyone sat in silence while this news sank in. Sheila got up and hobbled to a log near her pack where she sat down and started to undo her boots.

"The enemy is within," Paul said, breaking the silence.

"That's just the point," Frank snapped back. "We are tearing our own country apart."

"It's being recreated," Paul responded evenly. "Unfortunately, we are taking a very difficult route."

"What's wrong with you?" Frank cried angrily. "You're just like the nut I was talking to the other day. You make this sound like it's somehow positive."

Tomo spoke as though he were addressing some memory of himself. "Americans have always been too tolerant of their own excesses and too intolerant of the legitimate needs of others."

Frank looked over at Tomo, obviously evaluating the origins of his mixed blood. "So where are you from?"

"I'm an American."

Frank backed off as though he realized that this group had befriended him and his wife. Attempting to excuse his reaction, he said, "All nations are intolerant."

Kim spoke, eager to keep the conversation off a personal level. "The very land we are sitting on is being actively negotiated with the First Nations people of British Columbia. Their ancestral land claims throughout the province are being seriously recognized."

"Giving the land back to the Indians?" Frank scoffed.

"Canada has had a long history of tolerance and understanding," Celine said. "Two European settling nations maintain their language and cultures within this single country."

It appeared that Celine's accent convinced Frank that he was in way over his head. It was his turn to try and change the subject. "I can see no act of creation in an economy gone wild," he said, turning his narrow dark eyes back to Paul.

"We have denied the responsibility of making that economy reflect our deepest values," Paul said, looking to Celine. "As long as we could point to numbers that demonstrated our economic growth, we allowed ourselves to ignore the costs. We are facing the dark side of man-made systems, but a new reality is taking hold."

Frank looked at Paul as though he was suspicious both of what he said and the accent through which he said it. "By grinding the whole system to a halt?"

"This is the most chaotic means of effecting change," Paul admitted. "But it stems from a desire to live by principles that converge human will with all other parts of nature."

"There are no principles in a land without law," Frank said, sounding defeated.

"It's the opposite that is true," Tomo said. "There is no law in a land without principles."

"If you guys are going to argue philosophy with my husband, it will be a short discussion. Frank, could we please set up our tent?" Sheila pleaded as she inspected her feet with a flashlight.

Kim could see the blisters clear across the camp-site. "Come on, I'll help you move your pack wherever you'd like to set up," Kim offered.

Frank got up as though he had unpleasant business yet to finish. "Thanks for the grub," he said unconvincingly over his shoulder as he followed Kim and Sheila through the dark woods.

Lesson to a Culture: *The value ethos*

Kim returned a few minutes later. Approaching Tomo at the camp stove, she looked sad. He put his arm around her, and they walked over to the fire, joining the others. Zahir leaned toward the fire and Celine placed her hand reassuringly on his back. The group searched each other's faces with the concern of a family faced with bad news.

"This is an affirmation of all we have said, not a denial," Tomo stated firmly, apparently most clear about how the news from the outside had affected them all.

"But we've been speaking of a good world view," Celine said. "Who would have thought it could come to this?"

"You did, Celine," Paul responded. "When we spoke of establishing a new order, and how it requires an act of will towards what we know has to be done, you said it reminded you of the breakthrough that people in crisis make."

"And you suggested that the force that unifies will come about through both insight and reaction to a crisis." Celine brightened. "Maybe this is all about realigning to our values."

"There is no local ethic," Zahir said.

Paul stared at the bright yellow flame. "The greed that takes our natural systems beyond their ability to carry has hit our social system. The crisis has occurred. The question remains if it will inspire a global breakthrough of consciousness, a collective act of will to life-supporting values."

"An enhanced-value ethos," said Tomo, sounding distant. "Approach it the way we do the Chief."

Kim recognized this term from James' paper and was certain that Tomo had discovered some personal meaning in it. "Tell us what you mean," she urged.

"When James and I were sitting on the Chief last week, he said I should approach the distribution of my invention the way we were approaching the rock face we were climbing."

"Strategically—confidently—that kind of thing," Paul offered.

"No," Tomo said. "I realize he was asking about my motivations, not my plan of action. He was asking 'why,' not 'how' I have framed my goals."

"What do you mean?" Paul asked.

"James was questioning the way I perceive *my* invention," Tomo spoke as though a picture was coming to focus in his own mind. "He wasn't talking about *how* we technically master the Chief. He was talking about an attitude of ownership. He was talking about *why* the Chief can be brought to its best use as public domain, that everyone enjoys and no one singularly controls."

"Are you saying that you will surrender your product to the public domain?" Celine asked.

"I'm saying by never asking myself *why* I created the invention, I have become defeated by issues of how to control its use. What is really important to me is getting the invention out in society. That *'why'* goal is leading me to a completely different set of *'how to'* actions."

Tomo looked over at Zahir, who had his elbows on his knees and was staring into the fire with Celine's arm still draped over his back. Tomo could see a change in his facial expression, some new recognition in his eyes.

"Does any of this ring any bells, my friend?" Tomo inquired.

As Zahir looked up, a smile of affirmation broke across his face. It spread around the group as the connection was made.

"Zahir was pursuing an enhanced-value decision when he downloaded his organizing program on the Internet," Celine said, picking up quickly on what the two men had acknowledged.

"It just seemed to be the right thing to do," Zahir said.

"It was, but society has been asking you to question why you did that ever since," Tomo said.

"You're right," Zahir acknowledged. "And I've been spending all my time questioning how to do it the next time." The broad smile flashed across Zahir's face again. "I guess I'll do it the same way."

A spontaneous cheer went up as Celine pulled Zahir down into a big hug and new directions tumbled into place all over the camp.

"I've got just the project you're looking for, Zahir," Celine said.

"You're on," Zahir replied as Celine hunkered into her ideas about using their combined skills. Soon Tomo saw his project fit into the culture that was being created and he joined in.

The energy was kinetic, spreading from the aspirations of one to another. Like some undeniable movement towards a better state, the spirit of a new reality pushed forward.

As Kim watched the fire reflect enlarged human shadows on the wall of first growth that framed the campsite, she knew she was witnessing a lesson an entire culture was ready to learn.

Chaos to Order: *The network as life*

Sunbeams pierced through the opening of the tent, as splashing and spontaneous laughter broke out over intentionally muffled voices.

Celine stirred and ran her hand through a thick fold of hair covering her face.

"Sounds like our boys are playing in the water," Kim said, aware that Celine had awakened.

"Mmmm," Celine cooed as she sank deeper in her down sleeping bag. "They sound happy like the birds." Kim lay still listening to the layers of sound. The river crackling over the rocks like crushed ice, before entering the goblet-shaped ponds. The sporadic tones of the forest birds fused into a musical pattern, overlaid with a blanket of wind softly blowing through the high treetops and the harmony of men in carefree laughter.

The natural symphony played on as Kim started to consider the day and where it would take them. They were entering the toughest terrain where big ladders, rough trails and rugged shoreline all conspired against smooth crossings. The ocean tides and forest blow-down ahead defied setting any schedule for the progress they would make that day.

As Kim lay weighing the challenges and the unknowns, her feelings were being transferred to thoughts of the broader world that they would soon face. She examined the lump of anxiety that had surfaced in her chest and realized that the final demands of the trail would be replaced by the demands of their other lives, leaving no time to secure the new directions toward which each seemed to be moving.

Pushing these thoughts to the back of her mind, she reached into her pack and pulled out her cell phone. She pressed the clasp and punched the "on" button. The unit was now totally dead. Her doubts surfaced again, so she rose, washed and dressed quickly.

At the cook site, Kim picked up on breakfast preparations that had been started by the men. As she finished making the coffee and pancake batter, the three men showed up wet-headed, dressed in light shorts and shirts, their hands brimming with wild blueberries.

"Good morning Kim," they said. "Sorry to wake you up."

"It was a great way to wake up," Kim said, holding up the plastic bowl and thinking back to Celine's comment.

Her anxiety evaporated as the men poured their offerings into the bowl, and a subtle shared act started the day.

Celine joined the group as everyone performed the routines of the camp easily. As they sat over breakfast, Kim could tell of an awareness that the group's mind centered on the hike drawing to an end. A new confidence was being projected as though they were clear their personal sense of direction was about to intersect with the drifting external world. Things that had been viewed as "could be" the previous night were now being approached as "would be". A rush of optimism replaced a block of oppression.

Lingering as the morning sun filtered through the high forest into the camp, that optimism seemed challenged by its own isolation to the outside world.

"It's strange to speak of creating these kinds of opportunities when much of the structure in which they are housed is in a state of crisis," Celine said.

Kim looked over the mirror-smooth surface of Logan Ponds. "Crisis comes from the ancient Greek word *krino,* which means to evaluate, judge or decide." Then she remembered something said the previous night and turned to Celine. "Do you think this crisis signals a corrective judgment of society?"

Celine smiled at the question. "I was just thinking of what we said back at Hole in the Wall: A universal expectation that change must happen creates universal access."

"You're saying the run on world financial markets is a stakeholder revolt? I don't get it," Tomo interjected.

"Yes you do, Tomo," Celine said. "Matter of fact, you're the first one that got it. Back at Bonilla Point you said the awakening character means we can't help but listen. When we can't help but act is when we've made a commitment to The More."

"But the commitments we've made are other-centered," Tomo replied. "When everyone on the globe is trying to save his or her financial skin, I'd say that is pretty self-centered."

"The commitments we've spoken of may be serving others, but they are also deeply selfish in that they fulfill our quest for meaning." Celine paused to find Kim nodding at her. "As for the financial markets, it's logical that people would want to cut their losses, but it's not selfishness that caused the massive correction. It was a collective understanding that we are driving an economic machine to our own environmental and social demise."

Paul picked up on Celine's meaning. "An interconnected consciousness that acted simultaneously though independent of one another to produce spontaneous change."

"But the market place is the most interconnected network ever created by man," Tomo retorted.

"Yes, but for the network to survive, it must serve the whole of the system," Paul said. "The right-minded expression of free enterprise has been manipulated to a single-minded statement of greed."

"We are moving from man-made to natural structures. We are mimicking nature because we are part of nature," Zahir said reflectively. "We follow an organic pattern—the network is life."

"Seeing the network as life moves us from self-centered to other-centered values," Paul said. "It is a world view of cooperative, self-governing, self-sustaining ways of being."

"You think the chaos of self interest has been transformed to a network of equality?" Tomo asked.

"Chaos reigns in a self-centered view of the world," Paul said. "The order of the network is a pattern that serves the whole."

"So the crisis was necessary to clear away the old growth and allow the new dynamic to rise above," Tomo responded.

"With each generation, the voice has gotten louder," Celine interjected. "It appears that all generations are listening now. The function of our lives has been recognized to be more than the cumulative exchange of monies."

"If life-supporting values have arrested the system, it will be those values from which the new pattern will arise," Paul said. "A network of values supporting the whole of life is the organizing pattern that brings order out of the chaos."

"The network *is* life," Zahir confirmed with a smile.

"And here I though you were going to say 'Let's do it!'" Kim quipped.

"It's already done," Zahir concluded, laughing as he rose to his feet.

It was more a habit of efficiency than planning that found them packed and ready for the hike. They stood waiting for Kim, who was first on with her gear but had disappeared through the woods toward the Detroit camp.

"Sorry to keep you guys waiting," she said as she returned.

"Well, some of us still have heavy packs you know," Zahir teased.

"Yeah," Tomo chirped. "Some of us are probably traveling much lighter—say, down one pair of running shoes and one of the camp stoves."

Everyone smiled as Kim said defensively, "Well, the shoes fit Sheila and the stove fit the gas supply they're packing. I think the Detroit group will make it."

"To the top of Mike's lighthouse?" Paul posed.

"Don't listen to them," Celine interjected. "The caring that moves us from chaos to order starts right here."

The Caring Power: *Convergent wills*

The ladders that climbed Cullite Creek were pinned to a barren face of rock where there was once lush growth. The Garwood group ascended them carefully, studying the stainless brackets and bolts that held the scaffolding to the cliff with surgical accuracy.

At the top, they looked back at the man-made scar of ladders and cable car that spanned the open gorge, ignored an uneasiness that the view evoked, and turned to the trail and the calm of dense wood. By the time they had settled into a comfortable pace, they came upon Sandstone Creek that rolled out of the forest over gentle foot-hills.

Downstream of the wooden footbridge, they spotted a smooth plane of stone that curved its way to the hidden beach. A thin layer of water covered its surface, which was perfectly smooth except for random potholes carved out by harder rocks captive in pockets of the soft stone.

The Garwood group took a few moments to walk upstream, the water barely covering their Vibram soles. The potholes, sometimes as big as bath tubs, looked inviting, though it was still too early in the day for the indulgence.

They moved back along the path, marveling at the growth now denser than they had ever encountered. The trail seemed consumed by forest and was, in fact, more a part of the forest.

The treated wooden boardwalks and bridges on other parts of the trail had been replaced by fallen trees with the upper curve of the log sawed flat, then hatch-marked for a walking surface. In many places where the path had been left bare, the earth was worn down to a network of roots that crossed the forest floor. Here the group risked their balance on the twisting skeleton of roots rather than risk their luck in the unknown depth of the dark organic mud.

The forest trail left in its more natural state seemed scarred by the press of humanity that tore through its soft belly. Kim mused that the care they had taken throughout the hike seemed contradicted by the steady beating of footsteps. They moved along the inland trail for over an hour, saying little as they concentrated on defining their personal route down the tortured path.

The trail reached a high point and then descended, the forest thinning to what looked like a glade ahead. When they arrived at the open space, they understood the full impact of the forest blow-down. A colony of giant trees lay stretched across the route they were traveling. The scale of destruction left everyone speechless, both because of the acres laid waste and the curiosity of how they'd find their way through it.

Tomo slipped off his pack and climbed along two smaller fallen trees in order to mount a massive hemlock. The others followed, soon standing on the fallen trunk that resembled a downed aircraft. Broken limbs and snapped backs of both young and old growth lay crushed on the forest floor.

"What kind of storm could have created this destruction?" Celine asked, staring into the open space.

"A totally uninterrupted one," Tomo replied, pointing to the land on the far side of valley.

"What do you mean?" Celine asked, looking through the sparse fringe of trees that disappeared over the hill.

"See how the area immediately adjacent to this one has been clear-cut?" Kim said. "When they leave a ridge of forest standing next to an area that is logged off, there's nothing to protect it from blasts of wind that travel down the valley."

"Give me a couple of minutes," Tomo said in a cracking voice as he headed off down the tree.

As the others conveyed the packs up onto the big tree, Tomo studied the surface of the logs, looking for clues where other hikers had been. After several dead ends, he established a route through to the trail. Pulling some orange surveyor's tape from his vest pocket, he marked branches on his way back to the group.

Kim had encouraged everyone to stay put, and from the pallor in Tomo's face, she was relieved they hadn't crowded him. "I'm glad you brought the ribbon. Nice work," she said.

"There are lots of tree pits to fall into, so be careful," Tomo replied as Kim helped him on with his pack.

They moved down the body of one tree until it became buried in the tangle, then crossed over to another, zig-zagging their way across the devastation. Having become accustomed to the rich growth of the forest, they could feel a tangible loss of life and moved in silence through the broken mass of trees as if crossing a graveyard.

Nothing was said as they reached the standing forest again, and they marched off as if in memorial. Kim wanted to thank Tomo for guiding them through, but sensed he wanted to be left with his own thoughts.

They traversed along the shoulder of a steep ravine that headed back out towards the ocean. The forest below was so thick that only the descending tops of trees could be seen. As they came upon a decrepit set of ladders, they got their first glimpse of Camper Creek far below.

They descended the ladders carefully, avoiding rotten steps and wobbly sections where earthen footings had eroded away. Standing in the dank clearing at the bottom of the canyon, they looked back at the decaying infrastructure.

"Nature is certainly getting its revenge on that stretch of trail," Paul said as he wiped his brow.

Kim sensed as much emotional as physical fatigue. "We've made good time, would you guys like to stop for an early lunch?"

Having agreed, they avoided the trail to the cable car over the river and passed through the empty campsites directly behind the beach.

"How can you tell we are getting close to 'civilization' again?" Zahir asked as they stepped through paper, cans and garbage of a discarded campsite, none of which they had seen earlier on the trail.

When they moved from the forest onto the beach, an entirely different perspective opened up. Camper Creek swept from the base of the cliffs on the left, several hundred feet across the beach, to the cliffs on the right. The ocean had piled a rocky barrier in front of the creek, forming a large pool that reflected the towering cliffs.

They all took the opportunity to wash themselves and their boots before crossing the broad creek on steppingstones. Moving up the outer beach, they sat casually on the logs facing the open ocean.

Kim had brought out the remaining camp stove, and the water was nearly boiling before everyone was settled. With Zahir's help, she made rehydrated soup and sandwiches from thick rye crackers and cheese spread. They sat enjoying the warmth of the sun and soup, watching a wall of cloud that stretched like an endless barrier across the ocean.

The somber mood contrasted the morning's optimism. Zahir stretched out as he took a seat with the others. "It sure is a mess back there."

Kim wasn't sure what part of mankind's influence to which Zahir was referring. "It's a shame," she offered vaguely.

"It's more than that. It's a crime," Tomo said.

"You're referring to the blow-down," Paul clarified.

"The lands next to this trail are licensed to some timber company that validates thoughtless practices with a 'legal' contract," Tomo said bitterly.

"They are not even that legal," Kim replied as she rose to offer a second round of soup. "After thousands of infractions to environmental guidelines, a Forest Practices Code in B.C. set law that attaches up to a million-dollar fine to each infraction along with the power to revoke licenses."

"'We cannot establish our value goals by putting more complex control structures over existing control structures,'" Tomo recited. "It is something James told me when we were last together."

"He's probably right," Kim replied as she took her seat again. "These laws are not being enforced because the forest companies argue they are bringing economic benefit to the region and can't stand those kinds of charges against their industry."

"We've got the language of economics down pat," Celine said. "The trouble is, if you're not speaking their language, you're not heard."

"It appears the public has rejected that language and is seeking another way out," Kim added.

"Meanwhile, the most remarkable wilderness trail on the planet is about to be blown away," Tomo added in frustration.

"The forest that was cut down beside the trail measures as a benefit, but the mess we climbed over this morning does not register as an economic loss," Celine said. "The trail is a microcosm of the way we measure cost/benefit across the entire planet."

"But if the news we heard last night is accurate, the blow-down is not of a single forest; it's an entire economic system," Tomo said.

"And the voice is no longer that of a few protesters in the woods; it's the voice of countless," Celine said. "It's the convergence of many wills that integrate a global economy with a global social consciousness."

"The system based on securing our individual interests has led us to ignore our collective interests," Kim offered. "Individualism that measures itself by obsessive wants, gave license to exploitation that has led to our global problems."

"Cast in the role of the dominant predator, we compete for control of a limited environment," Paul said. "The resource dwindles, along with our quality of life, until we question what kind of pathology has delivered us to this questionable future."

"So we have learned that ecology is the only thing that matters?" Tomo wondered.

"Resolution does not lie in our being eco-centric, because that alone does not address the exploitation caused by a system that has rewarded us for being ego-centric," Paul said. "Humanity has learned there is no future in a system that pits us against one another."

"But if that is what has brought us to this standstill, what will move us forward?" Tomo persisted.

"We may not know what happened out there," Paul said, looking at the oppressive wall of cloud, "but we know the actions of many have imposed a new pattern. Some convergent will is addressing the problems we face collectively."

Tomo paused as though reframing Paul's words. "If the network is life, what does it mean when our will converges as a living network?"

"It means we see ourselves as part of the preservation of the whole, not simply as a preservation of the self," Kim said. "The network is the pattern in which we naturally set priorities based on our power to care for the whole."

"I think that is what the N-Gen was trying to tell us the other night," Kim said. "Seems they are trying to act out a broader caring power for which there is no common expression of understanding." She paused. "What did we say about spontaneous change?"

Paul recited the points they had discussed earlier in the week. "'Oppressive conditions, high degrees of feedback, an attitude of chaotic unrest, the emergence of a broader pattern, a spontaneous self-organization to a higher form, and group insight.'" He paused. Then, looking back to Celine then Kim, he added, "We are in the midst of spontaneous change to a convergent will."

"A will that causes us to act on our own greater capacity to care," Kim responded, letting the conclusion hang.

Paul's voice flowed in to fill the gap. "When conditions are right, the knowledge of many transcends to a judgment—a single unifying force—our wills converge to a caring culture."

"I'm thinking of how that single unifying force must hold within it a great capacity for wellness," Kim said, reflecting on Celine's statement the night they projected wellness to James. As if trying to see beyond the wall of cloud in front of them, she concluded, "Who among us is unable to feel it is time the world moved the source of its will to a caring power?"

To Better States: *'Net democracies*

"I haven't had the opportunity to use one of these since we started," Celine said as they passed the out-houses just before the cable car over Camper Creek.

"Well, if we are going to prepare ourselves to be back in civilization, we had better give it a go," Kim said.

Zahir looked at the sorry repair and said, "I'll take the bush any day."

"Easy for you to say," Celine retorted as they all headed in separate directions.

Several minutes passed before everyone congregated at the cable car.

"Where's Tomo?" Kim asked.

"I saw him head toward the beach," Paul replied.

"I'll go check it out," Zahir offered, jogging around the corner without his pack.

A few minutes later, the two appeared carrying green garbage bags. "I caught him red-handed trying to steal other campers' belongings," Zahir joked.

"No big deal. I brought the bags as pack covers in case it rained, so they might as well be put to use," Tomo said as he and Zahir tied the garbage bags to the outsides of their packs.

"There'll be lots of cleanup before we can move to any new standard," Kim concluded.

Moving up onto the platform, they took the short cable-car ride across to the rock bluff on the far side of Camper Creek. Just past a screen of giant trees at the riverside, they came upon the last big set of ladders they would encounter.

They knew from the maps that in less than an hour, they would be back on the beach, at the lowest tide of the day. In theory, this put them in a good position to make Thrasher Cove that afternoon. However, they had learned not to underestimate the trail, and no one speculated how the last leg of the trail would unfold.

Having ascended the ladders they walked into the shadows of a dank medieval forest. The twisted shapes of huge cedar trees stood like giant mutations. In other areas, fallen first growth nursed huge second growth that radiated from the nurse tree as if it were the earth itself. The forest floor was alive with greenery exploding from every nook in which it could grow or cling like a blanket of thick moss.

The forest reclaimed its noble character by showing another dimension of its personality. It occurred to Kim, as they passed over the bridge at Trisle Creek, the ethereal mood of this rich biosphere was captured in the reflection of the deep stream. The Garwood group stopped in silent reverence for this magic place. The perfection of the moment gave Kim confidence that the better states they had speculated upon were underway.

The forest and the mood lightened as the group made a steady descent towards the smell of the ocean. They traversed long stretches of boardwalk near the beach cliffs as the sun cast brilliant shards of light on the forest floor. Movement became so effortless that they traveled at a canter, nearly missing the last beach access at 'Kilometer 66.'

Moving out to the edge of the cliff, they could see that the low tide had exposed a flat shelf of rock extending in both directions. A long ladder took them down the rock slope onto the shelf; in the distance, they could see Owen Point, the physical turning point that would take them down Port San Juan Bay to Thrasher Cove.

Everyone seemed happy to be back on the beach with its solid footing and open vistas. They spread out to explore ridges of rock, tidal pools and long fissures slicing the rock plate.

Having moved some distance down the foreshore, they came together at a point where an eight-foot-wide surge channel cut up to the cliff wall. Across the span, some earlier hikers had felled a small log, which Zahir bent over and rolled back and forth in his hand.

"It's kind of wobbly," he said.

Kim scanned the headland for a passage up and over the channel. Glancing back, she was startled to see Tomo halfway across, Zahir holding firmly to the log.

"Okay, Celine, you're next," Tomo said, bending down and taking a firm grip on the other side of the log.

Kim was about to protest when Celine stepped up, without even a glance her way, and walked across blithely. As Celine hopped off the log, Tomo raised his hand, and she gave him a low five. The others followed, Kim last, before all headed down the beach without ceremony.

Kim walked beside Paul, wondering if only she had perceived the change. "Paul, have you noticed how fearless this group has become?"

"Nothing like a sense of purpose to overcome preconceived limits," Paul replied.

Kim knew Paul wasn't talking about the log crossing or any kind of physical bravery. She wanted to ask him exactly what he meant, but a more pressing question came to mind. "Paul, tell me about your sense of purpose."

Paul looked out over the ocean as if searching for an answer in the cloudbank off shore. "I guess before we started this trip, I thought I had achieved it. It seemed that everything we had created in the business was proving to be a blueprint for organizational change."

"And then a voice from the next generation reminded you there is a 'beyond.'" Kim said, thinking back to Carmanah Beach.

"Laurie," Paul said affectionately. "She certainly forced me to confront it, but it was the First Nations elder who made me see how subtle the loss of a culture can be."

"That's why you were so adamant with Frank that we are in a process of recreating through moral principle."

"Yes, and when I realized that our history of freedom has the flexibility to embrace a value ethos, I realized that North America was on that path."

"And you want to play a role in ensuring the Czechs are, also."

Paul smiled at her. "Not much gets past you, does it?"

"I've noticed the interests you have expressed would have you less operationally involved in your business and more involved in the affairs of your homeland."

"Yes, as a matter of fact, I'm going to ask the four division heads if they will accept a rotating CEO position. I think it will bring new ideas and opportunities forward in the company."

"And you will act as chairperson," Kim surmised.

"Yes, and I want to cultivate an advisory board, so the company develops a broader view of its potential role in society. But my gender balance for the board is a little off. So far, I've targeted five women and an unconscious man."

Kim laughed. "I shouldn't speak for James, but I'm sure he would love to do it."

"Speak for yourself, then," Paul said. "Would you love to do it?"

Kim was clearly taken aback. "I'm not sure I understand the business sufficiently well."

"Remember we talked about the importance of 'why' judgments, not 'how to' issues?" Paul queried. "Well, you're the most intuitive 'why' person I've ever met."

"Thanks, Paul," Kim said. "I'd love to join you. Who are the other women you're approaching?"

"I would want my wife's judgment at the table—she is in every sense my partner. Also, a company staff representative; the woman I have in mind has a great understanding of the company and is a tremendous communicator. I wasn't totally clear about all this the other day, so I approached Laurie about it more in terms of doing some consulting work for the company."

"That sounds great!" Kim said, remembering Paul had doubled back to the N-Gen camp. "Laurie will ensure we are all moving to a better state. Who's the fifth woman?"

"Well, I really shouldn't speak of it until I've had a chance to ask her. But it wouldn't do any harm to tell you it's another woman with whom I hiked the West Coast Trail."

"Right on," Kim said with a chuckle.

"I'm looking forward to Beerman making some interesting new contributions if Celine will help us."

They had moved quickly along the rock shelf and were approaching a sandy beach just before Owen Point. The others were ahead, having almost crossed the beach. Paul jumped off the sandstone ledge onto a log jammed against the rocks. He turned and gave Kim a hand as she took a large step down. As they lingered for a moment, Kim noted that his relaxed features complemented his tanned complexion.

"You feel very good about this, don't you?" Kim asked.

"I've never felt better. I think, because I hadn't imagined where I could go beyond what I had done, I convinced myself that I had arrived. Now, it's not a matter of identifying where I can go beyond, but of choosing the thing that really is my calling."

"Your caring that the Czechs enjoy what your parents once had is a deep passion for you," Kim observed. "If James were here, he would say this is The More for you."

"I suppose I carry that ideal forward from my father," Paul said. "When I told him I was leaving the country, he simply said, 'The Communist regime is nothing more than a momentary mistake in history. Go and learn the value of freedom.' I think it was his way of supporting the country and my decision at the same time."

"Sounds like he knew all along you would return."

Paul seemed to ponder this mix of destiny and decision making. "The Czechs have a democratic past. I think the value ethos of which we have spoken rests in the ideals of that country, but I couldn't be sure it extends to other nations."

Kim looked out at the Pacific Ocean, still obscured by cloud. "If a shift in the world view is underway, it can not be limited to the consciousness of a single group. The movement to better states must be compelling enough to tap the caring power of all people."

"A caring culture pervasive enough to correct social inequity world wide." Paul stated quietly.

"We'll find out soon enough if the tests we have applied can be extended to 'Net democracies, where global economies are networked to global consciousness." They moved down the beach, following the others around the rock outcropping where they heard Zahir's voice, "We've found a shortcut."

Looking up, they saw the others gathered on the beach immediately in front of the broad opening of a sea cave. The waves had drilled a 40-foot-deep tunnel directly through the land of Owen Point, revealing the beach on the other side. From the cliffs overhead, the green forest and ground cover spilled down toward the beach, framing the cave with a natural garden.

Kim and Paul approached the cave and dropped their packs on a slab of stone with the others. Tomo stood with his back against the outer wall of the cave and pointed in the direction they had come. "From here, you can see the headlands of Camper, Cullite, Logan and Bonilla. I bet way off in the distance that's Pachena Point." Then, pointing ahead, he added, "This way you can see straight up Port San Juan."

Paul and Kim joined him in the center of the open tunnel that looked down Port San Juan then back up the coast. The view reminded Kim of the one they had seen after crossing Adrenaline Surge, except now the clouds hung a couple of miles off shore and the headland stretched 40 miles back from where they had come.

"You're right, Tomo. That is Pachena Point Lighthouse off in the distance," Kim said.

"Our vision is certainly clear today," Tomo replied.

"Maybe caretaker Mike would have that different discussion with us now," Celine added.

Kim looked at them as they grinned. "You guys knew what I was talking about back there, but you didn't say anything," she said.

"Kim, we didn't have the language to describe our true desires," Paul said. "We've discovered it as we moved down the trail."

"So we are carrying them forward from here," Kim stated, as if answering her earlier anxiety.

"This journey has brought each of us to see the evolution to betterness," Zahir responded.

"Or, as James would say if he were here," Paul added, "The More."

Part 7: *Commitment*

You Heal With Words: *A universal language*

K im was aware of having responded as the group reorganized to get underway, but while they were passing over the flat shelf beyond Owen Point, her thoughts were absorbed in reviewing the trip from a new perspective. She played the last several days through her mind like a mixing tape, pulling out specific words and actions while fading others into the background.

She realized how consciously each member of the Garwood group had taken the journey. She thought of the turning points: Paul at Nitinat Narrows with the First Nations elder, Tomo at Carmanah among the giants, Celine at Adrenaline Surge through her rescue, and Zahir at Cullite Creek after Tomo had revealed his own transformation. Events that led to those turning points clarified the quest in each of their lives. Their destinations were all different, but they had been traveling down a common path.

"Are we arriving at the 'certain end'?"

Kim jumped at the sound of Tomo's voice.

"Sorry to startle you," Tomo added. "I was just thinking back to when we parked the car over at Port Renfrew last week. You said it was strange to be certain of the end point, and uncertain of the events that would lead you there."

Kim looked across the bay at the rolling south-island landscape, mostly bare from clear-cut logging. In the distance she could see markings on the waterfront that she calculated to be the settlement of Port Renfrew. "The end goal of reaching Thrasher Cove," Kim said, remembering the conversation. "But it's turned out to be so much more."

"Perhaps that's because you went without the leader and became the leader."

"We all became leaders," Kim replied.

"Why do you think that happened?"

"I think James set up a framework and then trusted us to explore it."

"I guess that was his plan—to awaken the change agents," Tomo said. "But I'm not sure we've solved the riddle."

"What are you talking about, Tomo?"

"He said that each of us has the ability to be change agents in the structures in which we operate, but the riddle was how to effect change on the broader systems level."

They stopped to wait for the others at the treed outcropping of Kettle Rock, now surrounded by the water of the incoming tide.

"We didn't have the language," Kim said, thinking back to their conversation at Owen Point. "It's what Paul said—we've discovered the words as we moved down the trail."

"The change evolved through language?"

"Each of us defined a pursuit of The More by creating a new frame of reference," Kim said. "But to share that reality, we needed to expand our language."

"There's a lot of folks out there with a new frame of reference," Tomo suggested.

"In the framework of caring, there is a universal language which translates our feelings to words and words to deeds."

"And what if there is a lack of will to translate?" Tomo responded.

"You heal with words," Kim said, as her mind extended out beyond their journey. "The desire for The More will translate a new system of belief."

"Is this not somehow the role of education?" Tomo inquired.

Kim looked at the virgin growth on Kettle Rock and then beyond to the stripped hillsides on the other side of the bay. "You're right, Tomo, but sharing that language represents a massive distribution problem."

"You don't have a distribution problem. You've got a value problem,"

Tomo said as Zahir caught up with them.

"Wow!" Zahir exclaimed as he studied the moonscape of boulders strewn on the beach ahead. "Kim, are you sure we can get through there? It looks impassable."

Zahir's words mirrored the doubts Kim was feeling about Tomo's comment. She heard herself saying, "No, it only looks impassable."

"Well, let's do it!" rang Zahir's battle cry.

Kim looked back and noticed that Paul and Celine were walking along deep in conversation. She realized Paul was recruiting and agreed to wait for them further down the beach.

They started off, picking their way around and over the house-sized boulders, seeking out the easiest route. Rounding the visual barrier, they could see that the larger boulders gave way to a long field of truck-sized stones. Kim, Zahir and Tomo scampered along the strip of moonscape towards a forested dome that stood off the mainland like a small planet.

As they moved towards the planet-shaped island, Kim knew they would have to enter the bay beyond it together—because it was Thrasher Cove. Her mind raced for closure as their physical journey drew to an end.

She thought of the capacity society has to educate and asked herself, "When does the universal desire for The More become arranged to a universal language? When do we practice as our norm the capacities we have at our best? When does a growing awareness of our magnificence transform to the ideal we long to live?"

Life to the Fullest: *Returning to wellness*

"That must be Thrasher Cove," Tomo said, looking down the short curve of sand beach. "There are the orange markers we saw from Port Renfrew." He pointed to the painted oil drums lying at the base of a large hemlock.

"Yes, we've come full circle," Kim confirmed.

Zahir turned and shouted back to Celine and Paul. "We have arrived!" They waved back and quickened their pace as the others studied the beach ahead.

"I'd like to spend our last night here rather than signaling for the boat to come and get us," Tomo said.

"It's four o'clock," Kim replied, looking at her watch. "I'm not sure they would respond to a signal this late in the afternoon, anyway."

"There's a welcome sight," Celine said as she approached, seeing the smooth sand beach with a fast flowing stream running through the middle of it.

"Looks like there's only one other group camped on the beach, so there's lots of room," Zahir said. "Let's lose these packs for the last time." He moved off the trailing rocks and onto the sand beach.

"It's a big group. Look at the size of the tarp they've rigged up," Tomo said, looking at the large tent supported in the middle with a rope that went back into the forest and then forward to a long pole lodged in the sand.

"It must be the park workers," Kim said. "See all the wood that has been cut and stacked up near the edge of the forest."

"It would be a lot more to the point if they'd hike into the blow-down and clear a proper trail," Celine said.

"I just hope they leave Tomo's markers as a guide and make everybody think about the damage by having to cross right over top of it," Kim said.

"Good point," Celine replied as they neared the stream.

"There's a good clearing for us to set up camp on the other side of the stream," Paul said as the sound of a hand-saw rang from behind the tent.

Passing by the front of the open fabric atrium, they could see sleeping and seating accommodation for several people inside. The large shelter looked inviting. A warm blue light shone over the driftwood benches and makeshift tables, suggesting a welcome transition back to civilization.

Just beyond the tent, Tomo and Paul saw a man bent over a log cradle, cutting driftwood rounds with a cross saw. He was wearing shorts, his shirtless, muscular back toward them. In the few moments it took the others to catch up, the man seemed to sense their presence.

As he turned, the faces of the Garwood group registered astonishment. "James!" they uttered.

A huge smile swept across James' face, as his alert blue eyes touched everyone and came to rest on Kim. They lunged towards one another, fusing in an embrace of joyful tears. A spontaneous cheer erupted from the group, now energized by the passion of the reunion.

"From now on, it's together," James said.

"Whatever it takes," Kim replied, suspended in his arms. James reached out one arm and pulled Tomo into their bear hug.

"Sounds like that knock on the head drove some sense into you," Tomo said, relaxing to the familiar grasp at the back of his neck.

"Thanks to you for bringing me back to earth," James replied.

As James lowered Kim to the ground, she opened her free arm wide and pulled in Zahir, while Tomo scooped in Celine and James, and Paul locked arms with Tomo and Kim. They held the embrace, tears flowing down their faces while kisses and greetings were shared in all directions.

Paul reached over some heads to shake James' hand, and the crowd parted. "How long have you been here?" he asked.

"I arrived yesterday," James said as Kim reached up and wiped the tears from his face, then hers. "I knew you were ending the hike at Thrasher Cove, but I really wasn't expecting you here until tomorrow."

Paul ignored the question and spoke searchingly. "When did you regain consciousness?" he asked.

"I came to three nights ago. The first thing I saw was the sun setting like a blazing orange ball outside the hospital window."

Paul dropped James' hand, and the excitement was suspended like the moment before a winning goal. Kim could tell by the look on each of their faces they were thinking of the night that they had projected wellness.

James seemed to feel obligated to fill the gap. "It's funny. When I awoke I thought I was in an after life. I felt so—well, I felt so much love," he said. Then, as though embarrassed by this admission, he looked at Kim and added, "Ever since, I've had an uncontrollable desire to get business cards printed with a Boston address."

"Now I *know* that bang knocked some sense into you," Tomo said, and they all laughed as Kim and James shared a look of confirmation.

"How was your journey?" James asked excitedly.

"We hiked it in your name," Celine said. "It was marvelous."

"What she is saying is, we took all the risks you would have," Tomo quipped.

"I can see that," James said, taking Celine's right elbow in his hand and turning her body to see the scar on her shoulder. "Let's get you guys comfortable," he added as he eased the pack from Celine's and then Kim's backs. Everyone responded as though they, too, had forgotten the weight they bore.

"You must have had a landing barge to get all this stuff over here,

James," Zahir said, looking more closely at the luxury of James' tent.

"I wanted you guys to have a comfortable last night. Make yourself at home. I'm going to clean up with a quick swim." The last comment was directed at Kim.

"I'm not letting you past your knees in the surf without me there," Kim said, as she disappeared behind the tent with her pack.

James helped the others into the tent with their gear, and Kim appeared in her Speedo before they had the beds rolled out.

James took her hand, and the two athletic bodies, seemingly chiseled by the same artist, turned toward the sea. "Don't bother putting anything on for supper," James said. "With any luck, it's out there."

With that Kim and James ran over the hard-packed sands into the calm waters of Thrasher Cove.

"That crazy man," Paul said. "You know, I think we were doing his work for him."

"What are you talking about?" Tomo said as he sat down on a log beside Paul.

"I don't know. It's just that every time I see James I seem to be at some point of exhaustion, and he blows in and defines a new benchmark to strive for."

"He compels us to live life to the fullest, and it's not easy at times," Tomo said, thinking back to the last time he had seen James.

Paul and Tomo looked at one another and laughed at the ironic truth. They watched James and Kim swim a good distance.

"Where the heck are those two going?" Paul asked, obviously concerned about how far off shore they were. A few moments later, the two figures stopped at what could barely be made out as a floating buoy.

They treaded water for a few moments. Then James started swimming a backstroke towards land, using only his legs and one arm. As they came to shore, Kim helped James lift a netted cylinder out of the water.

The remainder of the Garwood group had moved to the edge of the water, realizing they were carrying a crab trap. James and Kim delivered the trap to the group's feet, and in it were a half dozen large crabs. James lifted the two smaller ones out then turned to place them at the water's edge. As the crabs scurried into deeper water, he returned and said, "The others are ready for the pot."

Tomo bent over the net and pulled out the largest crab, lifting it from behind its back legs. "We believe that if you kill an animal with respect, its spirit is free to wander until it finds another body it can occupy." He stepped over to a sharp rock sticking out of the sand, and brought the front tip of the shell down with the desired results.

He turned and handed the still crab to James. "I've not known you to be an idealist, Tomo," James said, smiling.

"I remember someone telling me that a cynic is merely a fallen idealist." Tomo returned the smile.

As they turned to walk up the beach towards the fire that James had laid, Paul said, "Speaking of fallen idealists, what's the real state of the outside world?"

"You've obviously heard word of the crash," James said.

"Yes, a couple from Detroit were telling us what a mess things are in," Paul replied.

"Frank and Sheila," James said, as Paul nodded his head and rolled his eyes. "I waited with them on the dock at Port Renfrew a couple of days ago. Carl, who runs the shuttle, said the ocean swells were too large to land here at Thrasher that afternoon, but they insisted that he take them right away. They went to Gordon River and yesterday he brought me here."

"Ah, so you're the 'nut' who was trying to suggest to them that the chaos would lead to positive ends," Tomo said, as he located a large pot at the cook area and moved over to the creek to fill it.

"Yes, I would be that nut," James said as he lit the fire and took a seat with the others on the logs grouped around it. "They need not rely on my point of view. All the editorials are tracking the corrective changes that are now taking place in the system."

Kim wrapped a towel around herself and sat on one of the logs closest to the fire. "We acknowledged this was catastrophic, but suggested the desire to move to better ways was behind the apparent chaos."

"That's exactly the kind of sense the rest of the world is coming to," James replied.

"So which sectors have been affected?" Celine asked James.

"There's not a sector that is unaffected. It's bigger than any part; it's the whole of the system. In the sector you work in specifically, a special sitting of cabinet has moved to change the Bank Act to redefine the industry's purposes and power."

"Seems we are all learning a new definition of risk and reward," Celine said, looking over at Tomo.

"That's just the beginning. The whole notion of investment has changed," James replied, stepping over to the cooler and pulling out a dozen silver-wrapped potatoes to place in the fire.

"None of the international stock markets have reopened, because they are plugged with sell orders," James continued. "The only speculating going on now is that, when they do open, it will be under drastically different standards. There's an International Securities Exchange meeting taking place right now with a stated agenda of capping stock values to a multiplier of earnings."

"These kinds of actions will have major ramifications for financing growth and expansion," Celine said.

"It seems, now that much of the wealth held on paper has collapsed, there's a widespread call to examine how the whole system works," James said.

"A 'call' from all the world leaders?" Celine speculated.

"Yes, millions of them," James replied. "Until my cell went dead last night, I was logged on the 'Net visiting corporate websites across the globe. Multinational and transnational corporations are being stripped down and rebuilt from within."

James was clearly unable to contain his excitement. "The people are quite literally transforming our organizational way of being overnight."

"A collective consciousness that has transformed our ability to act," Tomo said, looking to Zahir.

"Unprecedented levels of social feedback, an explosion of communications and a new order emerges," Zahir confirmed.

"Yes," James said, doing a double-take over this exchange. "Media across the globe seem to be coalescing public sentiment that we redefine our notions of growth. There is a call for democratic principles that see capitalism within a habitat, rather than operating beyond the limits of all habitat."

"A dynamic that goes beyond the definition of old growth?" Paul posed without being specific. "But something must have set these events in motion. Frank said there was some strange market activity before it self-destructed."

"Subtle factors can move a system to a dramatically higher order," James replied, looking over to Kim. "Hammond Power Systems bought back all their stock."

"And the market went nuts, believing this was proof they had the power to change the world," Kim speculated.

"Yes. Every related industry went right off the chart," James said, through an impish smile. "That was the day Hammond announced they had broken all the cost constraints and would be providing the technology as an open system worldwide through collaboration agreements with national governments."

"They gifted their technology to the public domain," Paul speculated.

"Let's just say they ensured there were no distribution problems," James responded.

"They listened," Kim said.

"They acted," James replied. "The market didn't know how to respond to the news. It could see a higher-level play was underway, and a lot of buy positions seemed redundant."

"When the most valuable invention in the history of man is being redistributed across the world, it's no wonder the value of everything else is being reassessed," Paul asserted. "And now it has moved to a global situation."

"The reassessment is happening at the highest levels," James confirmed. "The U.N. has convened, and there has been agreement on a vast array of development programs aimed at providing the basics of civilization to the poorest of the poor."

"But that will cost billions." Tomo replied

"Yes, but not as much as six months of war and not nearly the cost of cleaning up after society has failed." James continued. "It would appear there has been universal agreement to adopt a broader set of economic indicators."

"Ones that redefine progress to include environmental and social well being will be difficult to enforce," Celine interjected.

"The irony is that people are embracing a socially restorative economy," James responded. "You can sense that the whole of society is self-regulating away from a monetary consumptive economy to one that aligns with the natural world. The U.S. Congress is in special session, and the reports are showing a total revamp of the tax system.

"They say the generators of human labor and capital will be taxed lightly, while activities that consume natural resources will go from a write-off to a tax-on status," James continued. "Capital-gains tax will be extreme for those who plunder, and light for those who preserve."

"By taxing activities that are consumptive, environmental accounting is built right into the price structure," Paul said. "Things become self-regulating when prices include environmental as well as social costs."

THE MORE: *A Journey to Sustainability*   167

"Things become self-regulating when your systems are aligned with your values," James clarified. "Besides, the enterprise that will be stimulated will resolve, not deepen, the problems we face."

The group sat in silence, considering how pervasive the changes had been.

"It's amazing to think that the status had to be knocked out of the status-quo before it could change," Paul said in astonishment. "All without one shot being fired. Maybe this wasn't the most difficult path we could have taken."

"We will never know just how tragic our suffering could have become if a new system of belief had not arisen at this time," James said. "No one can say what state of chaos humankind must reach before it transforms to a higher order, but transform it must. Our species was borne to a dark coma of aggression, but the light may now be bright enough to advance a new consciousness of caring."

"Perhaps we have learned that the power to change the world rests in us, not in our inventions," Paul replied.

"It seems we've awoken to the reason we are here," James confirmed, looking around at the group; then a smile cleared all the intensity from his face. "It is so great to be with you guys. Let me pull dinner together. I think we'd better eat under the tent—a change in the weather is coming. It will rain tonight."

"Can you sense a change in the weather?" Celine asked, obviously thinking back to the sensitivity of the First Nations elder.

James picked up a small black box from the cooking table. "Radio."

The group laughed as everyone dispersed to clean up, delighted in more than one way that James was there to spoil them.

Kim joined James at the cooler. "Can I help you with anything?"

"After they held me overnight at the hospital for observation, I didn't want to waste any time getting over here, so I just did a veggie and fruit shop on the way," James said as he pulled big Tupperware containers of freshly cut vegetables and fruit from the cooler. "We'll just do a quick stir fry and fruit salad."

"Great, but let's change first."

They entered the tent and changed quickly. As James pulled his shirt from his pack, a letter dropped into the sand. He picked it up and handed it to Kim.

"Kim, when I talked to your folks and told them I was coming over, they said there was a registered letter forwarded to you in care of their address. I picked it up thinking it might be important to you."

"Thanks for doing that," Kim said as she pulled a cotton sweater over her head, stood on her toes and planted a firm kiss on James's mouth.

"Well, I'll leave you to it," James said, stealing another embrace before he left the tent.

Pulling a wok from a canvas sack at the cook station, he took the container of vegetables and a premixed jar of sauce over to the fire and started cooking.

When Kim approached, James looked up from the steaming jumble of colors. "Everything okay?

"Fine," she said with a reassuring smile.

"Tomo's got the crab all cooked," James said. "Zahir has pulled the potatoes out and has them on the table, Paul has opened the wine. Celine has the table set, complete with stones to crack the crab. I think we are ready to go."

"Well, let's do it!" Celine exclaimed.

James stopped for a moment and turned to Celine with a puzzled look. "I haven't put my finger on it yet, but if nothing else, you all sound a lot more like Zahir than the last time I saw you.

"What can we say?" Celine responded. "His enthusiasm is contagious."

"It's the fuel of the future," James said as he converged with the others at the table, the steaming stir-fry in hand.

Taking seats, passing plates and pouring wine produced the din of a family table. The cathedral ceiling and the cloud cover layered a feeling of intimacy that cast an aura of light over the occupants.

In many ways it was like the meals they had shared at all the beautiful sites on the trail, but in many ways it was different. The moment arose before they started, a pause of unnamed thanks, and all eyes moved to James. He bowed his head.

State of Grace: *A system of belief*

Our Father, infinite mind, ultimate unity.

We thank you for the spirit you gave us to recognize a Godliness.

To understand the self-determined capacity of our lives.

To be as men and women might strive to be:

> our purpose contribution,
>
> our persons compassion,
>
> our passion companions.

Kim looked up at the serene faces gathered in a state of grace.

"Would it be premature to say 'Here's to The More?'" Celine asked, raising her glass.

"If not now, when?" Paul added with confidence as the clink of plastic goblets disappeared in a chorus of "The More."

"James, this is a great looking dinner," Zahir said, dishing Celine, then himself a liberal portion of vegetables. "You've been a busy guy around here judging by the size of that wood pile."

"Just doing a little care-taking," James said.

"Seems like that's where we started our journey," Zahir replied. "These guys spent 10 minutes in the dome with the care-taker at Pachena Point Lighthouse, and our trip moved out of the realm of the way things are and into the realm of the way things could be."

"Mike would be happy to hear you say that," James replied, as he placed a crab leg on the flat stone plate and cracked it using a round stone.

Zahir looked beguiled. "If you know him, you must know why he stuck himself out on that rock."

"I met him when I hiked the trail alone a few years ago," James replied. "I agree with his ends, not his means. Mike has a lot to offer as an educator."

"I don't think he was overly impressed with our visit," Paul said. "Earlier today, we speculated that, were we to have met him at the end of the trek, we might have had a different kind of conversation."

"What would you say to Mike now?" James asked.

Kim knew that would be James' question, just as she knew Paul would redirect it to her. As the Garwood group looked her way, she placed an empty crab leg on her plate and searched to express the end point of their journey.

"I think it set us on a search for a system of belief," she said, realizing that James would be more comfortable that the "it" was assumed to be their visit with Mike, rather than "it" being named as James' paper.

Kim noticed that James returned the sensitivity by not asking her the obvious question, and feigned that eating was the most important issue at hand. He picked up the largest crab claw off the platter, cracked it and placed it on Kim's plate, then took a bony knuckle and placed it on his own plate.

"We talked about attitudes driving change, and that led us to think about where those drivers are taking society," Tomo said. "Once we had a sense of what Kim has called a system of belief, I think each of us saw the potential for change in our own lives."

Kim could see the others were surprised by Tomo's definition of the experience they had shared, and it sparked more comments.

"I think we were all pretty clear that, as knowledge becomes a commodity, our collective judgment is the exchange—the liberating force," Zahir said. "But I had never considered how this dynamic breaks down the traditional structures of control and, by definition, leadership gets transferred across a very broad spectrum of people."

"If the form and substance of leadership has changed so that knowledge brings decision-making into many hands, what unifies our direction? What stops the anarchy of special interest?" James posed.

"You have to have taken the full journey to get that answer," Tomo quipped.

Kim laughed with the others, realizing Tomo was suspicious that James' question was Socratic. But she also sensed there was new ground to be covered, so she pressed on.

"We acknowledged that our growing sophistication has defined a new reality that fulfills our quest for meaning," Kim said. "This quest for meaning manifests itself as a humanizing force in which broad-based empowerment creates new patterns of thought and action."

Kim noticed that James looked over at Tomo, but Tomo seemed to be enjoying the thought of having a big fish on the line. "The example we used is in organizations such as Paul's, where the absence of formal structure allows people to exercise abilities that move them towards their ideal," Tomo offered.

"Because a broad spectrum of people exercise a movement towards an ideal, the change appears at times to arise spontaneously," Paul said. "Like the spontaneous shifting of order in parts of Eastern Europe as many souls there have exercised a natural will."

Zahir's engaging voice broke in. "Natural in the sense that there's an organic pattern beneath the surface of this change. It's a network of stake-holder activism."

James smiled. "Sounds like you bridged from seeing things happen beyond nature to seeing things happen through nature."

"Exactly," Zahir replied. "A nature that is capable of self-organizing and moving spontaneously to a higher order."

Paul paused from his feast and added, "Being immersed in the beauty of this place, it's easy to feel nature is part of you, literally internal to your being. Seeing the nature of things revealed that, as part of nature, we are similarly capable of self-organization to a higher order."

"As we pursue that order which nature has endowed us with, we realize we are acting on the voice from within," Kim said. "The voice is an endowed morality that speaks of moving beyond consumption, greed and self-centeredness to conservation, caring and other-centeredness."

The light was dimming as the last of the day reached through the thickening clouds. James stepped over to a box in the corner of the tent and returned with two candles he began to light.

"You're saying the voice leads us not only to an equality of rights but to an equality of spirit—it is the pattern of unity."

"As the conquest of nature is replaced by a co-dependence, we unify under a new world view that sees the protection of all living things as our ultimate spiritual goal," Paul confirmed.

"Man's alignment with nature is a predetermined stage of evolution we had to arrive at together," Tomo said. "Our convergent will is decreed by nature."

"It was as though being out here guided and, in some cases, pushed our insight," Celine admitted, looking quite abashed. "But once we had internalized your concept of spiritual determinism, it was like a magnet that drew each of us to a new destiny."

Kim could see that James was deeply moved. "We thought we'd lost you," she said. "It helped us realize we move to this new order through our caring power."

Tomo smiled at James and spoke of an agreement they had made in the past. "'Our beyond ideas of right-doing and wrong-doing is a field. I'll meet you there.'"

James smiled, nodding his head gently as his eyes pooled with emotion.

"The field is love!" Tomo confirmed, his eyes locked with James' before moving to Celine and Kim. "It is the force at the center of our caring power. It is the final word of the voice from within."

Beliefs to Actions: *The caring culture*

After Tomo had articulated a conclusion the whole group had arrived at together, silence of self-examination lingered until Tomo began to laugh softly, although clearly on the verge of tears.

"It all came together like this for me at Carmanah," he addressed Kim as he regained his composure. "But you would have thought I'd fallen out of a tree if I'd used those words."

Kim smiled, understanding his inspired awakening. "Who was it that said, 'The conclusion is always the same: Love is the most powerful and still the most unknown energy of the world'?"

"It was Pierre Teilhard de Chardin," Paul replied. "He also said, 'We are not human beings having a spiritual experience; we are spiritual beings having a human experience.'"

"It's the energy of the world that resolves us to better ways," Tomo said, as though the desire to act on the thought were universally evident.

"To understand that love is our human calling, is to see the end of the journey first," Kim said, constructing the conviction in her own mind.

"You really have come to a system of belief as you moved down the trail," James responded.

"We cheated a bit. We had some notes to follow," Zahir said, smiling at James.

"There were a few guides along the way," Paul added. "A First Nations elder at Nitinat Narrows confirmed the need for new ways and said our generation was the one destined to make it happen."

"How did he help you to that insight?" James asked.

"He spoke of a prophecy that seven generations after the arrival of Europeans there would be a Great Awakening," Paul replied. "Aligning with nature is the Awakening; living within her limits is the urgency."

"For me, the urgency hit when we spent the night with the 'Net generation at Carmanah," Tomo said.

"Some of us didn't see it until we heard of the crash and sort of rose out of the ashes," Zahir said, as everyone laughed at his self-recrimination.

"There are thousands of Prometheans that have risen from that crash," James said to Zahir, and then turned to Tomo. "Tell me more about N-generation."

"They made it clear that much of the change we speculated on is already a part of their reality. The N-gen is an awakening character and looking to us to clear the road." Tomo replied.

"It was kind of a wake-up call for us," Paul added. "These young people saw it as essential that our generation return to its earlier idealism."

Tomo looked at James as though reading his thoughts. "Yes, we are a generation of fallen idealists. But, traveling with this bunch, I've come to believe there is an awakening character upon which the boomers are acting."

"One that has transformed society towards a new idealism," James said.

As Tomo nodded back unflinchingly, Kim was thinking of the events after their time at Carmanah. "We were still unsure of how the ideal would transform our own lives, but the next morning at Bonilla Point, we understood enough to know that we were committing as a group to your definition of The More."

James set his lips as though searching for a way to acknowledge them. "You know the First Nations name for the sea stacks at Bonilla Point is '*i'weyl*,' or 'one who follows behind his sweetheart.' When I listen to how you all arrived at The More, the image seems appropriate, but I feel like the one who follows."

They laughed at James' modesty and their earlier interpretations of the sea stacks.

"The journey opened you up to the system of belief that brought transformation to your own lives. What sort of event brought that about?" James asked.

"It was different for each of us, wasn't it, Celine?" Zahir said with his familiar grin.

Celine smiled back good-naturedly. "I have the distinction of the most dramatic turning point," she confessed reluctantly. "It would have been marked by being crushed at Adrenaline Surge if it weren't for Tomo."

"He rescued her invincible spirit," Zahir joked as he and Celine launched into an animated account of what had taken place. Kim smiled as the feelings between these two shuffled together like a crisp, new deck of cards.

James laughed as Zahir finished by poking fun at himself being frightened up the rock slope by the large wave. "Nice work," James said to Tomo. "Have you fulfilled your quota for saving lives this month?"

"More than, my own included," Tomo replied, embarrassed but obviously happy to be recognized.

Celine rescued Tomo from the spotlight. "After all we had learned on the trail, the incident forced me not to be complacent about my own deepest desires. When I realized those desires matched the enhanced-value ethos Tomo seemed to be applying to his decision-making, I just pursued what seemed natural."

"Oh really!" James said, directing a surprised glance at Tomo.

Tomo, looking uncomfortable with all the attention, broke in. "Believe it or not, it was only last night that the Detroit couple came in with all the bad news. The threat of what was happening in the real world, compared to the vision we had discussed on the trail, made me realize what you were saying to me last week."

Kim knew how important this admission was to James. As she rose to retrieve the coffee pot, she could see, even in the dim candle light, the joy in his eyes.

"Sounds like you've been surveying your own intellectual property," James beamed.

"Yes, and I've found a lot of areas where I'm not building fences. You said we do not get closer to achieving our value goals by adding more complex control structures on existing control structures. I realized that the positive value I would like to affect by curbing crime was being restricted by my inclination to control my product's distribution totally."

James was clearly eager to coax a more specific definition. "And how do people access this public domain?"

"My distribution will be through the law enforcement network," Tomo replied. "The technology will be passed through to local police free of charge. They can set up agents or volunteers to perform the encoding service."

"That solves market penetration and distribution costs, but what about the raw manufacturing cost of the technology?" James asked as he handed Tomo's coffee cup to Kim.

"As I mentioned to you before, the technology is not expensive to produce, but in these quantities, there will be a substantial cost. That's where Celine comes in."

"The bank?" James queried, turning to Celine.

Celine smiled back. "There you go loading this public service project with a lot of front-end costs. We'll be working on some private funding for this effort."

"The stock market?" James responded incredulously.

"The private funds I'm talking about would view an effective deterrent to crime as both the investment and the return."

James studied Celine. "You're talking about a voluntary redistribution of wealth."

"That's right," Celine said matter-of-factly.

"The bank won't let you run that program," James said in a concerned tone.

"Given all the changes that have taken place, they probably would, but they won't have to. The agency will treat each project just like this one: evaluate its social merits, ensure there is no profiteering and submit donated funds to fiscally responsible recipients. If we can prove this test on each project, the agency will have no trouble attracting willing financial donors to its causes."

"What agency?" James said, clearly bewildered.

Celine smiled over at Zahir, who took his cue. "Celine is not going back to the bank. We are going to use her personal contacts in the financial world and her knowledge of social projects that need funding as the basis for an agency that would match the two."

As Zahir looked back to Celine, she picked up on the explanation without a pause. "Zahir will apply his expertise on the 'Net to establish penetration at our web site and security clearances for exchanges between the parties. Using the 'Net, we can attract concerned wealth to worthy causes anywhere in the world, so we are calling the agency 'Financing International Societal Health.'"

"Financing International Societal Health," James repeated as though he were weighing a business case. "Great idea. *www.fish.net* and you've already caught your first project."

"There you go. He's named the web site." Zahir laughed. "James, you have a few volunteer hours to help us pull this thing together, don't you?"

James smiled his confirmation. "Sounds like you've decided there should be a little more park space in the world of intellectual property."

"Cyberspace can accommodate both commercial and non-commercial objectives," Zahir paused. "The 'Net as public domain is like this trail: too many users and not enough caretakers."

James looked thoughtfully at Zahir, apparently understanding his metaphor. "Is that a caretaker speaking?"

"I was all pumped up about the role of technology to create a new collective consciousness," Zahir said, glancing at Tomo. "Then a good friend pointed out that we need to enter this new era with new attitudes, or we will simply end up with self-serving, information-based mega-structures."

"What are you leading to, Zahir?" James pressed.

"We have been making software applications user-friendly," Zahir said, looking to Kim. "But to advance our shared understanding, we need a new language—we need to make software creation user-friendly."

"The creation of software applications by many is externalizing consciousness," James pondered. "What's the platform for the application?"

"It's organic, residing on the public domain of the 'Net," Zahir replied. "By writing a tiny bit of code that mimics a computer and installing it on the 'Net, people can write their own applications."

"Zahir, you're destined to develop a billion-dollar mega-structure," Tomo quipped.

"These dollars will advance The More because they will promote social equality," Zahir responded.

"Advance The More because they will translate the language of a new reality," Tomo said.

"Advance The More because they will facilitate the Natural Economy," Paul said.

"Advance The More because they will enable the culture of caring," Celine added.

Kim looked from the smiling foursome to the look of sheer overload on James' face. She knew he could not believe the commitment that was unfolding in front of him.

"I think we should have a bottle of champagne to celebrate," she said, trying to bring James to the surface.

"I think this is more appropriate," Zahir said, raising his coffee cup. "Java is the champagne of the masses."

The clank of mugs sounded all around; then James spoke thoughtfully. "We have become unashamed of our magnificence," he suggested.

"It appears the world view has shifted to one of caring," Paul confirmed. "It is only natural we all move our beliefs to actions."

James simply raised his eyebrows. "I'm not surprised you're advocating to vote with your body," he said to Paul.

Paul smiled back. "Once we saw The More, it became very easy to see what forces facilitated our movement and what part of the structure held us back artificially."

"It becomes a little more complicated when you are the structure," James responded to Paul.

"That's why we called it Beerman & Associates. It's time the associates had a turn running the company," Paul responded. "We've been thinking of some ways to support a rotating President so that one person or set of ideas doesn't become the standard mantra."

"Is this to be the model for organizational change?" James queried.

"I once read that 'tomorrow's organizations will be self-policing and self-evaluative, recognizing how each member contributes to a dynamic of organic growth," Paul said, quoting James' paper. "I didn't know what that meant the first time I read it, but now I know this is the code of conduct that will let the members of the company grow beyond."

"That proves there is a beyond for you," James said, quite unaware of why it brought a smile to everyone's face.

"I'm going home," Paul stated simply.

"The Czechs have crucial federal elections next spring," James observed.

"And I'll be there," Paul said, grinning at James' insight.

"On a ballot card," James guessed.

"On a ballot card."

"There will be no hollow politics to your campaign slogan: 'Building the Natural Economy'," James said as he reached out and shook Paul's hand, prompting the others to follow suit.

As the din in the tent settled, James looped back through the conversations they had had over dinner. "Through the system of belief, you've explored how we converge to universal values."

"We explored through language," Tomo confirmed, glancing at Kim. "We've learned there is a common path, a universal language that speaks to each of us. In this way, Kim was our teacher. But how do you disseminate this kind of teaching?"

"It's not a distribution problem. It's a value problem," Kim said, returning Tomo's smile.

"Change the principles that guide the policies, and the process will change as a byproduct," James offered.

"In the great monolith of education, how do you position to change the principles?" Tomo pressed.

Kim smiled like a card player with a winning hand. "The More arises from the principles of the new reality, and I'm getting into the distribution business." Kim reached into her shirt pocket and handed James the letter he had given her earlier.

James unfolded the stiff white bond and held it up in the candlelight. A heavily-embossed crest cast a shadow at the top of the page as James began to read.

> *Dear Ms. Downing:*
>
> *It is with great pleasure that I notify you on behalf of the Government of British Columbia and the Ministry of Education, of our desire that you be appointed Deputy Minister of Education...*

James didn't finish reading, the excitement interrupting his thoughts. "Are you going to take it?"

Kim smiled back. "Do whales dance? Don't throw away your old business cards. We're staying right here in British Columbia."

An explosion of cheers went up as Kim pulled James into a hug and the first clap of thunder crashed overhead.

The More: *A global ethic shift*

Other than the embers of the fire and the odd wave that crested white at the edge of the beach, there had been no source of light beyond the tent. Kim had listened to the Garwood group speak of moving their beliefs to actions and had committed herself to The More. She had been watching the clouds thicken before they disappeared into the darkness of the night and was the only one who didn't jump when the first thunderclap occurred.

James was clearly too excited to sit down, and the thunder gave him an excuse to get up and pack the metal cooking items under cover.

When he returned moments later, the group had been affected by the energy in the air. They were aware Kim's appointment was the highest non-elected position in government, and they were equally aware of her will to effect change. The news galvanized the commitments they had made as individuals and deepened their understanding that a new system of belief was taking hold.

As the implication of these events sank in, the first tap of rain on the broad shelter punctuated the mood. Kim sensed that the silence that followed was deeper than the instinct of protection they shared.

Tomo looked to James. "Last week when we were standing on the ledge of the Chief, you said the riddle is how change comes about at a system level. The riddle is solved."

James smiled at Tomo, then looked across the faces of the Garwood group. "Yes, because you have shown me the system moves when we all become part of The More. It is clear now that countless others have initiated the journey you have completed."

"To sustainable ways of being," Tomo suggested.

"As the function and limits of nature become anchored in our personal and institutional life we move to sustainability through the Natural Economy," James replied. "It is our greater spirit connecting as a caring culture across the globe."

"It is still so unbelievable that the transformation has occurred," Tomo replied. "How can we be sure the changes off this trail will have the same motivation—will take a similar path?"

James looked past Tomo through the broad opening of the tent, and spoke in measured tones. "We have lived out of balance with life-supporting values. We have applied ever-increasing stress against our better nature. We witness the chaos with a growing sense of disease. We dream of a broader vision of wellness. We connect with others who are sharing this dream. We act on this understanding and the whole world acts with us."

Zahir's voice, charged with its own enthusiasm, broke in. "Disequilibrium, the maximum amount of energy into the system, an attitude of chaotic unrest, the emergence of a pattern, a network of collective insight, and self-organization to a higher order."

"We are in the midst of spontaneous change," Tomo said, retesting the idea as a global theory. "It's a shift..." He looked to James as though unsure about making the leap.

"To an ethic," James concluded. "One we long to live."

"But what if we...?"

"We cannot help but act," James said. "You've discovered we are compelled by nature to hear the voice. The enhanced pattern has emerged, our wills converge, the energy of the world now moves through our caring power."

Kim thought of her earlier questions, and her mind raced. When does the universal desire for The More become arranged to a universal language? When do we practice as our norm the capacities we have at our best? When does a growing awareness of our magnificence transform to the ideal we long to live?

She realized that what James had just said answered these questions. "The world has discovered The More," she stated emphatically.

"Free will has evolved within a predetermined capacity for unity," Paul added.

James smiled as if he, too, were feeling the change. "As the whole world acts, spiritual determinism delivers humanity to its caring power."

Celine's gentle voice rose above the sound of falling rain. "James, perhaps it is time you shared the journey to The More."

A look of insight registered on James' face. "The journey to a global ethic shift," he responded as though he saw it.

"You can make it a tale about rescuing a group of fallen idealists and showing them the way to the good world view," Zahir said good-naturedly.

"When you do," Tomo spoke over the heavy rain, "just make sure you include the highest statement of The More."

"And what statement is that?" James replied, with a look of admiration.

"It's the pronouncement I'll be rushing to my wife tomorrow," Tomo hollered as the rain pelted harder on the tarp.

"What's that?" James shouted back.

"It's time to have that baby!" Tomo exclaimed, beaming.

Kim heard James speak softly, as if forming some broad generalization. "Our statement of faith in the future." Then he looked at Kim in such a way that she saw in his eyes an endless field of light.

The light broke over her face as she turned and looked to each member of the Garwood group. Their smiles affirmed their understanding, and as her eyes left Zahir's and returned to James, she shouted above the pounding rain, "Let's do it!"